"BILLYBUCK DANCER, ARE *YOU* READY?"

The Dancer, arms folded loosely across his chest, looking more asleep than awake, nodded.

"Then, contestant," said Tojo, "the first move is yours. Let the battle begin!"

The Tilarban swiftly began bringing up the gun to where he could aim it. From fifty feet away came a sudden blur of motion, followed by the sharp explosion of a gunshot—and then three things happened almost simultaneously:

The Tilarban's pistol flew across the ring and wound up in the second row of the audience.

The Dancer twirled his own gun and replaced it in its holster.

And the Tilarban fell heavily to the ground.

"He's killed him!" cried Mr. Ahasuerus.

"The hell he has!" snapped Flint. "There was only one shot. It hit the gun!"

But there was no denying the evidence of the alien's body sprawled in the sawdust. And as the crowd became louder and uglier, Flint realized that what had happened or how it had happened wasn't important right now. What was important was saving all their necks . . .

SIGNET Science Fiction You'll Enjoy

THE BEST ROOTIN' TOOTIN' SHOOTIN' GUNSLINGER IN THE WHOLE DAMNED GALAXY

Tales of the Galactic Midway #4

by
Mike Resnick

A SIGNET BOOK

NEW AMERICAN LIBRARY

TIMES MIRROR

NAL BOOKS ARE AVAILABLE AT QUANTITY DISCOUNTS WHEN USED
TO PROMOTE PRODUCTS OR SERVICES. FOR INFORMATION PLEASE
WRITE TO PREMIUM MARKETING DIVISION, THE NEW AMERICAN
LIBRARY, INC., 1633 BROADWAY, NEW YORK, NEW YORK 10019.

SIGNET TRADEMARK REG. U.S. PAT. OFF. AND FOREIGN COUNTRIES
REGISTERED TRADEMARK—MARCA REGISTRADA
HECHO EN CHICAGO, U.S.A.

SIGNET, SIGNET CLASSIC, MENTOR, PLUME, MERIDIAN and NAL BOOKS
are published by The New American Library, Inc.,
1633 Broadway, New York, New York 10019

First Printing, October, 1983

1 2 3 4 5 6 7 8 9

PRINTED IN THE UNITED STATES OF AMERICA

To Carol, as always,

And to the very talented and generous writers who volunteered the cover quotes for the books in this series:

Marion Zimmer Bradley
Ed Bryant
Jack Chalker
Frank Robinson

1.

The Dancer could ride, the Dancer could fight,
The Dancer could draw with the speed of light.
With his pale-blue eyes and his killer's heart,
The Dancer at work was a true work of art.

Billybuck Dancer, Billybuck Dancer,
Firing those forty-fours.
Didn't rob, didn't loot,
But by God could he shoot!
The Dancer was bigger than all outdoors!

—from "The Ballad of Billybuck Dancer"

"The place looks pretty full," remarked Thaddeus Flint to the brightly clad, undersized hunchback standing next to him. "I guess it's time for Tom Mix."

"There are just a few more people to sit down at the back of the tent," replied his companion, speaking with a pronounced stammer.

"I don't know that I'd exactly call them *people*," said Flint. "But what the hell—their money spends as good as anyone else's. Give 'em a couple of minutes to get comfortable and then go to work. And Tojo?"

"Yes?" said the hunchback.

"Remember to plug the cotton candy. My idiot partner just bought five tons of sugar."

"Five *tons?*" repeated Tojo. "Why would Mr. Ahasuerus buy so much?"

"Why does he do anything he does?" snorted Flint. "His

computer told him we were getting a good price on it." He lit a cigarette. "Five'll get you twenty he never thought to ask the goddamned machine where the hell we were going to unload it." Flint checked the house again. "Okay. Go to work," he said, heading off to his accustomed viewing position in the lighting control booth, high above the crowded grandstand.

Tojo walked out across the sawdust floor of the tent and clambered awkwardly onto a small platform as the huge crowd of purple birdlike beings suddenly fell silent. He activated his translating mechanism, turned on the public-address system, waited for the recorded drumroll to be piped in, and began speaking.

"Ladies and gentlemen!" he cried, as Flint glanced at the audience and wondered idly if it even fell into those two categories. "Now for the moment you've all been waiting for. *The Ahasuerus and Flint Traveling Carnival and Sideshow* is pleased and proud to present, for the first time ever on Beta Epsilon IV, the one, the only, the fabulous *Billybuck Dancer!*"

"Actually," commented Flint dryly as a tall, bald, incredibly gaunt blue being climbed up to the booth and sat down next to him, "it's the third time ever, if you count the two shows yesterday."

"Poetic license, Mr. Flint," said the blue man easily.

"And he forgot to mention the cotton candy."

"This is neither the time nor the place for it," replied the blue man.

"Unless you've got one hell of a sweet tooth, Mr. Ahasuerus, this is precisely the time and place for it," said Flint.

"Do you know how rare sugar is in this sector of the galaxy?" inquired Mr. Ahasuerus gently.

"Not rare enough. We've got two hundred sacks of it piled up in the galley."

Further discussion was made impossible by the roar from the crowd, as the house lights darkened for a few seconds and then came on again to reveal a slender, blond young man standing in the center of the tent, his arms folded casually across his chest. His fringed cowboy shirt and pants glistened a brilliant silver, his Stetson was covered with the same material, and his boots and holster were a shining silver patent leather. He wore a red garter on his right sleeve, and a sheer black bandanna around his neck.

"A new outfit?" asked Mr. Ahasuerus.

Flint nodded. "Now that the strip show's closed, he's got a lot of bright material to choose from."

Billybuck Dancer touched the brim of his hat to acknowledge

the ovation. Then, as Tojo explained the principles of a projectile weapon to the audience, the Dancer walked over to a prop table, picked up three small plaster figurines, and threw them high into the air. He waited until they had reached the apex of their trajectory and were falling back to the ground before he even reached for his pistol. Then his hand became little more than a blur of motion, and three shots were fired so quickly that even Flint, who had seen the act hundreds of times, was sure that he heard only one explosion. The three figurines shattered into thousands of tiny pieces.

The Dancer spent another five minutes with his solitary display of marksmanship, then was joined by a scantily clad assistant.

"Isn't that Jenny?" asked the blue man.

"Yeah," replied Flint. "You sound surprised."

"I thought Priscilla was working with him yesterday," continued Mr. Ahasuerus, mildly perplexed.

"The girls have decided to start taking turns working with him every day instead of every planet. I guess they feel a little safer that way."

"But that's silly! He never misses."

"He hasn't missed *yet*," said Flint. "There's a difference." He snuffed out his cigarette and immediately lit another. "And for the five years we've been playing these jerkwater little worlds of yours, I've never once been able to make him practice. One of these days he's going to misjudge the gravity, or just get out-and-out careless, and we're going to have one less pretty girl on our hands."

"Do you really think so?" asked the blue man.

Flint shrugged. "No. But the girls do."

He turned his eyes back to the Dancer, who was preparing to shoot a cigarette out of Jenny's lips. There was no careful alignment of sights, no closing of one eye while he took aim, not even a request for her to turn slightly to her left so he could get a full profile view of her. There was just another blur of motion, and suddenly Jenny had only half a cigarette in her mouth.

Jenny then produced a deck of cards and had a member of the audience select four court cards. She showed them to the Dancer, then stood about forty feet away and hurled the entire deck into the air. Three shots rang out instantly; then the Dancer dropped to one knee as he peered at the falling pasteboards, and got off a fourth shot just as one of the cards was about to land on the sawdust. Jenny spent a moment gathering up the cards and

produced four headless jacks, as the audience roared its
appreciation.

A few more minor tricks followed, and then the Dancer
prepared for the stunt that always made the carny crew—including
Flint—wince with apprehension.

A pair of robots brought out a huge wheel, perhaps eight feet
in diameter, and attached Jenny to it, her arms and legs spread-
eagled and held tight with small straps. A card, the ace of
spades, was affixed to a spoke of the wheel no more than an inch
from her left hand, while the ace of hearts was attached a similar
distance from her left foot. The wheel was set erect and one of
the robots began spinning it so rapidly that it soon became
almost impossible to distinguish her features.

The Dancer stared calmly at her for a moment, then pulled a
knife out of each of his boots. Turning his back to the spinning
wheel, he displayed the knives to the crowd—and then, in a
single motion, he whirled and hurled both knives within half a
second of each other, one with each hand.

The crowd emitted the avian equivalent of a gasp, the wheel
was allowed to spin to a halt, and the Dancer casually walked
over and withdrew a knife from each card. As the birdlike
creatures fluttered their wings by way of applause, a robot
attached another card just to the left of Jenny's neck, while its
companion brought out a small contraption that looked very
much like a hassock with a tent pole sticking up from its center.
This was placed about fifty feet from Jenny, and the Dancer,
placing one knife back in his boot, crossed over to it, stepped
onto the circular platform, and took a firm grip on the pole with
his left hand.

"I hate watching this," whispered Mr. Ahasuerus, nevertheless unable to look away.

"It's not exactly my cup of tea, either," admitted Flint as the
first robot set Jenny's wheel in motion again. "Still," he added,
as the second robot touched a button on the Dancer's platform
and it, too, began spinning, "it fills up the tent." He glanced at
the Dancer, who was spinning faster and faster. "You know, if
he ever loses his grip on that post, he's going to wind up in the
fortieth row."

The two humans kept rotating with blinding speed as another
drumroll was sent over the sound system. Then, suddenly, there
was an extra blur of motion from the Dancer's platform, and the
lights reflected off his knife for the merest flickering of an
instant as it sped toward Jenny's wheel.

Again the robots allowed the wheel to slow down by itself, as the Dancer leaped off his platform and landed, seemingly not dizzy in the least, a good twenty feet away.

"I don't know how he does it!" said Mr. Ahasuerus, shaking his bald blue head in amazement as the Dancer once again walked across the sawdust and removed his knife from the center of the card.

"I don't know how *she* does it," replied Flint. "Whatever we're paying her, it's not enough."

This time the audience rose to its feet and filled the tent with weird hooting noises. The alien cheers persisted for almost five minutes before the Dancer could continue his act, and then they allowed him to proceed only after he'd doffed his Stetson a number of times and shaken the feathered claws of half a dozen of the more prominent spectators.

"And now, ladies and gentlemen," said Tojo, "Billybuck Dancer will put his life on the line while performing the most dangerous trick ever devised. May I call your attention to the device being moved into the ring at this time? We call it our Killing Machine, and it can hurl ten knives in less than three seconds, in random order and with deadly accuracy. You will notice that one of the robots is placing a dummy fifty feet away from the device. Now please observe what happens when the Killing Machine is activated."

Tojo himself pressed a button on the side of the machine, and ten knives flew across the ring and embedded themselves in the dummy's head and torso. A whisper of apprehension spread through the crowd as Tojo resumed speaking.

"Each knife has a bell on the handle, similar to the circular metal hand protector you see on this sword"—he held a fencing foil high above his head—"and should Billybuck Dancer fail to hit even one of the bells while the knives are in flight, this will be the last performance he ever gives. Each of his guns holds six bullets, so even disregarding the time factor he has almost no margin for error."

The Dancer drew his guns, twirled them until they were pointing towards the top of the tent, and fired one shot from each.

"Correction!" added Tojo, grateful that the translating device masked his stammer but unhappy that it also edited out the excitement and inflections he was trying to instill in his voice. "He has *absolutely* no margin for error!"

He waited for still another drumroll, then turned to the Dancer.

"Billybuck Dancer—are you ready?"

A slight, almost indiscernible nod was the only indication the audience had that the Dancer hadn't fallen asleep, so casual and relaxed did he appear.

"Audience—are *you* ready?"

A single sound was hooted in chorus.

"Then," cried Tojo, reaching once again toward the firing mechanism, "let the battle begin—Billybuck Dancer versus the Killing Machine!"

The Dancer's fingers inched downward toward his holsters.

"Look at him," said Flint, shaking his head. "You think he can keep awake for this?"

"The man is brave," commented Mr. Ahasuerus, leaning forward in his chair. "That much I will grant him."

"The man is *crazy*," responded Flint.

Tojo's finger reached the button no more than a tenth of a second before the Dancer's hands reached his pistols. Then they were out and blazing, deafening the crowd with their explosions. It was over in less than four seconds: not a single knife had come within twenty feet of him before the bullet found the bell.

This time nothing could contain the birdlike creatures. They stormed off their benches like some feathered purple wave and carried the Dancer around and around the tent on what passed for their shoulders. Finally, after fifteen loud and exuberant minutes, they allowed him to make his exit, looking—as he always did—slightly uncomfortable to be the center of so much attention and adulation.

"Ladies and gentlemen," cried Tojo, as the Dancer paused by a tent flap to take one last unenthusiastic bow, "I give you Billybuck Dancer, the best rootin' tootin' shootin' gunslinger in the whole damned galaxy!"

And then he was gone, and the crowd began filing out as Max Bloom, now seventy-five years old and slowing down almost daily, came out in his Emmett Kelly clown's garb and put on a brief pantomime entertainment for those members of the audience who had decided to wait until the aisles cleared out a bit before leaving.

"What was the count tonight?" asked Tojo, joining Flint and the blue man in the lighting control booth after the crowd had emptied out. Flint was drinking beer, while Mr. Ahasuerus was sipping coffee and studying a computer printout.

"Damned near six thousand," replied Flint. He turned to his

partner. "I think we're going to have to go to three shows a day until your friends at the Corporation deliver our new tent."

"*Another* new tent?" interrupted Tojo. "We've only had this one for a couple of months."

"You asked the wrong question," said Flint.

"I don't understand."

"The count is *always* damned near six thousand. The operative question is: how many purple birds did we have to turn away?"

"Well?" persisted the hunchback.

"About twice that many," said Flint.

"That's wonderful!" exclaimed Tojo.

"We've come a long way in five years," beamed Mr. Ahasuerus. "I can remember when we could barely afford fuel for the ship, to say nothing of not being able to meet our payroll."

"Nothing up here to spend it on anyway," muttered Flint, finishing his beer and pitching the can into a darkened corner of the booth.

"That's not the point," said the blue man. "We've turned a fly-by-night operation into a solid money-maker. It is not something I would have anticipated, based on our first meeting."

"I still remember the first time I saw you," said Tojo. "I was never more frightened in my life."

"I can safely say that the feeling was mutual," replied Mr. Ahasuerus, thinking back to a frigid October morning in Vermont.

"And now here I am," continued the hunchback, "talking and telling jokes to a bunch of aliens. *Me*—ugly, misshapen, fumblemouthed Tojo, the carny barker! It still seems like a dream!"

"Let's not forget who are the aliens on this world and who are the natives," said Flint. He shook his head. "Lord, but they're homely! I wonder if they molt?"

"They probably wonder if you shed your skin," said Mr. Ahasuerus.

"Probably," agreed Flint with a sigh. "I don't suppose it makes a hell of a lot of difference what they do, just so long as they spend their money."

"They were lined up before sunset, just to get into the specialty show," said the hunchback.

"I know," said Flint. "It seems that our friend Wyatt Earp is getting himself a reputation."

"It must be wonderful to be known and loved on hundreds of different worlds," said Tojo wistfully.

"I'll settle for just getting rich off him," responded Flint, lighting up another cigarette.

"Be truthful, Mr. Flint," said the blue man. "Wouldn't you like the admiration?"

"Not if I had to face the Killing Machine twice a day to get it," said Flint devoutly.

"Still," said Tojo, turning his homely face toward the flap through which the Dancer had disappeared, "he must be a very satisfied man. Just think of it: ten years ago he was doing God knows what in Texas, and five years ago we were all working for peanuts back in New England, and now he's the most famous entertainer who ever lived."

As they spoke about him, the handsome blond marksman walked down the Midway toward the carny ship, signing an occasional autograph. He entered the airlock, tipped his hat to two of the girls who were sitting in the mess hall, and walked to an elevator. He emerged on the fifth level, walked down the curved corridor until he came to his door, pressed the combination code on his computer lock, and entered the room. He sat down on a hard wooden chair, stared blankly at the posters of Jesse James and Doc Holliday and John Wesley Hardin that hung on his walls, and sighed deeply.

And then the best rootin' tootin' shootin' gunslinger in the whole damned galaxy, the most famous entertainer who ever lived, walked over to his bed and lay down on it.

And cried.

2.

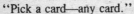

"Pick a card—any card."

Thaddeus Flint, who had been sitting about a quarter of a mile from the ship, propped up against a small, gnarly tree and thoughtfully sipping a none-too-cold beer, looked up and saw a dapper man in his fifties, wearing a derby hat, a white shirt, carefully pressed gray pants, a bright-red satin vest, and a pair of diamond rings that sparkled with the same intensity as Beta Epsilon IV's low-hanging sun. Flint stared at the proffered deck for a moment, then resumed looking at the barren brown landscape that stretched away from the Midway in all directions, highlighted here and there by the dull midday sun.

"Three of spades," he said in a bored voice.

"You're supposed to pick one, and *then* I got to guess what it is," Jason Diggs explained patiently.

"Rigger," said Flint—Diggs was in charge of the carnival's fifty-six games of chance, and had long since earned the sobriquet Digger the Rigger—"I hope to hell you didn't traipse all the way out here to show me a goddamned card trick."

"Of course not," replied Diggs, masking his disappointment and putting the deck away.

"And don't look so heartbroken," added Flint. "That's a stripper deck: it hasn't *got* a three of spades. What it's got is twenty-six queens of hearts, all shaven, and twenty-six other cards, all sevens and higher."

"Son of a bitch!" exclaimed Diggs, withdrawing the deck from his pocket and examining it. "I hadn't even noticed."

Flint snorted. "Yeah. It probably would have escaped your attention while you lost some one-dollar bets, and would have come to you in a flash the second we upped the stakes to fifty." He finished his beer and tossed the empty can out onto the sparse brown vegetation.

15

"You figure to leave a few cans on *every* planet in the galaxy?" asked Diggs.

"Ten minutes after we're gone, that's the only way they'll ever know we were even here."

"Well, I can see you're in a bright mood today."

"And I can only assume you're here to add to it," said Flint. "What seems to be the problem?"

"You got a mighty unhappy cowboy on your hands, Thaddeus." Flint chuckled.

"What's so funny about that?" demanded Diggs.

"Rigger, you aren't exactly a prime candidate for the Pulitzer Prize in journalism. We've been out here—what?—five years now, and you're just coming to the realization that the Dancer isn't the happiest person you've ever seen?"

"He's getting worse."

"He never talks to anyone, he's spent half his waking hours for the past ten years staring off into space, he probably hasn't had a woman in even longer than that, he doesn't drink, he doesn't smoke, and the next time he swears will be the first. How much worse can he get?"

"He keeps to himself all the time."

"He always did," replied Flint, lighting up a cigarette.

"Damn it, Thaddeus, I'm trying to tell you that your superstar is crazy!"

"I never said he wasn't," said Flint. "He's been crazy since the day I met him. So what? He's harmless." He turned and pointed to two figures that were walking down the middle of the Midway, engaged in animated conversation; one was human, one was very definitely inhuman. "You want to see someone who's *really* crazy? Try him."

Diggs squinted and peered off toward the Midway. "Which one do you mean—Jupiter or Batman?"

"Six of one, half a dozen of the other," Flint responded. "They spent eight months trying to kill each other in the ring and damned near wrecked the carnival. Monk'll never walk right again and Batman's wings look like a piece of cloth that's been shredded by the wind."

"But that's all over."

"You think so, do you?" said Flint. "You think it's perfectly sane for Jupiter Monk to give up training animals so he can spend the rest of his life working the Bozo cage with a refugee from Creature Features? Hell, they spend every penny they make trying to dunk each other, and I don't think either of 'em has said more than ten words to anyone else during the past year. Give me a pleasant, pixilated catatonic like the Dancer every time.''

"Maybe you'd better talk to him, then," persisted Diggs, pulling out a cigar and shielding his match from the warm breeze.

"I've known him for the better part of ten years and I haven't found any subject that interests him yet," said Flint. "Except Billy the Kid and the Younger Brothers and that whole crowd," he added wryly. "If you know anything about the O.K. Corral, *you* go talk to him. My experience with cowboys and Indians begins and ends with John Wayne and Clint Eastwood.''

"It's not my job," said Diggs defensively. "Hell, I've been with you longer than *he* has. I know what he's like."

"Well, then?"

"I'm telling you he's changed in the past couple of months, Thaddeus," said Diggs, puffing vigorously on the cigar. "He used to just stare off into space, and you knew just by looking at him that he was back in Dodge City or Tombstone, saving proper young virgins from outlaws and Indians. But now he spends all his time sitting around moping."

"How can you tell the difference?" asked Flint with a smile.

"Just look at him."

"He looked pretty animated in the tent last night."

"Sure. But that's the only time he ever comes alive."

"Look, Rigger, any guy who enjoys having a batch of knives shot out of a machine at him isn't playing with a full deck to begin with. As long as he does his job and shows up sober, he's two steps ahead of most of the people around here. What else is new?" Flint ground his cigarette out in the dirt and lit another.

Diggs rubbed his chin thoughtfully. "Well, now that you mention it, I'm probably going to have to fire three of the games workers—the ones from Zartaska."

"What do Zartaskans look like?"

"They're the big jokers, look kind of like fat orange orangutans."

"Didn't we just take them on a couple of weeks ago?" asked Flint.

"Yeah—and if we keep them for twenty years, there's no way they're ever going to learn how to make change. So next time you talk to your Corporation buddy Kargennian, tell him to send us three replacements."

"All right."

"Is he going to give you any trouble about it?" asked Diggs.

"Nothing personal, but it ain't exactly a secret that you two ain't the closest friends that ever were."

"No," replied Flint. "There won't be any trouble. In case it's escaped your attention, he's given us everything we've asked for lately. We're a money-making proposition these days." He shrugged. "I kind of liked things better when I had to bluff and cheat and blackmail him out of whatever it was that we needed." He picked up a small stone and threw it at the empty beer can. It missed.

"Yeah? Well, don't forget that we damned near starved to death a couple of times waiting for you to swindle that little bastard."

"Almost—but not quite."

Diggs paused and looked at Flint for a long moment. "What the hell's the matter with you, Thaddeus? If the Dancer isn't troubling you, what's got you down? The way we're raking in money, you ought to be the happiest guy in the world."

"In the galaxy," amended Flint with a ironic smile. "I don't know, Rigger. Maybe I just work better when I'm hungry."

"I've been hungry and I've been full," replied Diggs. "Full is better. The problem with you, Thaddeus, is that you're too damned used to adversity. You ought to just settle back and enjoy being rich and respectable for a change." He smiled and added, "Don't worry—if you can't adjust to it, there's always the Dancer. One of these days he's going to get tired of shooting at stuff that can't shoot back, and then you're going to wish you were fat and carefree again."

"Probably," agreed Flint.

They fell silent for a few minutes, and then Diggs withdrew the deck of cards from his pocket.

"Don't suppose you'd care for an honest, friendly little game of gin?" he asked innocently.

"I'd love one," said Flint, grinning and getting to his feet. "As soon as you find someone who can play an honest, friendly little game of gin, send him around." He began walking back toward the Midway, and Diggs, after uttering an insincere obscenity just for form, fell into step behind him.

They passed the game booths, the specialty tent, and the ring where their green alien wrestler, Julius Squeezer, challenged all comers, passed by the concession stands, circled the Null-Gravity Ferris Wheel and the other rides, paused for a moment to watch Monk and Batman in the midst of yet another heated argument at the Bozo cage, and finally reached the ship. Diggs took the elevator to his quarters, but Flint stopped by the mess hall, had the galley robots fix him a sandwich and another beer, and seated himself at his usual corner table.

The mess hall itself was the social center of the ship. The walls were covered with holographs of the Dancer in his cowboy outfit, Monk with his long-departed leopards, a pair of strippers back before the carnival found out the hard way that alien beings had very little visceral interest in watching human women undress to music, and, above Flint's own table, a very early holograph, taken by Mr. Ahasuerus, of Flint and the twelve carny workers he had induced to join him in his bold new venture. There were some twenty tables in the place, all but one deserted because of the hour.

The Dancer was on the opposite side of the room, sitting alone as usual, staring off into space at some vision only he could see, and Flint turned toward him, trying, in the light of his conversation with Diggs, to see if the sharpshooter looked any crazier than usual. After a few minutes he sighed, shrugged, and turned away, unable to make up his mind.

"Ah, Mr. Flint!" said a familiar voice, and he looked up to see his gaunt blue partner approaching him. "I have wonderful news!"

"I can always use some of that," said Flint. "Have a seat, Mr. Ahasuerus." He lit another artificial cigarette, tried not to wince as the smoke reached his lungs, and waited for the blue man to lower himself awkwardly onto one of the plain plastic chairs.

"I have solved our sugar problem," announced Mr. Ahasuerus, beaming with satisfaction.

"Oh?"

The blue man nodded happily. "I traded it to one of the Corporation's circuses on Gamma Eridani IV."

"Where the hell is that?" asked Flint.

"About forty thousand light-years from here," said Mr. Ahasuerus. "If it is clear tonight, possibly I can point out the star cluster to which it belongs."

"Well, good for you, partner," said Flint. "What did we get for it?"

"Two new rides."

"Very good," said Flint. "However, what we really need is a new tent for the Dancer."

"Of course," agreed the blue man. "But they would never

trade a tent with the dimensions we require for a mere five tons of sugar.''

"They probably feel that way too," said Flint, taking a bite of his sandwich. "Our job is to instill a more reasonable attitude in them."

"You have something in mind, no doubt?"

"What are they going to do with the sugar?" asked Flint with a smile.

"Manufacture cotton candy," replied Mr. Ahasuerus. "I had my computer open our records to them so they could see how much gross revenue cotton candy has generated during the past five years."

Flint's smile broadened.

"Surely, Mr. Flint, you are not suggesting that—?"

"Was a cotton-candy machine part of the deal?" asked Flint.

"No. But our robots can duplicate one in a matter of hours."

"Right," said Flint, finishing his sandwich and taking a long swallow of his beer. "And as soon as the tent is delivered, they'll do just that."

"But Mr. Flint!"

"Tell you what. You can soften the blow by tossing in our animal crates and training cage. Monk is never going to be needing them again anyway."

"I'll see what I can arrange," said the blue man dismally.

"Fine," said Flint. "And since you seem to feel so guilty about it, tell them we'll only need one of the rides—provided they pay shipping costs on both sides."

"They'll never accept it."

"Sure they will," answered Flint easily. "As things stand now, they've got even less use for the sugar than we do."

"But the Corporation will *give* you a tent if you'll just request one!" protested Mr. Ahasuerus.

"I don't like being given things. This way we'll earn it and dump the sugar, all in one fell swoop. There's a certain elegance to it, wouldn't you say?"

The blue man sighed deeply and made no reply.

"Speaking of your friends at the Corporation," continued Flint, "you'd better tell your pal Kargennian to send us three more games workers. The Rigger says they can't be Zartaskans."

"Some form of prejudice?" inquired Mr. Ahasuerus.

"He's downright bigoted when it comes to con men who can't count," said Flint. He lit another cigarette, and began coughing. "And when you talk to Kargennian, tell him to get me another fifty cartons of Parliaments. I could die of old age before your idiot robots ever learn how to manufacture a decent smoke.''

"I'm afraid that is out of the question," said the blue man.

"I thought we had a deal: I don't nag you about putting away thirty cups of coffee a day, and you don't nag me about cigarettes.''

"That has nothing to do with it.''

"Then what's the problem?'' demanded Flint irritably. "Mr. Romany is running seven or eight sets of tourists a year in and out of the freak show at my old carnival. Just tell him to send some Parliaments back with one of them. And maybe some Schlitz, too, while he's at it.''

"I had meant to tell you last week," said the blue man apologetically, "but it completely slipped my mind. Mr. Romany is no longer on Earth. His tour of duty ended, and he has been transferred to another station.''

"Fine. Then tell his successor.''

"He has none.''

"What are you talking about?''

"Earth has been removed from the tourist circuit," replied Mr. Ahasuerus.

"How come?'' demanded Flint.

"I suspect it has to do with you, Mr. Flint.''

"With *me?*''

"What's past is past, but the fact remains that you did recognize my group for what it was and kept us against our wills to exhibit in your own carnival. That your actions ultimately resulted in a very profitable endeavor not just for myself but for the entire Corporation does not in any way alter the fact that if one man of Earth could cause so much mischief and confusion, others may do so—and Earth, as you know, is not a member of our Community of Worlds and hence must not be allowed to know of our existence.''

"Bullshit!'' snapped Flint. "If that's their reason, why didn't they take it off the circuit five years ago?''

"Because of Mr. Romany," explained the blue man patiently. "He had undergone a very painful and complex operation in order to appear as an Earthman, and they allowed him to fulfill his contract before totally closing off the world.''

"Totally closing it off?'' Flint repeated. "That sounds ominous.''

"I certainly didn't mean to imply anything ominous," said Mr. Ahasuerus. "There is no question in my mind that at some point in the future Men will reach the stars and be welcomed into the Community with open arms." He paused. "But until that happy day, Earth has been ruled off-limits to Community members."

Flint frowned for a moment, then shrugged. "What the hell. We were never going back there anyway." He stared expressionlessly at his beer can.

The blue man watched him for a moment, then reached out and touched his arm. "I know how you must feel," he said gently. "I myself have not been back to my home world for more than thirty years, and I have no expectation of ever returning there again. Yet I would feel an enormous sense of loss if I were to be told that even the option of returning had been eliminated."

Flint continued looking at the beer can for a long moment, then turned to his partner. "It's no big deal," he said at last. He paused. "But I want you to do me a favor."

"Certainly."

"Don't tell the others. They might feel about it the way you do."

"I can't promise to lie to them," said the blue man. "But I see no reason why the subject should ever arise, and I certainly will not bring it up."

"Fair enough," said Flint.

"What about Billybuck?" asked Mr. Ahasuerus, gesturing to the marksman. "He may have overheard us."

Flint looked over to the Dancer, who was still staring blankly into time and space, his handsome face totally without expression.

"Not a chance. Hell, it would take something like Doc Holliday or Jesse James to shake him out of one of those trances."

Which was as close as Thaddeus Flint ever came to prophecy.

3.

The Dancer was quick, the Dancer was sly,
The Dancer just lived to see his foes die.
With his ice-cold gaze and his lust to kill,
The Dancer would fire and their blood would spill.

Billybuck Dancer, Billybuck Dancer,
Firing those forty-fours.
Nerves of steel, resolute,
And by God could he shoot!
The Dancer was bigger than all outdoors!

—from "The Ballad of Billybuck Dancer"

Tojo stuck his homely head through the open doorway. "Do you mind if I come in?" he stammered.

"Suit yourself," said the Dancer in his lilting Texas drawl.

The hunchback shuffled into the compartment. Billybuck Dancer, clad in blue jeans and a T-shirt, lay back on his cot, surrounded by posters and tintypes of famed lawmen and desperadoes he had accumulated on Earth. On his bedstand were two photos, one a sepia-toned picture of his parents, the other a print of a rather nondescript girl in a gingham dress. Both resided in cheap plastic frames.

"You ain't come visiting in quite a while," said the Dancer. "Got any special reason for it?"

Tojo nodded. "I stopped by to tell you that I'm your new assistant."

"Didn't know I needed another. Has Thaddeus got some new trick in mind?"

"No."

"Well, then?"

"It's the girls," said Tojo uncomfortably.

"What about 'em?"

"They don't want to do the wheel trick anymore—the one where you throw knives at them."

"Don't know why not," said the Dancer, genuinely puzzled. "I ain't never missed."

"I know," said the hunchback. "But they kept complaining to Thaddeus, and he finally gave in to them."

"If you're part of the act, who's gonna do the barking?"

Tojo shrugged. "I don't know. Swede, probably, or maybe Thaddeus."

"Well, don't just set up housekeeping in the doorway," said the Dancer, walking over to his refrigerator. "Come on in. Want a Coke?"

"That would be nice," said the hunchback.

The Dancer pulled out two cans, popped them open, and handed one to Tojo, who was busy adjusting himself on one of the spartan wooden chairs. "These ain't really Cokes, you understand," said the blond marksman. "The robots did the best they could, but like Thaddeus keeps saying, they ain't none too bright."

Tojo took a sip and managed to avoid making a face. "It tastes just fine, Dancer."

"You think so?" asked the Dancer curiously. "They taste pretty awful to me."

"Well, it *could* do with a little less carbonation," admitted Tojo.

"And a little more flavor," agreed the Dancer. He sat down on the edge of his bed, facing the hunchback. "You're looking kind of sickly," he said in an amused tone of voice. "Is it the Coke, or the thought of all them knives flying at you?"

"Neither."

"You sure?" persisted the sharpshooter. " 'Cause if you're worried about the act, you ain't got no need to be. I only hit what I aim at."

"I know, Dancer. It's just that I like being a barker." He paused, absently took a sip of his drink, and couldn't help showing his distaste for it this time.

"Even saying the same stuff night in and night out?"

"Even so."

"Funny," commented the Dancer.

"Not really. Ever since I learned to speak I've had this stammer. Other kids dreamed of being Mickey Mantle or Johnny Unitas. All I ever wanted was to be six feet tall and make myself understood. I can't do anything about my height, but the translating device hides my stammer from the audience."

"You want to be six feet tall, why not have one of them shape-changing operations like Gloria and Mr. Romany had?"

"I am what I am," said the hunchback.

"You sound like that sailor in the comic strips," said the Dancer with a smile. "If you think you're supposed to be a little bitty feller with a lump on his back, how come you don't think you should be tongue-tied in front of the audience, too?"

"Because I use the same device everyone else uses," said Tojo. He paused. "I spent my whole life being either teased or pitied or tolerated. Thaddeus finally gave me a chance to work, and now I'm good at what I do."

"So?"

"If I changed, it would make all the abuse and all the work seem meaningless. I've made my peace with what I am."

"You sure?" asked the Dancer. "Sounds to me like what you are right now is a target in my act. If being a barker is so all-fired important to you, tell him no."

Tojo shook his head. "It's for the good of the show."

The sharpshooter chuckled. "More likely, it's for the good of Thaddeus' love life. I can just about guess what Lori and Jenny threatened him with."

"Maybe," said the hunchback with a shrug. "But what's done is done. Is there anything special I have to know for the act?"

"Not really. I'd tell you not to duck, but that's why we got all them straps on the wheel. Just ask one of the girls what order I do my tricks in."

"All right," said Tojo. He looked around the compartment. "I haven't seen your posters in quite a while."

"You ain't come around in quite a while," replied the Dancer.

"I've meant to," said Tojo apologetically. "You're one of my only friends."

"I'd have thought you had lots of 'em, a friendly little guy like you."

Tojo shook his head. "Very few, really. Alma's back on Earth, and Gloria is dancing on Hesporite III, and Monk doesn't speak to anyone except Batman these days." He sighed heavily.

"No, there's just you, and Max, and Diggs, and Mr. Ahasuerus, and Thaddeus."

"I don't know that a friend would make you give up barking if it means all that much to you," offered the Dancer.

"If it wasn't for him, I wouldn't have been a barker in the first place."

The Dancer shrugged and said nothing. Tojo waited politely for him to resume speaking, and when it became obvious that he wasn't going to, the little hunchback clambered down off his chair and began inspecting the posters and tintypes.

"That's a mean-looking one," he said at last, pointing to an exceptionally villainous-looking portrait. "Who was he?"

"Canada Bill. He was a swindler and a card sharp." The Dancer smiled. "Kind of like the Rigger, only uglier."

"And this?"

"Tom O'Day. A real nasty character. Used to ride with Butch Cassidy's gang." The Dancer's face came alive as he reeled off his store of data.

"That one I know," said Tojo, pointing to a photograph of a young man supporting a rifle. "It's Billy the Kid, isn't it?"

"Good for you," said the Dancer. "Did you know he was born in New York City?"

"You're kidding!"

"Truth. I seen his birth certificate once when Thaddeus gave us a day off while we were playing the Connecticut circuit."

"Was he the fastest gun?" asked Tojo.

The Dancer shook his head. "The meanest, maybe. But the best? That'd be Johnny Ringo or Doc Holliday. The Doc, probably."

"Doc Holliday was the fastest gun of all?"

"Except for me."

"Really?"

The Dancer nodded. "Only difference is, he had a chance to prove it. I never did."

"You prove it every night," said Tojo.

"Lot of difference shooting at something that can't shoot back. Old Doc, he fought Billy Claiborne and the Clanton brothers. Me, I just shoot cards."

"What made him so good?"

"He didn't much care about living."

"I don't understand," said the hunchback.

The Dancer got up, crossed the room, pulled out another Coke, and opened it. "Most gunfighters, no matter how fast they are and no matter how mean they are, they start thinking about getting killed. Makes 'em hesitate, or get ready to duck, or wonder why they got into such a damnfool situation in the first place. Doc Holliday, now, he wanted to die.''

"Nobody wants to die," said Tojo.

"Don't you go betting your tiny little britches on that," said the Dancer seriously. "More people do than you might think—and Doc, he was dying from consumption anyway. That's why he went out West in the first place: for the dry air. He knew he wasn't going to live to see forty, so he just went out looking for trouble. He was so crippled up that he needed a cane to walk from his hotel to the O.K. Corral—but once he got there, he took care of business. Spent his whole life hoping someone would kill him and put him out of his misery, and since he was always less worried about dying than the next guy, he always came out the winner.''

"Then who finally killed him?"

"No one. Died in a sanitarium when he was thirty-five.''

"Really? I didn't know that.''

"Ain't real romantic, is it?" said the Dancer, downing his new Coke and sitting back on the bed. He placed the can on the floor, propped himself up against the headboard, and clasped his hands behind his head. "Still, he was the best for as long as he lasted, and a man can't ask for no more than that.''

"And now *you're* the best.''

The Dancer shook his head.

"But you are," persisted Tojo. "You're the most famous gunfighter who ever lived.''

"The most famous trick-shot artist. It ain't the same thing.''

"You wouldn't really want to kill somebody.''

"I did once.''

"You mean that story Monk and Thaddeus used to tell about Brazil?" asked Tojo.

"Argentina," corrected the Dancer. "His name was Miguel Perantes, and he was the most famous *bandito* in the country. I was down there with a show even smaller than the one Thaddeus had back in New England. Me and Perantes, we rented out a bullfight arena in a town called Rio Cuarto and sold tickets to the gunfight.''

"And you really killed him?"

The Dancer nodded.

"You must have felt terrible," said Tojo sympathetically.

A wistful expression crossed the Dancer's handsome face. "It was the last time in my life I felt happy," he said at last.

Tojo stared at him, unsure of what to say next. The Dancer seemed content to stare off into space, reliving that long-gone day, and finally the hunchback couldn't stand the silence any longer.

"Did the police come after you?" he asked, startled at how loud his voice sounded.

The Dancer returned to the present. "*They* wanted him dead more than anybody. Practically pinned a medal on me." He smiled at the memory. "Even asked me to join the force, but I hadn't heard of no other gunmen down there, so I went back to work for the carnival."

"How old were you then?"

"Maybe seventeen. I hooked up with you and Thaddeus a year or two later."

"And you were already that good with a gun?"

The Dancer shrugged. "It's just like pointing your finger."

"For *you*, maybe."

"I could teach you," offered the Dancer.

"No, thank you. Guns scare me."

The Dancer laughed.

"What's so funny?" asked Tojo.

"That guns scare you. I was just thinking that what scares me more than anything else is the thought of getting up and talking to an audience."

"It's all I ever wanted to do," said the hunchback, trying unsuccessfully to hide his disappointment.

"Yeah," said the Dancer. "Well, all I ever wanted to do was be a gunslinger." He frowned. "So here I am, a zillion miles from home, shooting at decks of cards."

"And ten knives at once," Tojo reminded him.

"It's all the same. There's only one thing in the world a gunslinger needs, and I ain't got it."

"And what's that?"

"Another gunslinger, standing maybe thirty feet away and looking to hit leather."

He fell silent again, and Tojo knew that in some country of the mind he was walking down a dusty street at high noon, ready to do battle against Doc Holliday and Johnny Ringo.

Suddenly the hunchback became aware of another presence in the room, and turned to see Mr. Ahasuerus standing just inside the doorway, looking extremely agitated.

"Tojo!" said the blue man. "I have been looking all over the ship for you!"

"I've been right here, talking to Billybuck."

The Dancer broke free of his reverie and turned to face his newest visitor. "Howdy, Mr. A. What brings you up here?"

"I have just been informed of Mr. Flint's decision, and it is totally unacceptable!" said Mr. Ahasuerus.

"It's not that important," said Tojo. "If that's where I'm needed, that's where I'll go."

"You shall do no such thing," said the blue man. "He may be an innately decent man, but sometimes he simply does not think before he acts."

"I'm sure he's just doing what he feels he has to do," said Tojo.

"I do not believe that, and neither do you. This is *my* show too, and I am not letting you perform!"

"Why does everyone sound like they think I'm gonna kill him?" asked the Dancer, mystified. "It ain't as if I ever miss."

"That is not the point," said the blue man. "Tojo is a barker and a fine one." The little hunchback's homely features lit up at that remark. "And he is not going to be part of your act unless he wants to be."

"Really, I don't mind," said Tojo.

Mr. Ahasuerus stared at him intently through his narrow orange eyes. "Answer me honestly, Tojo: which would you rather do—be an announcer or work in Billybuck's act?"

"Be a barker, of course. But—"

"Then it is settled."

Tojo shook his head sadly. "Nothing's settled until Thaddeus says it is. You know that."

"I will fight him on this," promised the blue man.

"Thank you for the offer," said the hunchback. "But when did anyone ever win a fight with Thaddeus?"

"Then maybe it is time that I tried," said the blue man uncomfortably. "You will not perform, and that is final."

"It won't work," said Tojo. "If you promise me that *I* won't be in the act, and Thaddeus has promised the girls that *they* won't be in the act, then who is the Dancer going to use?"

"We will simply have to eliminate those particular tricks from the performance," said the blue man.

"You can't just get rid of them and not replace them with something," said Tojo. "Not only are they what the audience pays to see, but the show is running short anyway, now that Jupiter isn't performing anymore.''

"Then we shall just have to come up with some alternative," replied Mr. Ahasuerus firmly. "Possibly Max Bloom can expand his comedy routine.''

"He's too old," said Tojo, shaking his head. "He can barely get through what he does already.''

"Can I say something?" asked the Dancer politely.

"Of course," said the blue man.

"I got a suggestion that may solve everyone's problems.''

"I should be more than happy to hear it.''

"I ain't been too pleased with the act as it stands anyway, like I was just telling Tojo here," said the Dancer. "So how about getting rid of the wheel and the Killing Machine altogether?''

"What would you replace them with?" asked Mr. Ahasuerus.

"I got a couple of million credits of back pay coming to me," began the Dancer.

"They are in an account bearing your name," affirmed the blue man. "But what has that to do with the act?''

"What if I was to offer a million credits, cash, to the man who could beat me to the draw?''

"Are you suggesting that you would challenge members of the audience to a gunfight?" asked Mr. Ahasuerus in disbelief.

"Yep.''

"It is absolutely out of the question. I cannot condone cold-blooded murder. I am truly shocked that you would even suggest such a thing.''

"I wouldn't kill no one," said the Dancer. "I'd just shoot the guns out of their hands.''

"What if you missed?" asked the blue man.

"You ever seen me miss anything I aimed at?''

"And what if one of them shot you?''

"Then I'd be out a million credits, and you'd still have enough of my money left to bury me," replied the Dancer with a smile. "Don't worry. Ain't nothing ever been born, hatched, or spawned that can beat me to the draw.''

"It *would* be quite an attraction," admitted Tojo.

"I do not like it," said the blue man.

"You'll like it when you see how much money it brings in," the Dancer assured him. "You can send movies and some practice pistols ahead to the next world so the local boys can try to get ready for me. Maybe even run it on television.''

"Video," the blue man corrected him absently. He lowered

his lean, totally hairless head in thought for a moment, then looked up and waved his strangely jointed fingers across the front of an imaginary poster. " 'Billybuck Dancer Takes On All Challengers.' " He bared his teeth in his equivalent of a smile. "It has certain commercial possibilities at that. In fact, it is not unlike what Julius Squeezer does in the wrestling ring."

"Except that a gun is a mighty powerful equalizer," interjected the Dancer. "Some of them guys, they take one look at all three hundred pounds of old Julius, and they know there's no way they're gonna whip him, so they don't even try. That ain't the case with a gunfighter. And," he added, his eyes bright with excitement, "when they climb into the ring with Julius, they know there's no chance of anyone getting killed."

"You're *sure* you can just disarm them?" persisted Mr. Ahasuerus.

"You been watching me for five years now. What do *you* think?"

The blue man sighed as he lost a final battle with his sense of caution. "I think there won't be a tent big enough to hold the crowds that this will draw." He paused. "I wonder what Mr. Flint will say?"

"If I know old Thaddeus, he'll probably be mad that he didn't think of it first," chuckled the Dancer. "It's the kind of thing he'd of come up with if his head was on right these days."

"Are you implying that something is wrong with Mr. Flint?" asked Mr. Ahasuerus.

"He's the only guy on the ship who's unhappy—except for me, and I'm getting happier by the minute."

"I myself have noticed that his behavior is perhaps a little more aggressive than usual," admitted the blue man. He looked at the blond sharpshooter. "But I simply assumed this is because he is a naturally competitive man."

The Dancer shrugged.

"He has wealth, and fame, and security, and everything he ever wanted," persisted Mr. Ahasuerus. "Why should he be unhappy?"

"Maybe because he's got wealth and fame and security and everything he ever wanted," replied the Dancer. He seemed to lose interest in the conversation. "Anyone want a Coke?" There was no response. "I got some milk in there, too." He waited for an answer, then shrugged again. "I had some booze that I kept for company," he apologized, "but Thaddeus drank it all."

"As long as we seem to be discussing the subject of emotional stability," continued the blue man hesitantly, "I think you should know that I take an interest in *all* my associates."

"That's nice," said the Dancer pleasantly. "By the way, how's old Jupiter doing these days? He don't hardly talk to me no more."

"Jupiter is the same as usual. As long as he and Batman can take turns dunking each other in the Bozo cage and hurling abuse at each other, he seems content. I must confess that I do not understand him at all."

"What's to understand?" said the Dancer. "He's happy with what he's doing."

"And what about you, Billybuck?" asked the blue man, wondering exactly how to phrase the question. "Has facing the Killing Machine every night put any undue strain on you?"

"I don't know what you mean."

"Well," said the blue man awkwardly, "a number of our people place their lives in your hands at every performance, and now it seems that members of our audience will be doing so as well."

"Yeah?" said the Dancer expectantly.

"I just want to make sure that your emotional state is . . . ah . . . all that we might hope it to be. I mean," he continued, "that if anything were bothering you, I hope that you would feel free to confide in myself or Mr. Flint."

"Like what, for instance?"

"Anything at all," said Mr. Ahasuerus helplessly.

"I'll keep it in mind," replied the Dancer.

The blue man looked plaintively toward Tojo for help, but the hunchback simply shrugged and shook his head.

"All right," said Mr. Ahasuerus with a sigh. "I shall speak to Mr. Flint about your proposal, and if he approves we will incorporate it on the next world we play." He paused in the doorway. "You're *sure* no one can outdraw you? There are some very unusual races out here."

"That's a promise."

The blue man took one last look at all the posters of all the gunfighters who knew no one could outdraw them. "Then I hope that this attraction proves to be as successful as you anticipate."

"You got the best owner and barker and gunslinger in the galaxy," said the Dancer, flashing him a boyish smile. "What could go wrong?"

4.

He never drank, he never swore,
He never laid up with a whore;
He never smoked, he never wed.
He had one goal: to mete out lead.

—from "The Ballad of Billybuck Dancer"

Thaddeus Flint looked up at the ominous, overcast sky.

"If I didn't know better, I'd say we were due for one hell of a blizzard," he remarked to his hunchbacked companion.

"I asked Mr. Ahasuerus about that," replied Tojo, "and he says that Tilarba's annual snowfall averages only thirty-one point seven centimeters."

"I don't know from centimeters," said Flint. "I just know what it feels like." He tucked his hands into his pockets. "Tilarba," he repeated. "Some world my partner picked. Even the name sounds like an Eskimo village."

"It *is* chilly," agreed Tojo. "And it will get colder when the sun sets in a couple of hours. Do you think it will affect Diggs or any of the other game workers?"

Flint shook his head. "I've already told him not to set up anything where our people have to deal cards or do any careful manipulating, and to offer overcoats to anyone who needs one. By the way, do you know if the skeleton remembered to move some heat blowers into the specialty tent?"

"Yes, he did."

"Good. I checked with Julius, since he looks like he'd be right at home sunning himself in a swamp, and he tells

me that the cold won't bother him, so I guess we'll let him
keep on wrestling the marks—at least, until he starts losing.''

Flint lit a cigarette and started walking down the Midway,
checking the layout of the games, making sure the electric
calliope had been attached to the sound system, stopping at an
occasional booth to rearrange the prizes that were on display.

"What about Monk and Batman?" asked Tojo when Flint had
finished his rounds.

"What about 'em?"

"They'll freeze to death if they have to work the Bozo cage."

"It's a possibility."

"Then shouldn't you stop them?"

"You wouldn't have any suggestion as to how, would you?" said
Flint. "Short of killing them, that is?"

"No, but—"

"If they didn't like what they were doing, they wouldn't be
doing it."

"I still think you should talk to them," stammered the
hunchback.

"What the hell," shrugged Flint. "I've got five or ten minutes to waste."

"You'll do it?"

"If that's what it takes to shut you up, you little bleeding-
heart dwarf." He headed off in the direction of the Bozo cage.
"Come on. Let's get it over with."

Tojo remained where he was. "I think I'll go back to the
ship."

"Forget something?" asked Flint with an amused smile.

"No," replied the hunchback uneasily. "But I'm sure I'd just
be in the way."

"And that's your only reason?"

"They make me uncomfortable," admitted Tojo.

"They make everyone uncomfortable."

"Well, then . . ." Tojo looked plaintively at Flint.

"All right," laughed Flint. "Go on back. I'll take care of it."

Tojo shot him a grateful look, then retreated in the general
direction of the spaceship. Flint watched him for a moment,
ground his cigarette out on the rocky loam, and made his way to
the cage.

Batman, the tall reddish native of Sabellius III, sat on a
platform above a small pool of water. The platform was attached
to a lever which stuck out one side of the cage and culminated in

a plastic bull's-eye. Monk stood perhaps fifty feet away from the cage, next to a huge container of hard rubber balls.

"Cold day," said Flint, blowing on his hands and rubbing them briskly.

"I've seen worse," said Monk. "You should have been with me back when I was hunting bears in the Klondike."

"Still, I think maybe you ought to pack it in for today."

"Horseshit!" snapped Monk. He picked up a ball, whirled, and threw it at the bull's-eye, and grinned when it struck its mark and dumped Batman into the water. "He loves the water. Don't you, you furry bastard?" he yelled at the Sabellian, while taking a credit out of one pocket and putting it into another. "Don't look so outraged, Thaddeus. I pay when I play." He turned back to Batman. "You ain't getting no towel until you ask for one."

The Sabellian muttered something in his native tongue. It sounded like gibberish to Flint, but Monk's face turned bright red and he hurled another ball at the target. This time it missed, and Batman uttered a harsh laugh.

"What are you going to do when he comes down with pneumonia?" asked Flint.

"Laugh myself sick," answered the burly former animal trainer.

"When do you switch places?"

"Tomorrow, like always. Why?"

"He'll never make it," said Flint. "That water's got to be forty degrees."

"You want us to knock off for the day, we'll knock off for the day," said Monk. He raised his voice again. "Only *he's* got to be the one to ask."

"Well, what about it?" said Flint, turning to Batman. "Are you ready to sign a truce until the weather gets better?"

"Certainly," said Batman in English.

"Good. Then it's settled."

"Monk must request it first."

"And if he doesn't?"

"Then we shall see if his skin keeps him as warm as my fur keeps me," said Batman with a grin. "Mr. Ahasuerus says it will be even colder tomorrow." He stared unblinking at Monk. "I look forward to it with great anticipation."

"Do you at least want a towel?" asked Flint wearily.

"Will Monk use a towel tomorrow?"

"I ain't using nothing you don't use!" bellowed Monk.

Batman turned his level gaze to Flint. "Does that answer your question?"

"Perfectly," said Flint, wondering why he had let Tojo talk him into this. "But if it snows, I'm closing you down."

"If Monk wants to quit, I will be more than happy to take the night off," said the Sabellian. He paused. "But we work tomorrow."

Monk transferred three more bills from one pocket to the other, picked up three balls, and hurled the first of them, dunking Batman again. "Why the hell should I quit?" he said with a sudden intensity. "I'm having the time of my life!"

As the Sabellian was pulling himself back up to his perch, an early arrival walked over. A typical native of Tilarba, he was perhaps five feet tall, covered by leathery orange skin with occasional tufts of bright orange hair. His eyes were quite large, his mouth broad, his nose almost nonexistent, his ears small and circular.

"What can I do for you, son?" asked Monk after flicking on his translating device.

"This game," said the Tilarban. "How do you play it?"

"Nothing to it," said Monk, bouncing a ball on the ground. "See this ball? You just pick it up and . . ."

Flint turned and began walking away. He heard a splash a moment later, resisted the temptation to look back, and returned to the ship. He walked into the mess hall, took his coat off, tossed it over the back of his chair, and told one of the galley robots to bring him a cup of black coffee.

When the coffee arrived he pressed his hands against the cup, warming them for a few minutes. Finally he took a sip, made a face, pulled a small flask out of his pocket, and poured a shot of artificial gin into the cup. Then he took a spoon, stirred the mixture vigorously, and took another taste, this time nodding his head in silent approval.

Tojo passed by the entrance to the mess hall, saw Flint sitting alone at his table, and walked over.

"Did you speak to them?" he asked.

"Yeah, I spoke to them."

"They're not going to stop?"

"What did you expect? They wouldn't stop when they were taking turns cutting each other to ribbons in the ring. Why the hell should a little cold weather slow 'em down?" He took another swallow of his coffee. "How's the Dancer doing?"

"The same as always," replied Tojo.

"And Ahasuerus remembered to rig the place for a video

recording?" persisted Flint. "We're going to need something to show on the next world so the marks will know what to expect."

"He says that everything is taken care of."

Flint frowned. "I'll just bet it is."

"What's the matter, Thaddeus?"

"What makes you think anything is the matter?" demanded Flint irritably.

"You seem disturbed about something."

"Do I, now?" Flint finished his coffee, brought out his flask, and took a long swig of the gin. "I've got two guys working the Bozo cage who want to kill each other, I've got a dipsomaniac bossing my games crew, I've got a cowboy who's stark staring mad and tonight I'm going to be letting him take pot shots at the customers, I've got a barker who stammers, I've got a wrestler who has to be reminded not to eat his opponents, and I've got a partner who spends more time being concerned about things than fixing them. Why the hell should you think anything is the matter?"

Tojo stared silently at him for a long moment. "I thought the translator hid my stammer," he said at last.

"It does," said Flint in a more gentle voice. "It's just that sometimes I feel like a pro football player who suddenly finds himself coaching a grammar school. He can see what has to be done, he can explain all the strategy to them, but he can't go out onto the field and play the goddamned game for them." He paused. "I was the best barker this show ever had."

"I know."

"And when Julius Squeezer got uppity a couple of years ago, I bet the shit out of him."

"I remember," said Tojo softly.

"The one time Monk was in real trouble back on Earth, I jumped into the cage and pulled his damned cats off him with my bare hands. And I taught the Rigger more scams than he ever taught me."

"There's only one Thaddeus Flint," said the hunchback.

"Well, sometimes I get the feeling that one isn't enough. Every carny carries its share of loonies and misfits, but I can't help feeling that we've got more than most."

"You wouldn't really rather be back in Vermont, would you?" asked Tojo.

Flint shook his head. "No. But at least I was in control of things then. And I knew who worked for me. Look at the

fucking Midway, Tojo—I don't even know *what's* working for
me.''

"I never heard you complain about it before."

"Who's complaining?" snapped Flint. "You asked me a
question. I answered it." He shrugged. "Maybe getting here
was more fun than being here." He glared at the hunchback.
"And you've got two seconds to get that expression off your
face before I rip your hump off and shove it down your throat."

"What expression?" asked Tojo, startled.

"Never mind," said Flint. "It's gone." He took another
swallow from his flask.

"Thaddeus . . ."

"Now what?"

"I've been thinking about tonight."

"Bully for you."

"And I think maybe *you* should do the barking. I'd like to
hear you do it once, so I can get an idea of the best way to go
about it."

Flint seemed to consider it for a moment, then shook his head.
"You're the barker."

"But—"

"Damn it, Tojo! You've been with me longer than any of
them. If you haven't learned what to do by now, one more night
isn't going to change anything." He paused, then briefly flashed
a tired smile. "Besides, I might like it . . . and how long do you
think this show could run with the skeleton making decisions all
by himself?"

"You're sure?" persisted Tojo.

"You ask me one more time and you're going to find out just
how hard it is to bark with a couple of split lips," said Flint,
getting to his feet. He took a final swallow of gin and put the
flask away. "Enough of this shit. Let's go hunt up the local
constabularies and make sure they understand that no one is
going to get hurt tonight. I can just picture them slapping cuffs
on the Dancer the second he challenges someone in the audience
to a gunfight."

They spent the next two hours indulging in the carny's particular brand of public relations—greasing palms, mollifying officials, making sure that the games boasted some big winners early in
the evening. Then, as showtime neared, they returned to the
ship, where Tojo donned his candy-striped jacket and straw
boater, and Flint had a couple of lukewarm beers and a sandwich.
Finally they walked over to the specialty tent, where Tojo went

backstage to go over the details of the new act with the Dancer, and Flint climbed up to his accustomed spot beside his partner in the lighting control booth.

"All set?" he asked, unzipping his coat and lighting a cigarette.

The blue man nodded. "My understanding is that three members of the audience have agreed to challenge him. At least, three Tilarbans have been taking target practice for the past hour."

"I didn't hear them."

"Diggs suggested we use silencers, so as not to alarm those potential spectators who have never heard the explosive report of a pistol before," answered Mr. Ahasuerus.

"Makes sense," said Flint with an approving nod. "Have we got any holsters that'll fit 'em?"

"I asked Billybuck about it," said the blue man, "and he told me not to worry about it."

Flint chuckled. "That's like telling the ocean not to be wet." He stretched his arms, grunted pleasantly, and leaned back in his chair. "Well, we'll just have to wait to see what he has in mind."

"You don't seem very concerned."

"Piece of cake," said Flint. "I don't know if he's the fastest draw or the best shot who ever lived, but he's sure as hell the fastest and best who's going to be standing in the ring tonight." He looked around the nearly full tent. "Where the hell is Stogie?"

As if on cue, Max Bloom, carrying the cigar stub that had given birth to his nickname, walked into the ring with Schnoozle, his miniature schnauzer, and began his routine. The dog leaped up and grabbed the cigar out of his mouth, and the next three minutes consisted primarily of a number of pratfalls as Stogie fruitlessly chased the small animal around the tent. This was followed by an old Harpo Marx routine, in which he managed to drop about two hundred pieces of silverware from his baggy overcoat, capped off by a huge coffeepot. Then he was back behind a tent flap, and Tojo was introducing the Dancer.

"What's going on?" demanded Flint, as the gunfighter appeared in his denim jeans and shirt. "Where's his costume?"

"He says that gunfighters don't dress like whores," replied Mr. Ahasuerus.

"Yeah?" said Flint irritably as he settled back in his chair. "Well, they don't get paid like whores, either. Remind me to discuss that little point with him."

The Dancer went through his preliminary routine, was joined by a scantily clad Jenny after a few minutes, and quickly performed his version of a card trick.

Then the house lights lowered, a prerecorded drumroll was played over the public address system, and Tojo once again activated his microphone.

"And now, ladies and gentlemen," cried the little hunchback, "for the first time anywhere, Billybuck Dancer challenges any and all members of the audience to a gunfight!"

The crowd seemed puzzled, and Tojo continued:

"The object of the contest is this. A member of the audience will be given a pistol, the very same weapon Billybuck Dancer has been using during this performance. Billybuck Dancer will begin with his pistol in his holster, the leather container that is at his side; his opponent will begin with the weapon in his hand. If the contestant from the audience can fire his weapon and shoot Billybuck Dancer, he will not only leave here with the certain knowledge that he has defeated the greatest gunslinger of all time, but he will be given a prize of"—he paused for effect— "one million credits!" There was a roar from the crowd, and Tojo waited for it to die down. "For his part, Billybuck Dancer will not reach for his weapon until his opponent has begun to aim and fire, and he will only disarm his opponent. I have here in my hand"—he held up a sheet of white paper covered by barely legible handwriting—"a release signed by Billybuck Dancer absolving his opponent of all liability or responsibility should this contest result in his death. Now, for one million credits, who will be the first to challenge Billybuck Dancer, the fastest gun in the galaxy?"

"Am I to understand that the Tilarbans will begin with their weapons already drawn?" asked Mr. Ahasuerus, as three members of the audience walked down the aisle into the ring.

"He doesn't believe in making things easy for himself, does he?" commented Flint, leaning forward in his chair.

Tojo arbitrarily selected one of the three Tilarbans to be the Dancer's first opponent. The slender Texan watched the orange being as Tojo positioned him some fifty feet away and placed a gun in his hand.

"Contestant, are you ready?" said Tojo from his announcer's platform.

The Tilarban muttered something Flint couldn't hear, but obviously it was an affirmative.

"Billybuck Dancer, are *you* ready?"

The Dancer, arms folded loosely across his chest, looking more asleep than awake, nodded almost imperceptibly.

"Then contestant," said Tojo, "the first move is yours. Let the battle begin!"

The Tilarban eyed the Dancer cautiously, then swiftly began bringing the gun up to where he could aim it. From fifty feet away came a sudden blur of motion, followed by the sharp explosion of a gunshot, and then three things happened almost simultaneously:

The Tilarban's pistol flew across the ring and wound up in the second row of the audience.

The Dancer twirled his own gun and replaced it in its holster.

And the Tilarban fell heavily to the ground.

"He's killed him!" cried Mr. Ahasuerus.

"The hell he has!" snapped Flint, starting to clamber down the stairs. "There was only one shot. It hit the gun!"

Flint raced across the ring and knelt down beside the Tilarban, while the Dancer stood where he was, staring curiously at the alien's body as it lay sprawled in the sawdust.

Flint turned him over and placed his ear next to where he assumed the Tilarban's heart was.

"Is he alive?" asked Tojo, who had run over to join him.

"Not if he's supposed to have a heartbeat," said Flint. "He doesn't seem to be breathing, either."

"Where was he hit?"

"He wasn't!" said Flint, examining the body for a bullet hole and finding none.

"Then what happened?"

"I don't know. But you'd better have Mr. Ahasuerus get the cops here before the audience starts turning mean."

"What about the Dancer?" said the hunchback. "We'd better get him out of here."

"I can't think of a quicker way to start a riot than to look like we're sneaking him away," said Flint, still searching fruitlessly for a bullet wound. "After Ahasuerus calls the cops, hunt up Julius Squeezer and get him in here on the double. Maybe he can scare off any heroes who want to kill the Dancer."

The crowd, which had been whispering in shock, became louder and uglier, and the Dancer approached Flint.

"All I hit was his gun, Thaddeus," he said calmly.

"I know," replied Flint, massaging the Tilarban's chest and wondering if he even *had* any lungs.

"Got any plans if his friends and relations come on into the ring?"

"Just one," said Flint. "Don't pull your gun out."

"They ain't taking me without a fight," said the Dancer.

"Just once, will you try to remember that we're not in the goddamned Wild West?" snapped Flint. "The cops will be here any second. Your job is to not kill anyone else until then. Got it?"

"I didn't kill *this* one," said the Dancer with a shrug. He turned and faced a portion of the audience, his arms once again folded across his chest.

Flint finally gave up working over the body, walked to the announcer's stand, and explained to the crowd that the police had been summoned and that everyone should remain seated, then had to do the whole thing over again when he realized that he hadn't activated the translating device.

Julius Squeezer entered the ring just as he finished, and took up a position next to the Dancer. A moment later the police arrived, two of the Tilarban's copiously weeping relatives were allowed to remain with his body, and the rest of the crowd was dispersed.

The police doctor made a brief examination, closed what passed for his little black bag, and announced that the Tilarban had almost certainly died from heart failure.

"I hope you'll make a public announcement to that effect," said Flint.

"If you wish," replied the doctor.

"I just want to make sure everyone knows that the Dancer didn't kill him."

"I didn't say that," replied the doctor. "I said that the victim died from heart failure."

"*Victim?*" repeated Flint. "What the hell are you talking about?"

"*Something* precipitated the deceased's heart failure. Possibly it was the explosion from the weapon; I understand that he practiced with a silent version. Possibly it was the shock of having his own weapon shot from his hand. Possibly it was something else. But whatever the actual cause was, there can be very little doubt that your entertainer precipitated it."

"You're crazy!" said Flint. "This guy volunteered. The whole thing was explained to him before he stepped into the ring."

"Then doubtless a jury of his peers will find your entertainer innocent," replied the doctor coldly. "In the meantime, it is my opinion that he should be taken into custody."

Suddenly the Dancer was surrounded by four policemen. He slowly unfolded his arms and lowered his fingers lazily toward his pistols.

"Thaddeus?" he said questioningly.

"Shut up and give them your guns," ordered Flint.

"I don't like jails, Thaddeus."

"Then don't kill any of them, and maybe I can get you out," replied Flint, turning off his translating mechanism. "Just spend the goddamned night there while I find out who to pay off."

The Dancer reluctantly handed his holsters and pistols over to the police, and was led out of the tent a moment later.

"What are we to do, Mr. Flint?" asked the blue man, literally wringing his hands in dismay.

"Go to bed, Mr. Ahasuerus," said Flint wearily. "I'll take care of it, just like I always do."

"But a sentient being has died here!" persisted Mr. Ahasuerus. "Surely we bear some moral responsibility. We must find a way to make restitution!"

"Yeah. Well, a sentient being is also on his way to the hoosegow, in case that little tidbit of information has already slipped your mind."

"But what shall we do about the dead Tilarban?"

"Mr. Ahasuerus?" said Flint softly.

"Yes?"

"*Shut up!*"

"But Mr. Flint—"

"Carnies take care of their own first, and in case you haven't figured it out, the only reason the Dancer gave up his guns is because he's still got a knife hidden in each boot." Flint paused and sighed. "So if you want to make yourself useful, stop worrying about a corpse that's already on its way to the morgue and hunt me up a map of whatever city they've carted the Dancer off to."

"I'll do more than produce a map," said the blue man firmly. "I'll go with you."

Flint shook his head. "Mr. Ahasuerus, I'm going into town to bribe my way up the ladder of justice. If I let you try to spread a little money around where it might do some good, I'll wind up having to get *two* carnies out of jail instead of just one."

"But surely there must be *something* I can do."

"Besides dithering, you mean?" he said sarcastically. "Yeah, there's one thing that pops to mind."

"Yes? And what is that?"

"Try just as hard as you can not to come up with any more bright ideas for a new act while I'm gone."

"That was an unfair remark, Mr. Flint," said the blue man reproachfully. "You know it was Billybuck's idea."

"Well, I'm in an unfair mood tonight," said Flint. "The sooner you get the hell out of here and hunt up that map, the sooner you won't have to listen to me."

Ten minutes later Flint was climbing into the poorly heated landcar, an inadequate map in one pocket and a roll of bills in the other. As he punched the ignition combination and headed off to bully a bunch of orange aliens into releasing a demonstrably certifiable gunfighter, he concluded—for perhaps the hundredth time—that he was definitely getting too old for this kind of shit.

5.

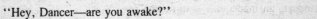

"Hey, Dancer—are you awake?"

"Is that you, Thaddeus?"

"Right," answered Flint, as the attendant unlocked the door to the Dancer's cell. The young Texan emerged into the brightly lit corridor a moment later, rubbing his eyes.

"What time is it?" he asked.

"It's seven-thirty in the morning, ship's time, and I've been freezing my ass off all fucking night finding out what strings to pull to get you out of here," growled Flint. He looked at the sharpshooter. "You didn't use your knife while you were here, did you?"

"I was in solitary."

"Not a bad place for a killer who's making headlines on all the newscasts."

"Really?" asked the Dancer, suddenly interested.

"Well, I don't know about *all* of them, but you were on the two I happened to see." Flint stuck his head into the darkened cell. "Got anything in here?"

"Nope."

"Good. Then let's get the hell out of here, before someone decides not to stay bought."

"No trial?" asked the Dancer.

"None. You're a free man—and a damned expensive one." He rubbed his hands together. "Jesus, you'd think a race that can travel through space would know how to heat their god-damned jails."

"How much did it cost?"

"More then they needed and less than you're worth," replied Flint. "Let's go."

"Do you have any money left?"

Flint stared at the young marksman. "Why?"

"I got a friend in here. Can you make his bail?"

"I thought you were in solitary."

"He's in the next cell," explained the Dancer. "We talked all night."

"How?" asked Flint skeptically. "You didn't bring a translator."

"He speaks English."

"Horseshit! Nobody on this dirtball speaks English."

The Dancer met Flint's gaze. "If I were you, Thaddeus, I'd be real careful who I called a liar."

Flint glared back at him. "And if I were you," he responded, "I'd think twice before threatening the one man who could get me out of this pigsty."

The Dancer walked back into his cell and folded his arms across his chest resolutely. "I ain't leaving without him, Thaddeus. It ain't right to leave a human being all alone in a place like this."

"Except for Earth, there's a grand total of thirteen human beings abroad in the whole damned galaxy," said Flint. "You want me to name 'em for you?"

"Him and me, we go together or we stay together," said the Dancer firmly.

"You haven't even seen him!" yelled Flint. "Even granting for the sake of argument that he speaks English, how do you know he isn't some feathered dragon with five heads?"

"Six," said an amused voice from the other side of the cell wall.

Flint jumped, startled, and stared at the wall. The Dancer smiled, and finally Flint walked over to the attendant, switched on his translating device, and asked him to find out the charges and the bail for the Dancer's unseen companion. He stood in the doorway, glaring silently at the marksman, until the alien returned and whispered to him in low tones.

"Three thousand credits," announced Flint, turning the translator off again. "That's an awfully high bail for a guy who's only charged with impersonating an officer." He paused. "Maybe I ought to let the pair of you rot in here."

"You won't, though," said the Dancer.

"You're dead sure of that, are you?"

The Dancer nodded. "It ain't because you got a generous nature," he said. "But whatever me and my friend cost you, you're still going to make more money taking me back than leaving me here."

"I might get more satisfaction leaving you here," said Flint.

"Suit yourself," said the Dancer, sitting down on a strangely shaped cot and leaning back against the wall.

"You've got about five seconds to get off your ass and on your feet or I really *will* leave you," said Flint disgustedly.

"And my friend?" asked the Dancer.

"Yeah, him too. Nobody who speaks English belongs in a hole like this. We'll turn him loose when we get out of the city."

The Dancer stood up and stretched. "I *told* him you'd make his bail," he said with a satisfied smile.

"Wait here," said Flint, following the attendant down the hall. He went up to the Tilarban equivalent of a magistrate, posted three thousand credits and signed a pair of papers that he couldn't read, and then returned to the Dancer's cell.

"You ready?" he asked.

"Yep." The Dancer stepped into the corridor.

Flint nodded to the attendant, and a moment later the door to the adjoining cell was unlocked.

"Well, damn it, Dancer!" boomed a loud, friendly voice. "You look just the way I had you pictured!"

Flint peered into the darkness, became aware of something moving toward him, and stepped back just in time to avoid bumping into the man who emerged from the cell. He was a bit under six feet tall, with clear blue eyes, black hair that was turning gray at the sideburns, a broad mustache, and a ruddy complexion. He was dressed in a long suede coat, a white silk shirt, a brocaded satin vest, carefully pressed pin-striped pants, and ornately embellished boots.

"*Just* the way I pictured you!" he repeated, stepping forward and shaking the sharpshooter's hand. "Pleased to meet you in the flesh, Billybuck Dancer!" He turned to Flint. "And you must be Thaddeus Flint. I heard all about you last night. I guess my friend Billybuck convinced you to pay my bail. How much do I owe you?"

"Three thousand credits," said Flint. "Whatever the hell *that* comes up to in dollars and cents."

"I'm afraid you'll have to settle for my heartfelt thanks until I can get a grubstake together."

"We'll worry about that later," said Flint distractedly. "Who the hell *are* you?"

"I'm the Dancer's friend and I'm a man who's grateful to you for setting me free," came the answer. "Take your choice."

"Have you got a name?"

"Lots of 'em. What name do you like?"

Flint stared at him. "Where do you come from? How did you learn a word like 'grubstake'?"

The man smiled. "I come from that airless little room," he said, gesturing toward the cell, "and I know lots of words. Seems to me that as long as I'm beholden to you for my bail, maybe you and me and the carny can work something out. You ought to see me with a crowd of marks and a bottle of snake oil!"

"How about just seeing you with a couple of straight answers?" persisted Flint. "Who are you and where do you come from—and why do you sound like a cowboy?"

"I'll be happy to answer all your questions," replied the man. "But I feel just a mite uncomfortable standing here in the middle of a jail. What say we go on back to the carnival and talk there?"

The attendant prodded Flint on the shoulder and said something in his native tongue.

"He's telling us to leave," said the Dancer's friend.

"You speak *his* language, too?" asked Flint suddenly.

"Piece of cake," he replied, and started walking down the corridor.

"That's one of *my* expressions," muttered Flint. "What the hell is going on here?"

"Don't worry about nothing, Thaddeus," said the Dancer easily. "I told you: he's my friend."

"Yeah. Well, when we pick up your guns on the way out, I want you to pull one of them out of its holster and keep it pointed at your friend all the way back to the ship."

"Not a chance, Thaddeus."

"You do it or I'm leaving both of you here," said Flint. "I'm not kidding this time, Dancer."

The Dancer stared at him for a moment, then shrugged. "Whatever you say—but he ain't gonna hurt you."

"What makes you so sure of that?"

"I passed him my knife through the air vent last night," said the Dancer. "If he wanted to slice you, he'd have done it already."

"You gave him your knife?" repeated Flint incredulously.

"Why not? I had another, and if you didn't make his bail he was gonna have to find some other way of getting out."

Flint shook his head in disbelief, then began walking down the corridor. When he arrived at the magistrate's office, there was no sign of the mysterious man. He picked up the sharpshooter's pistols and headed out the door. When he reached the groundcar he found the man sitting comfortably in the back seat.

"Sorry to rush off like that," he said pleasantly, "but jails depress me."

"Right," agreed the Dancer, climbing into the car.

"And speaking of things that depress me," he added as Flint hit the ignition combination, "so does poverty. Billybuck tells me you might be able to use a person of my talents, Mr. Flint."

"And just what *are* your talents, besides ducking questions?" asked Flint as he began driving back toward the carnival.

"Well, I can juggle, I can do card tricks, I'm pretty good with a knife—though not as good as Billybuck here—I've worked with wild animals, I'll wager I can play a game of three-card monte every bit as good as your friend the Rigger, I can sing a song and tell a story and play a musical instrument or two. You just name what you want done and turn me loose."

Flint smiled in spite of himself. "I think we'll want to know a little bit more about you before springing you loose on an unsuspecting public," he said, veering to avoid hitting a small domestic animal that had darted out between a pair of decrepit buildings.

"All in good time," said the man. "Right now I'd just like to luxuriate in being free. Ah! Smell that fine fresh air!"

"Smells like dead fish to me," said Flint, turning sharply onto a bumpy road that passed for a Tilarban boulevard, and vaguely wondering why all the houses and stores looked as if they had been made from cheap brown plasterboard.

"Well, it's not clean Texas air, I'll admit that—but on the other hand, it sure as hell beats what I've been breathing the last three days. I want to express my gratitude to you once again."

"How about being a little less grateful and a little more forthright?" said Flint. "And while you're at it," he added, "choose one accent and stick to it. You're driving me crazy."

"With no disrespect to my friend Billybuck, I think I'll use this one," came the answer. "It seems more functional, even if it is a bit less poetic."

"What does your *real* language sound like?" asked Flint, spotting the highway that led out of town and back to the carnival and heading for it.

"You couldn't pronounce it, let alone understand it," replied the man easily. "Stop worrying so much, Mr. Flint. I've got a lot more to fear from you than do you from me. I've never harmed a soul in my life, and I don't plan on starting now, not with two such interesting and pleasant companions."

"That must have been one hell of an impersonation," remarked Flint dryly, trying to assimilate what he had just heard.

"Oh, it was," replied the man with a chuckle. "You should have seen me."

"Was it as good as the job you're doing now?"

"Better," admitted the man. "I didn't mix up my dialects."

Flint reached the highway and increased his speed. "We'll be out of the city once we pass those three ugly-looking buildings on the left," he said. "Now that the masquerade is over, do you want me to drop you off there?"

"Life is an unending masquerade, Mr. Flint. I prefer to remain as I am—and I really do want a job with your carnival."

"You haven't answered any of my questions. Why the hell should I put you on my payroll?"

"Because you need me, Mr. Flint. Jupiter Monk is no longer a viable performer, Gloria Stunkel has left the show, Max Bloom's health is deteriorating, and there is no call for strippers in a galaxy filled with nonhumans."

Flint turned to the Dancer. "Did you give him your home address and the combination to your safe, too?" he asked sardonically.

"He asked about the carnival, so I told him," answered the Dancer.

"I thought you were supposed to be the strong, silent type," muttered Flint.

"Please don't blame my good friend Billybuck," said the man. "I nagged him mercilessly."

"Someday you must tell me exactly how you did it," said Flint. "It took me the better part of three years just to find out his social security number."

"Kindness is usually repaid with kindness."

"Yeah. Well, I wouldn't know about that."

"You can say that again," chimed in the Dancer.

"You got any platitudes about loyalty?" asked Flint wryly.

"Half a hundred of 'em," came the reply. "Take me along and they're all yours, gratis."

"You've already told me why I need you," said Flint. "Why do *you* need *me?*"

"Because if you leave me on Tilarba, I will almost certainly die here," said the man seriously.

"Horseshit. You seem to be handling the air and the gravity as well as any of us."

"It will not be the atmosphere or the gravity that kills me, but the inhabitants."

Flint pulled the vehicle off the road and came to a stop. Then he turned in his seat and faced his passenger.

"All right," he said coldly. "You seem as friendly as the next guy, but in a carnival the next guy is probably a child molester. If you don't want me to leave you right here, you'd better tell me why the Tilarbans want to kill you and why you think I won't. *Dancer!*" he bellowed suddenly. "Will you please stop looking at the goddamned sky and pay attention?"

"What's the matter, Thaddeus?" asked the Dancer.

"Depending on what this so-called friend of yours says in the next couple of minutes, we're either going to take him along or return him to the cops or maybe have to kill him. If it's the second or third alternative, I might need a little help, since he's probably not a hell of a lot more anxious to die or go to jail than most people." He paused. "Do you understand what I'm telling you?"

"Yep." The Dancer smiled pleasantly and resumed staring at the sky, as Flint shook his head in disgust.

"Relax, Mr. Flint," said his passenger. "I already told you that you have nothing to fear from me."

"I know what you told me. What do the Tilarbans have to fear from you?"

"Nothing."

"Then why will they want to kill you?"

"Racial bigotry," came the answer. "I believe it is not unknown to people of Earth."

"What particular reason have they got for hating you more than the rest of us?"

The man shrugged eloquently. "Absolutely none." He paused and smiled. "Who ever said that bigotry was logical?"

"Just what race is it that you belong to?"

"You're going to find out sooner or later," said the man with a sigh. "I am from the planet Jimor, of the star system Pirelliate."

"Never heard of it," said Flint.

The Jimorian smiled. "Then you have no reason to be prejudiced against me, have you?"

"I don't know. What do you look like when you don't look like this?"

"You name it. I am a master of disguise."

"Are you trying to tell me that this is a makeup job?" said Flint with a sarcastic laugh.

"No. I am trying to tell you that I would like to be your friend, and that I mean no harm."

"What were you doing on Tilarba in the first place?"

"Hiding," replied the Jimorian.

"From who?"

"There are many bigoted races in the galaxy, Mr. Flint."

"What is it about Jimorians that seems to bring this little character trait out?"

The Jimorian shrugged. "Since I'm not a bigot, I can hardly be expected to tell you what makes a bigot tick, can I?"

"You'd damned well better make the attempt if you want to come along."

"We frighten people."

"Why?"

"What difference does it make? I obviously don't frighten you or Billybuck."

"Not acceptable," said Flint. "Try again."

"I would love to, Mr. Flint," said the Jimorian, "but I feel I must point out that there is a Tilarban police car approaching us. Possibly they are merely going in the same direction, but there is every possibility that they wish to, shall we say, repossess either Billybuck or myself."

"I've been watching him," replied Flint calmly.

"Shouldn't we try to get away?"

"What for? I've paid your bail, and the charges against the Dancer have been dropped."

"They may have changed their minds," the Jimorian pointed out.

"They may have," agreed Flint. "But we're beyond the city limits now."

"But—"

"If I run, they might arrest me too. We'll wait and see what they want. Besides, what have I got to worry about? They're supposed to be scared to death of you, and I've got the greatest bodyguard in the world sitting right next to me—if he hasn't gone blind from staring at the sun."

The police car came to a stop about fifty feet behind Flint's vehicle, and a Tilarban officer got out and began approaching them.

"Why are you smiling, Mr. Flint?" asked the Jimorian.

"Either you're as harmless as you say, or he's so goddamned scared of you he's afraid to pull out his weapon."

The policeman arrived a moment later and leaned against Flint's door.

Flint activated his translating device. "What can I do for you?"

"Our sensor devices had indicated you had come to a stop," replied the policeman. "I'm here to make sure nothing untoward has happened to you."

"Nothing has," Flint assured him.

"And to make sure," continued the officer, "that you proceed directly to your ship."

"Me, personally?" smiled Flint.

"What *you* do is a matter of complete indifference to us. But we want *them* out of here." He paused. "I will follow you the rest of the way to make sure that you get there without further delay or interference."

"We've been run off planets before," said Flint with a wry smile as the Tilarban returned to his car, "but never with police protection." He started his vehicle and pulled back onto the road.

"I realize that you have your doubts about me," said his passenger after a moment's silence, "but all I can do is assure you that they're totally groundless. No Jimorian has ever harmed a member of another race."

"Our conversation isn't over, just suspended," said Flint, increasing his acceleration and starting to pull well ahead of the police car.

"Just the same, I want you to know that I'm extremely grateful, and that I'll never give you cause to regret taking me in."

"That's what they all say," muttered Flint as the cold, bleak Tilarban countryside sped by.

6.

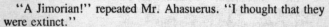

"A Jimorian!" repeated Mr. Ahasuerus. "I thought that they were extinct."

"Well, either you were wrong, or I found an awfully weird Earthman doing time in a Tilarban jail," commented Flint. "Take your choice."

They were sitting in the blue man's office on the top level of the ship. Mr. Ahasuerus sat behind his desk while Flint tried unsuccessfully to adapt his body to the awkward contours of one of his partner's decidedly inhuman couches. The walls were covered with the prints and holographs displaying the blue man's taste in art; Flint tried as hard as he could to keep his eyes averted. None of the pictures made sense, and quite a few of them imbued Flint with the fervent desire never to meet their creators.

Mr. Ahasuerus held a cup of coffee in his long, oddly jointed blue fingers, and was stirring it thoughtfully with an intricately embossed silver spoon, while Flint sipped from a stein of artificial beer—Mr. Ahasuerus had long since requested that he not drink directly from the can, a request Flint honored only in his partner's office—and tried to pretend that it tasted better than lukewarm dishwater.

"There are no other Earthmen," announced the blue man at last. "He *must* be a Jimorian." Suddenly Mr. Ahasuerus got up from his desk and began pacing excitedly around the office. "Then they are not extinct after all! What splendid fortune, Mr. Flint! I've never even seen a holograph of one."

"He looks just like me, only uglier," said Flint sardonically.

The blue man seemed not to hear him. "What a fabulous opportunity we have before us! I have a very close friend back on my home world who has been studying and writing about Jimorians for almost half a century, and yet I'll wager even *he* has never seen one in the flesh. You should feel very lucky indeed, Mr. Flint.''

"I'll settle for just being lucky enough to get you to tell me what a Jimorian *is*," said Flint.

"A member of an ancient, ancient race," replied the blue man. "No one knows very much about them."

"People seem to know enough to be scared shitless at the mention of them," replied Flint. "Why?"

The blue man sighed. "It is very difficult to separate truth from legend."

"Make the attempt," said Flint dryly. "And while you're at it, try to sound a little less like a B movie."

"What is a B movie?" inquired the blue man curiously.

"Never mind," said Flint. "Just tell me about Jimorians."

"I really don't know where to begin." He returned to his desk, seated himself on the edge, and picked up his coffee again.

"Start with what our friend looks like when he's not decked out like an overripe frontier dandy."

"I don't know," said Mr. Ahasuerus. "I doubt that anyone *does* know, except perhaps another Jimorian."

"Why don't we just pull off his mask and hold him up to the light?" asked Flint, shifting vigorously on the couch but failing to find a comfortable way to position his body.

"He is not wearing a mask," said the blue man. "At least, not in the normal sense."

Flint snorted. "Yeah? Well, suppose you tell me where he came up with that outfit he's wearing."

"He is not wearing an outfit of any kind," replied Mr. Ahasuerus. "Indeed, my guess is that he's quite naked."

"What are you talking about? You shook his goddamned hand when I brought him on board. Didn't you bother looking at what it was attached to?"

"What you and I saw and what he was wearing are two different things," explained Mr. Ahasuerus patiently. "The Jimorians are feared because they can supposedly cast illusory images of themselves: they can appear to be virtually anyone or anything at all." He paused, fascinated by the thought. "I wonder if we can convince him to let us watch while he's establishing an identity."

"Are you saying that he looks like a man to us because he's controlling our minds?"

"No. I am sure that if he had the power to read or control your mind, he would have been able to assuage all your doubts. I am merely stating what I have been told about Jimorians, and what your experience with one would seem to support: that they have the ability to appear in any guise that they choose.''

"If he *can't* read minds, how did he know about you and me and Tojo and Monk and everyone else in the carnival?" demanded Flint. "How did he learn English, slang and all?"

"I am not an expert on Jimorians," said Mr. Ahasuerus. "But if I were to guess, I would say that picking up languages is probably a survival trait. After all, many of our nonhuman employees have learned English with very little difficulty. I seem to remember Kargennian remarking that he had mastered it in a single evening."

"Kargennian says a lot of things, most of 'em lies."

"I myself learned English in little more than two days," added Mr. Ahasuerus, taking a sip of his coffee and trying not to look too smug. "It is a very simple language, really—far easier to master than, say, Rabolian or Canphorian."

"What about his knowledge of our personnel?" persisted Flint.

"Billybuck told him, obviously."

"The Dancer wouldn't give the time of day to a clock," said Flint, finally giving up on the couch and walking over to an equally uncomfortable chair.

"Come now, Mr. Flint. Merely because *you* find it difficult to speak with him doesn't mean that others do. Didn't Billybuck himself tell you they had spoken all night? Surely the Jimorian would have asked some rather pointed questions if he had planned on impersonating a human and asking us for employment. One of the reasons they arouse so much opposition is that they are so thorough in their impersonations."

"Then how do you know *I'm* not one?" asked Flint.

The blue man flashed his teeth in his equivalent of a smile. "No Jimorian would be so rude." He chuckled hoarsely, and then spoke again. "Absolutely nothing I have heard about the abilities of Jimorians would indicate that they can read minds, so while he might know in general how a sentient entity or even a Man might react to certain questions or situations, he couldn't possibly know how Thaddeus Flint would react. And he certainly couldn't match your capacity for abusing your body with alcohol and tobacco."

"You're sure this isn't just some fairy tale your mother invented to keep you in line after you came in from a hard day of pinching all the little bald blue girls in the neighborhood?"

"I am only repeating what I have heard," replied Mr. Ahasuerus seriously. "Very little is known about them."

"Well, if it's true, I can see why everyone counts their teeth when a Jimorian comes into the room."

"They are really more to be pitied than feared," said the blue man. "They spend their lives in constant danger, they are hated and feared everywhere except their home planet, they are frequently slaughtered for no reason other than being Jimorians. Indeed, the prevalent view is that they had been totally eradicated from the galaxy. For all we know, this specimen may be the last surviving member of his race; at any rate, he is certainly one of the last."

"I wonder what the hell he ever left home for," mused Flint.

"Why do any of us?" said Mr. Ahasuerus gently. "To see the next world, to meet beings we had never imagined existed, to—"

"Spare me the bad poetry," interrupted Flint. "Most of us left just to make a buck. There's no reason to assume this guy is any different. So the question isn't whether to pity him or fear him, but how best to *use* him."

The blue man shook his head. "People—especially planetbound people—hate and fear what they cannot understand. If you put him on display, or concoct some scheme to utilize his special talents, you are very likely inviting his death at the hands of our customers."

Flint stared at his partner. "What did you think I was going to do—turn him into a one-man freak show? He juggles, he does magic tricks, ask him and he'll probably swear that he can do a buck-and-wing. Stogie is slowing down and the Dancer's act has gotten shorter, so I say we put him to work in the specialty tent."

"An excellent suggestion," agreed Mr. Ahasuerus. "Forgive me, but I naturally assumed that—"

"I know what you naturally assumed," said Flint. "But we're rich, successful men these days, so we take something like a Jimorian and turn him into a third-rate entertainer." He paused. "Do you know what I could have done with him back on Earth, or even the first couple of years out here?"

"I know," said Mr. Ahasuerus distastefully.

Flint shook his head sadly. "What a fucking waste. I almost wish we were starving again, just so I could use this guy the way he *ought* to be used." He lit a cigarette, exhaled two streams of smoke from his nostrils, and turned to his partner. "You know, success isn't everything it's cracked up to be. I'm worth how many million credits—forty? fifty?—and I still can't get a decent beer or a hamburger that isn't blue; I'm going to see the same four women for the rest of my life, and just between you and me I'm getting sick of the sight of them; those bastards at the Corporation are even less lovable when they grovel and kowtow than when we used to have to bamboozle 'em out of every little thing we needed; and when I get something like a Jimorian, a guy who was *born* to be a carny, I turn him into a second-rate version of W. C. Fields.'' He smiled wryly. "I don't know—maybe Karl Marx knew a little something about capitalism that J. P. Morgan missed.''

"The names are unfamiliar to me," replied Mr. Ahasuerus.

"No great loss," said Flint. "Neither of 'em was worth the powder to blow him to hell." He shrugged. "I guess I'll hunt up our new employee after he's had a couple of hours to get used to the ship and figure out whether to let him juggle or do card tricks—or who knows, I might just have the robots whip up some snake oil and see how good he is at selling it.''

"Snake oil?" repeated the blue man in a puzzled tone.

"Don't worry your pretty little head about it," said Flint with a smile.

"But we have no snakes aboard the—"

The blue man was interrupted by a knocking at the door.

"Come in," he said, pressing a button on his computer console that caused the door to slide back into the wall.

"Diggs said that you wanted to see me," said Tojo, stepping into the office. "Hello, Thaddeus."

"Yes, I did," replied Mr. Ahasuerus. "Please sit down."

"If it's not going to take too long, I'd rather stand," said Tojo. "I don't want to offend you, but your chairs are, well . . .''

"Torture racks," offered Flint.

"Probably it's just because of my back," said Tojo apologetically.

"This won't take long at all," replied the blue man. He opened a desk drawer and withdrew two gaily wrapped packages. Then, standing up, he carried one over to Flint and handed the other to Tojo.

"What's this all about?" asked Flint.

"I realize that we haven't celebrated any of your holidays since leaving Earth," explained the blue man, "but according to my calendar, today is the last Thursday in November."

"So?"

"Happy Thanksgiving!" said Mr. Ahasuerus, contorting his lips to form a smile.

There was a momentary silence.

"I'm afraid you've got it all wrong," said Flint. "On Thanksgiving we slaughter innocent birds and forget to abuse Indians. Christmas is when we defoliate forests and exchange gifts."

"Oh?" said the blue man, suddenly upset. "I am terribly sorry. I must have—"

"Then it's time for a new tradition," stammered Tojo. "And I, for one, want to thank you for being so thoughtful." He held the small package in his hand, staring at it. "What is it?"

"Open it up," said Mr. Ahasuerus, his enthusiasm returning.

"I will," said the hunchback, peeling off the wrapping paper. He came to a small box and lifted the lid.

"Well?" said Flint.

"It looks like a whistle," said Tojo, holding up a small glistening object.

"It is," said Mr. Ahasuerus, beaming like a proud parent. "It is gold-plated."

"Just what a ringmaster needs," said Tojo. "It was very thoughtful of you, Mr. Ahasuerus."

"There is an inscription," said the blue man with childlike eagerness.

"Oh. I see it now," said Tojo, holding the whistle up to the light. *"To Tojo,"* he read, *"the finest barker in the galaxy. With appreciation, from the Ahasuerus and Flint Traveling Carnival and Sideshow."* The little hunchback looked up with moistened eyes. "Thank you," he said sincerely. "I will cherish this forever."

Mr. Ahasuerus glowed with satisfaction, as Tojo carefully replaced the whistle in its box.

"I'll find an appropriate chain for it before tonight," said Tojo, "and I'll wear it at the performance."

"Good!" said the blue man. "I'm so glad that you're pleased with it."

"I just may go into insulin shock," remarked Flint dryly.

"Aren't you going to open yours, Thaddeus?" asked Tojo.

"Later," said Mr. Ahasuerus. "Mr. Flint's present is of a more personal nature."

Flint cocked an eyebrow, but said nothing.

"If it's all right with you," said Tojo, "I'm going to hunt up a chain now."

"Hold on," said Flint. He removed a thin gold chain from his neck. "Wait'll I pull this thing off"—he detached a life symbol—"and you can have the damned thing."

"Are you sure?" said Tojo hesitantly.

Flint nodded. "Yeah. Alma gave it to me just before we left Earth. I don't suppose it's going to hurt her feelings at this late date—and besides, it occasionally gets in the way, if you know what I mean."

"I think we all know what you mean," said Mr. Ahasuerus disapprovingly.

"Thank you," said Tojo, taking the chain and attaching the whistle to it. He paused at the doorway. "It's funny, your mentioning Alma just now."

"Yeah?"

"Yes. When I was down on the third level a few minutes ago, I could have sworn I saw her out of the corner of my eye. It must have been one of the other girls, but it sure fooled me for a second." He shrugged awkwardly. "I guess I've been working too hard."

"If you have been," said Flint, "you're the first. Probably you've been hanging around the Dancer too much. Living in the past might be contagious."

"I guess so," said Tojo. He thanked Mr. Ahasuerus again and left.

"That was very generous of you, Mr. Flint," said the blue man when the door slid shut.

"What was?"

"Giving him a chain that was given to you by a woman you loved."

Flint toyed with his present for a moment. "I never loved her," he said at last. "Besides, it was a long time ago." He paused again. "Hell, if anyone loved her, it was Tojo."

"Still, it was a decent thing to do."

"*What* was a decent thing to do?" asked Flint distractedly.

"Giving him the chain, as I just explained," said the blue man patiently.

"Yeah. Well, I always try to do at least one humane thing a year."

The blue man stared at him curiously. "Why do you continually pretend to be colder and less caring than you are?" he asked at last.

"What makes you think I'm pretending?" asked Flint.

"Because over the years I have watched you continually try to appear callous and uncaring, and yet your actions ultimately prove that you are not.''

"It's your imagination."

"It is not, and I think I deserve an answer."

Flint walked over to the blue man's refrigerator and pulled out another beer. He opened it, stared at it for a moment, and sighed heavily. "There's a room on the third floor of a tenement building in Trenton, New Jersey, that's been waiting for me to come back since I was twelve years old," he said slowly. "It hasn't been painted in half a century, and I don't think it's *ever* been heated. At night, you can shine a flashlight on the floor and watch the cockroaches fight the termites. I've spent my whole goddamned life getting as far away from that room as I can, and something deep down in my gut tells me that the day I stop running and start caring is the day I'll find out that someone has moved my bags back into it.'' He looked directly into his partner's narrow orange eyes. "Does that answer your question?''

"You're a very unusual man, Mr. Flint."

"So are you, Mr. Ahasuerus. Isn't that why we became partners in the first place?''

"I suppose so," sighed the blue man.

Flint took a long swallow of his beer. "This is really pretty awful stuff," he commented.

"Then don't drink it."

Flint smiled. "It's not quite *that* awful.''

"By the way, I haven't made my ledger entries yet. How much did you spend to get Billybuck and the Jimorian out of jail?''

"Three thousand credits for the Jimorian," said Flint. "If I'd known then what I know now, I'd have charged them to take him off their hands.''

"And Billybuck?''

"You don't want to know."

"I must have a figure."

"Twenty-two thousand."

"That much?'' asked the blue man, surprised.

"They'd hit him with a murder rap. I had to grease a lot of palms.'' He finished his beer. "Don't worry about it. We'll make it all back on the next world.''

"You have a plan," suggested Mr. Ahasuerus dryly.

"You'd better believe it," said Flint. "We've got a real live killer on our hands. They arrested him for murder the last time he appeared in the ring, and ran us off the planet.''

"I don't see how—"

"We're putting a notorious killer on display!" interrupted Flint. "We're giving a whole world a chance to put up their champion against the Dancer! We're going to run ads on every videocast, we're going to boost the prize to five million credits, and we're going to triple the admission to the specialty tent."

The blue man looked his surprise. "I rather assumed that Billybuck would go back to his original act, now that we've had this unfortunate occurrence."

"Not a chance."

"But we can't make a profit from that poor being's unfortunate death!"

Flint laughed. "Two weeks from now you're going to be so grateful to that poor Tilarban asshole for having the good sense to die in the ring that you're going to be shipping flowers to his grave."

"And if another sentient being should die from heart failure during the next performance?" demanded Mr. Ahasuerus, so upset that he inadvertently spilled most of his remaining coffee onto the saucer.

"Relax," said Flint. "We're not that lucky."

Mr. Ahasuerus stared at his partner for a long moment, then sighed and turned his attention back to his coffee.

"Can I open my present now?" asked Flint.

"I had quite forgotten about it," said the blue man. "Yes, by all means."

Flint ripped the wrapping paper off and found himself holding a paperback book in his hands. "What the hell is this?" he demanded.

"I had Mr. Romany ship it to me just before he left Earth."

"Your Body and How to Care for It," read Flint. He looked up at his partner. "This is some kind of a joke, right?"

"Absolutely not," said Mr. Ahasuerus seriously. "I have every hope that this book will help persuade you to cut down on your drinking and give up cigarettes altogether."

"I'll cherish it forever," said Flint mockingly.

"I would be satisfied if you merely read it."

"As soon as I work my way through Monk's stack of pornography," said Flint.

There was another knock at the door.

"It's probably Tojo, back to find out how a whistle works," commented Flint.

Mr. Ahasuerus opened the door and Billybuck Dancer entered the office, a disconcerted expression on his handsome face.

"I hope I ain't bothering you or nothing," began the Dancer, tipping his hat.

"Not at all, Billybuck," said Mr. Ahasuerus pleasantly. "What can we do for you?"

"I just want to make sure I still got a job here."

"Why shouldn't you?" asked the blue man, puzzled.

"Well, you know—that guy dying in the ring and all," said the Dancer.

"I was with you all morning," said Flint. "How come you just started getting worried now?"

"I just bumped into the new guy."

"The Jimorian?" asked Flint.

"No, the other one."

"What other one?" demanded Flint.

"The one who's dressed up like a gunfighter," said the Dancer. "Looks an awful lot like Doc Holliday."

"Where did you see him?"

"On the third level. I was just getting off the elevator, and he was coming down the hall. Real thin fella. All in gray, too, just like the Doc used to wear." He paused. "So I figured maybe you hired another trick-shot artist to take my place."

"We didn't."

"Good. 'Cause it wasn't my fault, Thaddeus. You saw it—he just keeled over and died."

"I know."

The Dancer looked puzzled. "Then who was that guy in the corridor?"

"Probably just Diggs playing a joke," said Flint. "I'll talk to him about it."

"Okay," said the Dancer, visably relieved. "I knew you wouldn't fire me for something that wasn't my fault." He touched his Stetson with his fingertips and walked back out the door.

"I had no idea Jimorians were so adaptive!" exclaimed Mr. Ahasuerus excitedly.

"You also had no idea they could read minds," said Flint.

"They can't. Billybuck obviously told him about Doc Holliday while they were in jail."

"Uh-huh," grunted Flint. "And when do you suppose Tojo told him about Alma?"

"That's right," mused the blue man. "I had forgotten all about that."

Flint got to his feet. "I'd better have my little chat with him right now, and find out what else he can do that you don't know about."

"I'll go with you."

Flint shook his head. "This isn't a field trip for a general science class," he said. "Has it occurred to you yet that a guy who can read minds and appear to be anyone he chooses just might constitute a potential danger?"

"All the more reason why we should both go," persisted Mr. Ahasuerus.

"Have it your way," said Flint with a shrug. He walked to the door. "Let's go."

"Haven't you forgotten something?" said the blue man.

"Give me a for instance."

"Your present," said Mr. Ahasuerus, picking it up from the chair and handing it to him.

"Now, how could that have slipped my mind?" said Flint apologetically. He stepped aside to allow the blue man to pass through the doorway first, quickly flipped the book onto a couch, and walked out into the corridor.

7.

Flint and his partner checked the Jimorian's room, and when they found it empty, they began methodically going through the ship's public rooms. They finally found him in the otherwise-deserted mess hall, sitting at a table with Diggs.

"Hi, Mr. Flint," he said, looking up. "Good afternoon, Mr. Ahasuerus. Won't you join us?"

"Yeah, do," said Diggs with the hungry look of a predator. "I was just explaining the finer points of blackjack to our friend here."

"Thanks," said Flint, walking over and pulling up a chair.

"How about Mr. Ahasuerus?" asked the Jimorian.

"He'll be along," said Flint. "He's got to load up with a gallon or two of coffee first."

"Billybuck says it tastes best cooked over a campfire," offered the Jimorian.

"The Dancer never drank anything stronger than milk or Coke in his life," replied Flint. He turned to Diggs. "You got a deck with you, Rigger?"

"Always," replied Diggs, producing one from a vest pocket.

Flint examined it, then tossed it onto the table. "How about an honest deck?"

Diggs shrugged, then fished around in his pants pocket for a moment and produced another one. Flint examined it, then nodded and slid it across the table to the Jimorian.

"Okay. You say you can do card tricks. Do one."

The Jimorian began shuffling the deck. "Does this mean you're taking me along?"

"It means I'm considering it."

The Jimorian gave the deck one last shuffle, then had Flint pick a card. He did so, replaced it in the deck, and waited while the alien mixed the cards again. Finally he spread them out in front of him and pulled one out.

"Is this it?"

Flint looked at the card. "Not even close."

"Well," said the Jimorian easily, "it'll take some practice."

"Maybe you've got another trick or two you can do," said Flint, as Mr. Ahasuerus, carrying three cups of coffee on a plastic tray, joined them. All conversation came to a halt while the blue man poured cream and sugar in one cup, cream in the second, and sugar in the third, and began carefully stirring each in turn.

"Maybe we ought to put *him* on exhibit," said Diggs, jerking a thumb in the blue man's direction.

"It is hardly my fault if you have no appreciation of your national beverage," replied Mr. Ahasuerus austerely.

"I always thought my national beverage was Schlitz, or maybe Budweiser," said Diggs.

"Getting back to the subject," said Flint, "what other tricks can you do?"

"I've got a little confession to make," said the Jimorian with a smile. "I just said that to get you to take me along. Actually, my talents lie along other lines." He paused. "And I really *can* sing and dance."

"I don't doubt it," admitted Flint. "But I've got a feeling that you're being modest."

"I don't follow you."

"I'll lay plenty of eight-to-five that you've got a bushelful of tricks you can do if you want to."

"Truly, Mr. Flint," said the Jimorian, "I've never seen a deck of cards in my life until today—though, of course, Billybuck told me about them."

"I wasn't referring to card tricks."

"Then what?"

"Something more in the way of illusions," said Flint.

"You mean magic tricks?"

"I don't know," said Flint. "Do I?"

"How should I know?"

"Tojo says you can do them. So does the Dancer."

"They say I can do magic tricks?"

"At the very least. How about mind reading?"

"I give up," said the Jimorian. "How *about* mind reading?"

"What's all this about, Thaddeus?" asked Diggs restlessly. "I thought we were going to play a friendly little game of blackjack."

"Keep out of this," said Flint. "I'm talking to my friend here."

"You're making me nervous," said the Jimorian. "Just tell me—what am I supposed to have done?"

"May I interject a word?" asked Mr. Ahasuerus, looking up from his coffee.

"Shoot," said Flint.

"It would seem that Tojo and Billybuck both saw you on the third level," said the blue man gently, "and in both cases, your appearance was different than it is now."

"Maybe it was the light," suggested the Jimorian.

"I doubt it," said Mr. Ahasuerus. "In at least one case you appeared as a person you couldn't possibly know about."

"Then it couldn't have been me, could it?"

"Damn it!" Flint exploded. "I'm getting fucking sick and tired of hearing you answer every question with another one!"

"Don't yell at me," said the Jimorian.

"Are you threatening me?" demanded Flint, rising to his feet. "Because if you are . . ."

"You're making me lose my concentration!" cried the Jimorian.

"Then concentrate on giving me a straight answer!" snapped Flint.

"Don't frighten me!" screamed the Jimorian.

And suddenly he didn't look like a Western dandy any longer. His outline blurred and faded, and then he was . . . something else.

"What the hell is going on here?" said Flint, staring at him.

"Just stop yelling at me," said the Jimorian. He seemed to make an almost physical effort to calm himself, and an instant later he was once again the overdressed Westerner.

"Most unusual!" exclaimed Mr. Ahasuerus, his face alight with interest.

"So now you know," said the Jimorian wearily.

"Know what?" said Flint. "We already knew you weren't human."

"Exactly what did you see, Mr. Flint?" asked Mr. Ahasuerus suddenly.

"The same as you: a big shaggy heap with a face like a green gorilla," replied Flint.

"I didn't see that," said Mr. Ahasuerus. "How about you, Diggs?"

Diggs was still staring disbelievingly at the Jimorian.

"Huh?" he said at last, when the blue man had addressed him a second time.

"What did you see?" Mr. Ahasuerus repeated.

"Well, it's the strangest damned thing," said Diggs, a wistful expression on his face, "but for just a second there I thought I saw . . . well, a girl I knew a long time ago."

"Ah!" said Mr. Ahasuerus happily. "It's a defense mechanism, isn't it?"

The Jimorian nodded.

"And when you're startled or scared, people see . . . what?"

"What they most want to see," said the Jimorian. "Usually a loved one."

"Fascinating," enthused the blue man. "Absolutely fascinating!"

"You think so?" said the Jimorian bitterly. "This is usually the point where people start throwing stones at us. They don't much mind that we can disguise ourselves as strangers. It's when we appear as their fondest dreams and wishes that the massacres start." He paused. "Nobody wants to know that his most secret self is no longer secret. That's why I tried to hide it from you."

"There was no reason to," replied Mr. Ahasuerus. "We are not barbarians here. You may very well find that carnival people, having lived and worked with oddities all their lives, are more tolerant of differences than you imagine. By the way, am I to assume that you have no conscious control of the images you produce when stressed?"

"None," said the Jimorian. "I know that I appear as each of you wants me to appear, but beyond that I don't know anything about how it works." He smiled ruefully. "And I really wouldn't call it a defense mechanism, since most of the time what it does is make people want to attack me."

"Yes," mused the blue man. "I can appreciate the anomalous effect of the phenomenon."

"Just a minute," said Flint, finally sitting back down. "Would someone tell me just what the hell it was that *I* saw?"

"Evidently you saw me as I really am," said the Jimorian.

"I thought you said we each saw our heart's desire," continued Flint. "Believe it or not, I'm not exactly enamored of your charms. So why did I see you?" He paused. "Better still, why did I see the real, unadorned, undisguised you?"

"I don't know. To the best of my knowledge, no one—except, of course, for other Jimorians—has ever seen my true form before."

"Maybe what you most want to see is the truth," offered the blue man.

Flint seemed to consider the statement for a minute, then shrugged. "How about you, Mr. Ahasuerus?" he asked at last. "What did *you* see?"

"I would prefer not to say," replied the blue man.

"Probably a bald blue lady skeleton," said Flint. He turned back to the Jimorian. "And this happens whenever you're scared?"

"Or startled," said the Jimorian. "I've been under a lot of stress, wondering if you would take me with you, and I'm not totally familiar with my characterization yet. In a few days I'll be able to do it with almost no conscious effort, but not yet. After all, I have never even met a human being until last night, and I never saw one until this morning. That's why I stood in the shadows at the back of the cell: so I could get a good look at you before I created an identity. Billybuck told me how tall he was and what he weighed, but until I could examine one of you for a minute, I had no working idea how long an inch was, or how much a pound weighed." He smiled. "You would have been surprised at my initial conception of your appearance—and, of course, I'm still not certain that I've got the genitalia right." He paused. "Anyway, I was worried and preoccupied when I was walking in the corridor, and Tojo is so misshapen that he momentarily shocked me."

"And the Dancer?"

The Jimorian shrugged. "I was tired. Probably I just wasn't concentrating."

"Well, that answers a lot of questions," said Flint, relaxing.

"And it gives him a name," added Diggs.

"Yeah?"

Diggs nodded. "A man works in a carny, sooner or later he gets a carny name. In this case it's sooner." He paused. "How's Jiminy Cricket sound to you?"

"It's a natural," said Flint with a smile.

"Jiminy from Jimor," said the alien. "I like it."

"Good," said Flint. "Because from now on you're stuck with it."

"What does it stand for?" asked Jiminy curiously.

"Dreams and wishes," replied Flint. "That ought to be right up your alley." He paused. "Now tell me the truth: can you juggle?"

"No," said Jiminy.

"How about pantomime?"

"I've never tried, though I modestly admit to being pretty good at impersonations."

Flint shook his head. "I think we'll turn you over to the Rigger and let him whip up some patent medicines for you to sell."

"Thank you," said Jiminy. "I'm truly grateful."

"And I think," continued Flint, "that we're going to have to alert the other carnies to this little trick of yours."

"Oh?"

He nodded. "Otherwise they'll all start thinking that they're going crazy." He grimaced and added: "And except for Dancer and Monk and Batman and about half the others, they'll probably be wrong."

"If you think it's best," said Jiminy dubiously.

"It is," said Flint. "Unless you want the Dancer hollering at you to slap leather because you look like a killer out of the Wild West."

"That's what Billybuck saw?" asked Jiminy.

"You've got to understand that he's not exactly playing with a full deck," said Flint. "His job is shooting things with a gun, and he's so damned good at it that he's never been tested. So when *he* sees his heart's desire, it's Doc Holliday calling him out for a shootout at high noon."

"Then by all means pass the word," agreed Jiminy.

"Well," said Flint, leaning back in his chair. "I guess that takes care of business. Check with Mr. Ahasuerus after he's finished his paperwork and told the ship where it's taking us, and you can haggle out your salary with him."

The blue man checked his intricate timepiece. "We'll be taking off in about two hours," he said. "Come seem me about an hour after that." He exposed his teeth in what passed for a pleasant smile. "And please plan to spend some time in my office. There is so much I wish to learn about Jimorians!"

"Three hours from now," Jiminy promised.

"In the meantime," said Diggs, clasping Jiminy's arm firmly, "he's working for *me* now, and the first order of business is that he's got to learn to play certain games of chance."

"How to lose at them, you mean," said Mr. Ahasuerus disapprovingly.

"Well, those are the kinds of object lessons that are best remembered," replied Diggs with a smile.

"He has no money," said the blue man.

"He's working for the carny. His credit's good with me." Diggs began shuffling the cards. "Besides, this is *business*."

Mr. Ahasuerus sighed. "I'm delighted to have you with us," he said to Jiminy as he rose from his chair. "I'll speak with you soon." He drained the last of his three coffee cups and began walking from the mess hall.

"It'll be my pleasure," Jiminy called after him.

Flint watched the card game for a few minutes, made sure that Diggs wasn't out to fleece the Jimorian too badly, and then went out to find the Dancer and assure him that Doc Holliday really had been dead and buried for an even hundred years.

8.

❖

Two arms or four,
Big or small,
Yellow or green,
Short or tall,
Billybuck Dancer
Fought them all.
He was the best
Rootin'
Tootin'
Shootin'
Gunslinger in the whole damned galaxy!
He was the
Leanest
Meanest
Killer of them all!

—from "The Ballad of Billybuck Dancer"

On Pelegoris II, the Dancer faced forty-seven different opponents from that barren world's dominant species of gold-skinned humanoids, disarming each of them without incident. Flint had holographic films taken of the contests, and forwarded them to the next four worlds on their agenda.

When the carnival hit Aguella VI, the Dancer began facing his foes three at a time. Again, the performance went off without a hitch, and the demand for tickets was so great that Flint finally negotiated a deal to air a pair of his shows on local video.

By the time they touched down on Delta Zeta III, they had international networks bidding for the right to broadcast the notorious gunman's fights. The Dancer responded by facing six Delta Zetans at once, and emerging unscathed, as usual.

The small, four-armed green beings inhabiting Klokanni II gave the Dancer the key to their capital city, then requested the right to face him with pistols in two of their hands. He insisted that they use four guns apiece, took on three of them at once, and disarmed them before they could get off more than two shots, both wild.

On Leonachim, a hot, humid world circling Pi Delta, he allowed five opponents to hide behind various barriers, took them all on at once, and won the contest before they could fire a single shot.

Flint had watched the young sharpshooter continue stacking the odds against himself with a growing sense of unease. *Someday* the Dancer had to show up for work with a headache or an upset stomach, someday he had to get a cramp in his hand or a cinder in his eye, someday he simply had to miss—but he never did, and so Flint continued to collect the huge amounts of money that entire populaces were shelling out to watch his gladiator in action, and idly wondered if the gravy train would end when the Dancer inadvertently killed an opponent or when the gunslinger himself lay dead on the sawdust floor of the specialty tent.

Not that the Dancer was his only problem. The Null-Gravity Ferris Wheel wasn't working properly; two of the Cinbellites had quit with no notice, leaving the games crew short-handed; Julius Squeezer had come down with something resembling the flu, and wouldn't be able to wrestle for at least a week; Max Bloom's schnauzer, Schnoozle, was slowing down almost as much as his owner; and the officials of Roboden III, where the ship had just touched down, had presented Mr. Ahasuerus with a number of highly restrictive regulations concerning the way the Midway was to be constructed.

Even payday, he reflected, was getting to be a problem. Most—but not all—of the crew were content to have the money credited to their accounts. But Diggs insisted on getting his pay in cash every week so he'd have a little something to bet with, Lori and Barbara didn't trust the blue man's computer, Monk and Batman wanted cash so they could continue to spend every last penny of it buying balls at the Bozo cage, and even Stogie preferred hiding his wages in his compartment to leaving them in the carnival's bank.

Flint walked out of the ship and stepped into the cool, dry Robodenian air, a number of pay envelopes stuck in his pocket.

He found Barbara and Lori setting up their booths, handed them their money, then walked over to where Diggs was screaming in exasperation at one of the robots.

"Thaddeus, I want you to fire this bastard!"

"We can't fire him," said Flint. "We *own* him."

"Well, have him work somewhere else from now on," continued Diggs. "Ten worlds in a row, I've told him that this tent takes five goddamned support posts, and ten worlds in a row he keeps using eight."

"Big deal."

"It's a big deal when we reach the last tent and come up three posts short."

"We've got more posts in the ship," said Flint wearily.

"It's the *principle* of the thing!" snapped Diggs. "Either he takes orders from me or he doesn't."

"You," said Flint to the robot. The machine turned and faced him. "Buzz off." The robot turned on its heel and walked away. "Talk to Mr. Ahasuerus about it," said Flint to Diggs. "He's in charge of the robots."

"Things worked a lot better when *you* were," said Diggs.

"Damn it, Rigger, I can't keep my finger on *everything!*" said Flint irritably. "When we came out here, we had twelve humans and six game booths and nothing else. Now we've got ninety people of various shapes and sizes, and maybe fifty booths. What the hell do you want me to do—drop everything else and spend my whole fucking day giving orders to robots?"

"Take it easy, Thaddeus," said Diggs, startled by Flint's outburst. "I'm mad at the robots, not at you."

"Just keep it that way," said Flint. He withdrew an envelope, checked the name on it, and handed it over to Diggs. "Here's your pay." He paused. "Should I hand Jiminy's over to you, too?"

Diggs smiled. "Nope. I'm all through gambling with him."

"Don't tell me he beat you?"

"No. But he's making so much money selling snake oil that I want to keep him happy."

"Yeah. The skeleton told me he was doing pretty good."

"He's a born con man, Thaddeus," said Diggs. "I haven't heard someone with a line of gab like his since the old days, back when you were barking for the meat show."

Flint stared at the distant horizon. "I *was* pretty goddamned good, wasn't I?" he said wistfully.

"The best," agreed Diggs.

He stared off into the distance for another moment, then turned back to Diggs. "That was a million years and a trillion miles ago."

"It doesn't alter the fact that you were the best of them all," said Diggs. "But this Jiminy Cricket, now, he's no slouch either. I think if we ever run out of junk for him to hawk, I'll stick him in a Psychic game, or maybe let him run an auction scam." He looked out across the Midway and saw Tojo laboriously walking toward them. "Good afternoon," he said pleasantly. "Don't tell me *you've* joined the ranks of people who don't trust the carny's bank?"

"Okay, he won't tell you," said Flint. He turned to Tojo. "What's up?"

"I think we've got another little problem with the Dancer," stammered the hunchback.

"What is it *this* time?" demanded Flint.

"He wants to face five Robodenians at once, and—"

"He's taken on five at a time before," interrupted Flint.

"But he wants to do it with just three bullets," said Tojo.

"He may be crazy, but he can count," said Flint. "What's the catch?"

"He says he'll use two knives."

"In a pig's asshole he will!" exploded Flint. "If any of those bastards can shoot straight, he's going to be dead before he pulls either knife. And even if they can't shoot, how the hell do you knock a gun out of a man's hand with a knife? For all we know, Robodenians are chronic hemophiliacs." He shook his head, stared at the ground, and spat on it. "What the hell's the matter with him, anyway? If he's so goddamned set on committing suicide, why doesn't he just put his gun against his head and pull the trigger?"

"I don't think he wants to die, Thaddeus," offered Tojo. "I don't think he can even conceive of himself dying."

"Then what is it?"

"He wants to prove that he's the best," continued the hunchback. "He sits in his room and stares at pictures of Doc Holliday and Billy the Kid and Bat Masterson all day and all night, and he feels cheated because he never gets to prove himself in a gunfight."

"What are you talking about?" said Flint. "He proves himself every night."

"More to the point," added Diggs, "he does it under conditions that none of his heroes ever faced. They went out to kill or be killed; he goes out to *disarm* or be killed."

"Yes," admitted Tojo. "But he does it because no one has ever presented a real challenge to him, so he keeps trying to even the odds."

"I don't understand a man like that," said Diggs. "He's got money, he's got fame, he could have any woman in the show he wanted—no offense, Thaddeus, but it's the truth—and he sits around and mopes because he's not shooting it out with Billy the Kid."

"Sometimes it takes more than sex and money to make a man happy," said Flint.

"I can't imagine why," replied Diggs.

"Be that as it may," said Flint, turning back to Tojo, "you tell him that he walks into the ring with six shells in each pistol or he doesn't walk into the ring at all. You got that?"

"Yes, Thaddeus." The little hunchback sighed. "I feel so sorry for him."

"Because he's not allowed to go on a killing spree?" asked Diggs sarcastically.

"That was a pretty stupid thing to say, even for you, Rigger," said Flint.

"Weren't *you* the one who was bitching because he's crazy?" demanded Diggs defensively.

"Yeah. But that doesn't mean I don't feel sorry for him too—when I'm not wishing he was someone else."

"Well, that's a new one!" laughed Diggs. "Thaddeus Flint with feelings. God must have dropped everything else He was doing to come up with that one!"

Flint glared at him silently for a moment, then turned back to Tojo. "Tell him what I said."

"I will, Thaddeus," replied the hunchback, heading off toward the ship.

"Three bullets and a pair of knives," mused Diggs as he watched Tojo walk away. "Do you think he'd have won?"

"In a walk," said Flint. He began walking over to the Bozo cage, stopped off long enough to give Stogie his pay, and was soon standing next to Monk and Batman as they erected the huge chain-link enclosure.

"Payday," he announced, handing an envelope to the winged Sabellian. "Don't spend it all in one place," he added sardonically.

"Got mine too?" asked Monk, taking his shirt off and mopping his face with it.

"Yeah," said Flint, handing it over. "You look a little short of breath, Jupiter."

"I'm getting a little old for this," panted Monk.

"Then why not have the robots do it?"

"Don't trust 'em," said Monk. "Besides, it's the only exercise I get."

"Except for throwing balls and falling into the water," remarked Flint.

"That's not exercise," replied Monk. "That's business."

"A subtle distinction." Flint lit a cigarette and offered one to Monk, who refused it and instead pulled a cigar out of his shirt pocket. "Did the galley robots make that?"

Monk nodded. "Same shitty tobacco as your cigarettes, but this way I remember not to inhale it."

"Take a five-minute break while you're smoking it, Jupiter."

"Any particular reason?"

"We're going to have a little talk."

"If it's about that fight in the gymnasium, talk to *him*," said Monk, jerking a thumb in Batman's direction. "All I was doing was defending myself."

"That is a lie," replied the Sabellian coldly.

"It's not about the fight in the gymnasium," said Flint. He turned to Batman. "Take a walk."

"Why should I?"

"Because what I want to talk about doesn't concern you."

"How do I know that?" demanded the Sabellian.

"You don't," said Flint. "Now, beat it."

Monk caught Batman's eye and nodded, and the Sabellian walked off toward the Midway. "Okay, Thaddeus," said the burly former lion tamer, stroking his long handlebar mustache. "What's on your mind?"

"You were the Dancer's closest friend back on Earth," said Flint.

"I suppose so," admitted Monk. "But that's kind of like being a starving tiger's least favorite dinner."

"I'm having a little problem figuring him out."

Monk laughed. "Lots of luck."

"For example," continued Flint, ignoring his remark, "you used to risk your life every night in the lion cage."

"I never looked at it that way."

"Neither does the Dancer," replied Flint, "but the fact remains that both of you faced the possibility of death every time you walked into the ring."

"If you say so . . ." sighed Monk.

"I do. But *you* never took any chances you didn't have to take. You always had a whip, and someone riding shotgun just outside the ring, and—"

"Hold it," said Monk. "You're making me sound like some kind of fucking coward."

Flint shook his head. "No. You were just a guy who tried to see to it that the odds were in his favor."

"Not all the time," protested Monk. "What about all the times I was in the cage with Batman?"

"The one night you went at it with all the wraps off, you both wound up in the hospital for a month," Flint reminded him. "Or maybe you forgot that you walked without a limp and could see out of your left eye before that night?" Monk offered no answer, and Flint continued. "So I thought maybe you could give me a little insight as to why the Dancer goes out of the way to stack the odds against himself."

"Why do you care?" asked Monk. "Forgive me for saying it, but sympathy was never your strong suit."

"He's pulling in more money than the rest of the carnival put together, and he's trying as hard as he can to get himself killed. I need to know why."

"He's always been kind of nuts."

"But he's never been suicidal."

"Who knows?" shrugged Monk. "I never watch him anymore."

"You must have heard what he's been doing lately," persisted Flint.

"Batman and me, we keep pretty much to ourselves," replied Monk. "I see bigger crowds at the specialty tent than there used to be, but that's all I know."

"The Dancer is taking on four and five guys at once."

"He's good enough to do it," said Monk with an approving nod. "How many has he killed so far?"

"Just one."

"Call *that* an act?" scoffed Monk. "He ought to get in the cage with Batman if he's looking for a little action."

"I have a feeling that we're not connecting," said Flint wryly. He tossed his cigarette onto the ground and stepped on it. "Break time's over."

"Not until that goldbricking bat gets back, it isn't," said Monk.

Flint smiled, shook his head, and walked back to the ship. He stopped by the mess hall for a sandwich, then went up to his room to ponder the Dancer's behavior and promptly fell asleep.

He awoke to the sound of bodies scurrying down the ship's corridors as his crew went out to meet the crowds that had flocked in from three nearby cities. His clothes were moist with perspiration, and so he showered and shaved before heading back to the Midway. Diggs had things well under control, and all Jiminy needed was a swaybacked horse and a fancy painted buckboard to complete the picture of an old-time huckster on the make. Monk was in the Bozo cage, and Batman seemed mildly irritated that the crowd was so large that he himself had almost no opportunity to throw balls at his partner. Julius Squeezer was trying to make himself useful by selling candy at one of the concession stands, but after Flint saw him sneeze on the food a couple of times he sent the green wrestler back to bed.

Finally he wandered over to the specialty tent, climbed up to his accustomed position in the lighting booth, and watched as Stogie and Schnoozle warmed up the crowd. Mr. Ahasuerus arrived just as the Dancer was being announced.

"Tojo tells me you had another problem today," remarked the blue man as the Dancer went through his preliminary routine.

"It's taken care of," said Flint, staring at the sharpshooter. "It least, it had damned well better be."

Finally the act reached the point the audience had been waiting for, and five Robodenians—bright-pink bipeds covered with scales—walked to the center of the ring. Tojo announced that they had been practicing with the guns they were carrying all afternoon, and that they would shortly be trying to win a million credits by killing the Dancer with these weapons.

Evidently the five beings had discussed the situation, for at a signal from one of them they began fanning out to form a large semicircle around the Dancer, who stood watching them, his arms folded loosely across his chest, a mildly amused smile on his handsome face.

"If he goes for a knife, I'll shoot him myself," muttered Flint.

Finally one of the Robodenians raised his pistol and pointed it at the Dancer, and the Dancer went into action, drawing both pistols and firing them as he whirled around to face his various targets.

"Son of a bitch!" said Flint in amazement. "He missed!"

The Dancer suddenly spun around, and a small red spot

appeared on his left shoulder. He kept firing, though, and in another instant all five Robodenians had been disarmed.

The crowd roared its applause as the Dancer tipped his hat, congratulated his opponents, and made his exit. Then Stogie was back in the ring, entertaining the Robodenians as they made their exit, while Flint and the blue man headed back to the ship. They found the Dancer sipping a glass of milk in the deserted mess hall.

"How bad are you hurt?" asked Flint, walking over and looking at the marksman's arm.

"Just a scratch," said the Dancer. "I'll be all right, Thaddeus."

"You're sure?" asked Mr. Ahasuerus solicitously. "I can call for the doctor."

The Dancer shook his head. "It ain't necessary."

"Well, if you had to miss," said Flint, obviously relieved, "at least you did it against a bunch of people who couldn't shoot straight."

The Dancer finished his milk. "I didn't miss."

"I heard seven shots," said Flint.

"Nine," corrected the Dancer.

"Then you missed *four* times. You're one goddamned lucky gunslinger."

"I didn't miss. They were blanks."

"I don't quite follow you," said Mr. Ahasuerus.

"*I* do," said Flint furiously. "And I just may bust his idiot head open for it!"

"Will someone please explain what happened?" persisted the blue man.

"Five men, five bullets," replied the Dancer. "The rest were blanks. I spun 'em just before the fight, so I wouldn't know where they were."

"But *why?*" asked Mr. Ahasuerus.

"To make it more interesting," said the Dancer.

"And did it?"

The Dancer shook his head unhappily. "No."

"Then," said Mr. Ahasuerus, "may we assume that we'll have no more contests involving blank shells?"

"Yep." The Dancer stared at a wall for a long moment, while Flint and the blue man exchanged troubled glances. "I'll have to find something else."

"I've been asking everyone else about you," said Flint at last, "so maybe it's time to get it straight from the horse's mouth. Just what the hell is it that you want, Dancer?"

"You wouldn't understand, Thaddeus."

"Try me."

"I want to be the best."

"You are," said Flint decisively.

"Being told isn't enough. I want to *know* it."

"How? By killing yourself?"

"By challenging myself."

"Isn't there some way other than what you have been doing in the specialty tent?" asked Mr. Ahasuerus gently.

"A few weeks ago, for just a second or two, I thought there was," said the Dancer quietly. "I was wrong."

"What happened a few weeks ago?" asked the blue man.

But the Dancer, oblivious to his question, was staring off into time and space, an expression of infinite sadness on his handsome face.

9.

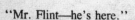

"Mr. Flint—he's here."

Flint reached over Priscilla's sleeping body and activated the intercom speaker on his night table.

"Tell him to keep his pants on," he said sleepily. "I'll be there in a couple of minutes." He ran his fingers through his disheveled hair. "What time is it, anyway?"

"A few minutes after noon," replied Mr. Ahasuerus' voice.

"Figures," grunted Flint. "That son of a bitch never did learn the difference between real time and carny time."

"Please, Mr. Flint," protested the blue man. "He's sitting right here in my office. He can hear every word."

"Good. Then tell him that we don't close up the show until sunrise."

Flint flicked off the intercom, got out of bed without disturbing Priscilla, quickly slipped into his clothes, and walked over to the bathroom, where he brushed his teeth and made a halfhearted attempt to comb his hair. Then he walked softly to the door, opened it, and a moment later was taking the elevator up to the blue man's office. As he entered, a small, rotund, reddish alien got to his feet.

"Mr. Flint, what a pleasure it is to see you again!"

"How's tricks, Kargennian?" muttered Flint, walking directly to his partner's coffee pot and pouring himself a cup.

"I trust you've been well," said Kargennian with polite formality.

"Until about ten minutes ago," replied Flint, flopping down on a couch and trying unsuccessfully to make himself comfortable. His gaze fell on his partner's latest acquisition, an abstract montage consisting primarily of bright-pink wire and yellow ferns, and he winced.

"I apologize," said Kargennian. "I had forgotten that you keep"—he paused disapprovingly—"rather unusual hours."

"It's okay," said Flint, turning back to Kargennian and deciding that he didn't notice much of an improvement. "Until this year you'd have pissed blood before you apologized to me for *anything*, so I guess we're even."

"What's past is past," said Kargennian coldly. "I was just telling Mr. Ahasuerus how pleased the Corporation is with your balance sheet for the last half year."

"Maybe you ought to tell the Dancer," said Flint. "He's the guy who's responsible."

"In point of fact, Billybuck Dancer is the prime reason for my visit."

"Shucks," said Flint sarcastically. "And I thought it was just because you liked to shoot the breeze with us."

"That too," said Kargennian, wondering why Flint always seemed to remind him of a bomb about to explode.

"Yes, sir," said Flint. "Things sure have changed since the days when you couldn't stand the sight of me."

"We're all working for the same team," said the round little alien emotionlessly. "Such personality conflicts as we may have had are inconsequential under the present circumstances."

"Yeah. Well, I guess money spoils everything sooner or later, even a lovely hatred like ours." Flint finished his coffee. "How about getting to the point, Kargennian? Ever since we heard you were stopping by, we've been making bets on what it is that you want."

"And what is your conclusion?" asked Kargennian, forcing a smile to his lips.

"Same as the last ten times. The Dancer's not for sale."

"I never thought he was."

"I thought you just said he was the reason you're here," noted Flint.

"He is." The rotund alien leaned forward, not quite able to mask his excitement. "We have received a most amazing proposition back at Corporate headquarters."

"Oh?"

"Have you ever heard of Darbeena?"

"It sounds like a laxative," remarked Flint, putting his feet up on a delicately carved hardwood coffee table.

"Isn't that a planet in the Albion Cluster?" interjected Mr. Ahasuerus.

"Correct," said Kargennian. "It is the home of a very unusual race, as violent in their way as the people of Earth."

"I'll assume that's a good thing to be," said Flint dryly.

"For the purpose of this proposition, it most definitely is," said Kargennian, ignoring Flint's undisguised animosity. "They have a culture that worships weaponry fully as much as yours does."

"I don't know that we actually *worship* it."

"Perhaps I used the wrong word," replied Kargennian. "But the fact remains that their history and cultures are as fully committed to firearms as your own. To this day, most of them carry hand weapons, as barbaric as the concept may seem."

"How much did they offer?" asked Flint.

"I beg your pardon?"

"That's the deal, isn't it?" he said. "Their champion against the Dancer?"

"I *knew* you would understand them!" said Kargennian. He paused for effect, then continued. "I've worked out the preliminary details with them. Each side will put up ten million credits, for a duel to the death!"

"But that's dreadful!" exclaimed Mr. Ahasuerus.

"That's all the money they could raise, and all we can afford to lose if worst comes to worst," apologized Kargennian.

"That is not what I am referring to," continued the blue man. "I am reluctantly willing to let Billybuck disarm his opponents in the specialty tent, but a duel to the death is out of the question." He paused, trying to control his emotions. "This is not what sentient beings do to one another!"

"We should have nothing to worry about," said Kargennian confidently. "I've seen Billybuck Dancer in action a number of times, and I can't imagine anyone ever defeating him."

"That is not the point!" protested Mr. Ahasuerus. "I will not stand idly by and be a party to murder!"

"I thought you would be happy with the proposition," said Kargennian, obviously bewildered.

"One of us is," said Flint. "Why don't you go on down to the mess hall for a while and let Mr. Ahasuerus and me discuss this in private?"

"There is nothing to discuss," said the blue man firmly.

"Fine," said Flint. "Then we'll talk about the weather." He turned to Kargennian. "Go on. We'll call you when we need you."

"But this is a chance to make ten million credits in a single evening, not to mention subsidiary rights!'' said Kargennian to the blue man. ''Think of what you're refusing!''

''Kargennian, you're about as subtle as an elephant in heat,'' said Flint. ''Will you please get the hell out of here and let me talk to my partner alone?''

''This was *my* idea!'' protested Kargennian. ''I really should remain and explain all of its implications.''

''There is only *one* implication that I am concerned with,'' said Mr. Ahasuerus.

''Kargennian!'' said Flint ominously.

The rotund little alien looked into Flint's eyes, sighed, shrugged, and walked out the door, which slid shut behind him.

''Well, Mr. Flint?'' said Mr. Ahasuerus, staring coldly across the office at him.

''Well, Mr. Ahasuerus.''

''I cannot condone premeditated murder,'' said the blue man firmly. ''What happened on Tilarba was tragic, but it was an accident. This is a totally different matter.''

''This is a unique situation,'' said Flint, picking up an alien artifact that his partner had set aside for use as an ashtry and studying it absently.

''We are doing very well as it is. We do not need the money.''

''You're going to find this hard to believe, but I don't give a damn about the money,'' answered Flint.

'' 'Hard' is an understatement,'' said Mr. Ahasuerus. ''I find it impossible to believe.''

Flint smiled wryly. ''I've already got more money than I ever dreamed of, and I haven't got a damned thing to spend it on. What do I need more for?''

''As you yourself have pointed out many times, you view it as a means of measuring success,'' retorted the blue man harshly. ''I, on the other hand, view dead bodies as a means of measuring not just failure, but immorality.''

''Why not look at it from the Dancer's point of view?'' suggested Flint.

''Because Billybuck Dancer is not a rational man.''

''He's not a rational blue skeleton,'' said Flint. ''There's a difference.''

''Come now, Mr. Flint. You yourself have remarked countless times that you consider him to be crazy.''

''Of course he's crazy,'' acknowledged Flint. ''So what? This is a whole different ball game from what's been going on lately.

He'll be fighting to win, and the competition will be hot enough so that he won't have to do anything stupid to give his opponent what he considers a fair chance.''

Mr. Ahasuerus shook his head. "No matter how you try to justify it, the end result is that someone is going to die.''

"People have been dying for eons.''

"That is not an answer,'' said the blue man.

"It's the best answer you're going to get. This is good for the Dancer, it's good for the Darbeenans, and it's good for business.''

"Murder is *never* good,'' replied Mr. Ahasuerus, the muscles in his face twitching as he tried to control his emotions.

"I agree,'' said Flint. "But murder implies an unwilling victim. Do you think you'll have to twist the Dancer's arm to get him to accept the fight?'' Mr. Ahasuerus glared at him but made no reply. "Do you think there aren't half a million Darbeenans hoping and praying right this minute that they'll be the one who is chosen to fight for their side?''

"And what if Billybuck dies?''

"He won't,'' said Flint confidently.

"But *if* he does?''

Flint shrugged. "Then he'll die rich and happy. There are worse things.''

The blue man shook his head gravely. "There is nothing worse than a meaningless death.''

Flint smiled a bittersweet smile. "I envy you for thinking so.'' He picked up his coffee cup, noticed that it was empty, and walked across the room to pour himself some more. "Why don't we call the Dancer up here and ask *his* opinion?''

"I already know what his opinion will be,'' replied Mr. Ahasuerus.

"You pride yourself on being a moral man,'' said Flint. "Isn't it immoral not to let him know the opportunity he's been presented with?''

"It would only frustrate him,'' said Mr. Ahasuerus, not without a note of compassion. "I will not allow him to accept the proposition.''

"Do my ears deceive me,'' said Flint with a smile, "or do I detect a note of totalitarianism in your voice?''

"He is not capable of making this decision rationally,'' replied the blue man.

"Well, if push comes to shove, neither are you.''

"I resent that remark, Mr. Flint,'' said Mr. Ahasuerus, stirring his coffee so vigorously that a goodly amount of it spilled out onto his desk.

"Resent away," said Flint. "The fact of the matter is that you're as single-mindedly committed to life as he is to death. What gives you the right to decide his fate based on your prejudices?"

The blue man shook his head in amazement. "I often wonder why your bed is never empty. Then I am subjected to your powers of persuasion, and I know." He took a deep breath and released it slowly. "However, this is not a debating society. Killing is *wrong*, and nothing you can say will make it right."

"All I say is that we should let the Dancer know what's going on."

"You insist?" asked Mr. Ahasuerus.

"I do."

"And if we do not tell him together, I presume you will tell him alone?"

"Yes."

The blue man sighed. "Then I shall summon him here. But I hope you know that the only change this will precipitate will be to make a very confused young man even more unhappy than he already is."

"Relax," said Flint, walking over to the communication console. "I'll do it for you."

He activated the intercom, tried without success to get a response from the Dancer's room, and then called the mess hall. Tojo answered, informed him that the Dancer was not there, and volunteered to hunt him up.

"I would imagine that Billybuck is in his room and simply did not bother to activate his intercom," declared the blue man.

"Makes sense," agreed Flint. "That means he should be here in a couple of minutes." He paused thoughtfully, then looked at his partner. "If you don't believe that I don't care about the money, you're never going to buy this next statement either—but I really don't like arguing with you, Mr. Ahasuerus. Let's call a truce and just keep quiet until the Dancer arrives."

They sat at opposite sides of the room, sipping their coffee, for the better part of five minutes. Then there was a knock at the door, and Mr. Ahasuerus opened it to reveal Tojo and the Dancer standing in the hall.

"What the hell are *you* doing here?" Flint asked the hunchback.

"You said to bring the Dancer up here as soon as I found him," replied Tojo.

"I said to *send* him up here," said Flint.

"I'm sorry," apologized the hunchback, turning to leave. "I must have misunderstood you."

"What the hell," said Flint. "As long as you're here, you might as well stick around. This isn't going to take all that long."

"But if I'm intruding—"

"Shut up and sit down," said Flint. "You've been with this carnival since before I bought it. You've got a right to put in your two cents' worth."

The blue man stared at Flint curiously, but said nothing.

"What's all this about, Thaddeus?" asked the Dancer, tipping his hat to his two employers and seating himself on an arm of one of the office's sturdier sofas.

"Kargennian's got a proposition for you, Dancer," said Flint.

"Who's Kargennian?"

"The Corporation guy—the one who looks like a little red butterball."

"I don't know him."

"Why should you?" muttered Flint. "You've only seen him twenty or thirty times." He shook his head, then continued. "He's got a pretty interesting offer from a planet called Darbeena. We've just been discussing whether to accept it or not."

"It don't make no difference to me where we go," said the Dancer.

"It might this time," said Flint. "It seems these Darbeenans have a lot in common with the National Rifle Association."

"What does that mean?"

"It means they carry guns, and they know how to use them." Suddenly the Dancer's face brightened, and he leaned forward eagerly. "They've offered us ten million credits if you'll go up against the best gunfighter on their planet."

"Love to," said the Dancer.

"There's a catch," said Flint. He paused for effect. "This is a fight to the death."

The Dancer laughed and slapped his leg. "Do you really mean it, Thaddeus?"

"I wouldn't kid you about something like this," replied Flint seriously.

"How soon do I get to do it?" asked the Dancer, barely able to contain his enthusiasm.

"First we've got to decide *if* you get to do it," said Flint.

"What are you talking about?"

"I'm talking about killing someone who's never done you any harm."

"That's a chance he takes. Besides, his people probably think he's gonna win."

"And the taking of a life doesn't disturb you?" asked Mr. Ahasuerus.

"He's gonna be trying to take *mine*, ain't he?" responded the Dancer.

"Not if we don't allow the fight to occur," said the blue man.

"Where's this here Kargennian guy?" asked the Dancer suddenly.

"Downstairs, in the mess hall," said Flint. "Why?"

"Thaddeus, you and Mr. Ahasuerus have always been good to me and treated me decent, but I been waiting all my life for something like this," said the Dancer without rancor. "If you don't go along with it, I'm gonna hunt up this butterball guy and make my own deal with him."

"Even if it means you can never come back?"

The Dancer nodded gravely. "Even so."

"You'd never see another human being again," Flint pointed out.

"This is more important," said the Dancer. "Besides, maybe I'll take Jiminy along. He can look as human as the next guy."

"Jiminy works for *us*," said Flint.

"Then I'll buy him off after I win," said the Dancer firmly.

"In other words, you plan to participate in this gunfight whether you do it as a member of the carnival or not?" asked Flint.

"I got to," said the Dancer. "Please believe me, Thaddeus: I don't want to hurt your feelings none, and I'd like to stay with the show—but this is what I was put here to do, and there ain't nothing gonna stop me from doing it."

Flint turned to the blue man. "Your witness," he said with a smile.

"I know Billybuck's feelings on the matter," replied Mr. Ahasuerus calmly. "I think what I would like now is some input from Tojo."

"From one bleeding heart to another," said Flint sarcastically.

"From one sensitive sentient entity to another," corrected Mr. Ahasuerus.

"He's just going to back you up."

"I'm sure he can think for himself," said the blue man.

"*How* sure?" demanded Flint suddenly.

"What are you driving at?" asked Mr. Ahasuerus.

"Do you have enough confidence in Tojo's sensitivity to let *him* make the decision?"

"Just a minute—!" stammered the hunchback.

"Yes, I do," replied the blue man firmly.

"Done," said Flint. He turned to Tojo. "Just for the record, had you heard anything about this gunfight before you came into the office?"

"No, but—"

"Then it's up to you."

"But I don't *want* it to be up to me!" protested Tojo.

"Well," said Flint easily, "nobody can have everything they want, can they?"

"It's not fair, Thaddeus!" continued Tojo.

"I know," said Flint softly, "but it's the only way we're going to keep peace aboard this ship."

"Dancer, say something!" demanded Tojo.

"Ain't nothing to say," replied the Dancer pleasantly. "I'm fighting no matter what you guys decide."

"Don't ask me to do this, Mr. Ahasuerus," pleaded the little hunchback, turning to the blue man.

"Mr. Flint and I have irreconcilable differences on this subject. I have confidence in your judgment and character; I will put my trust in them."

"But you're not a *Man!*" said Tojo, stammering so badly he could hardly force the words out. "Thaddeus is. He *knows*."

"What are you saying?" asked the blue man, blinking his narrow orange eyes very rapidly.

"That if the decision is mine, the Dancer is going to fight on Darbeena," said Tojo miserably.

"But *why?*" demanded Mr. Ahasuerus in disbelief.

"Because he's my friend, and I care for him."

"But a *gunfight . . .*"

"It's all he's lived for," said Tojo, "all he's ever wanted. If it will make him happy, then I want it too."

"Even if it means he must kill a Darbeenan?"

"I don't *know* any Darbeenans," replied the hunchback. "I hope he changes his mind, but if he doesn't, and the Darbeenan voluntarily faces him, then I can't tell him not to do it."

"And if the Darbeenan should win?" persisted the blue man.

"Not a chance," said the Dancer easily.

"Even if the Dancer loses, isn't it better to die doing what he thinks he was born to do than to live for however many years he's got left without once getting the chance?'' asked Tojo.

The blue man sank back in his chair, totally deflated.

"I gave my word," he said at last. "So be it."

"Thanks, Mr. Ahasuerus," said the Dancer, standing up and tipping his Stetson again. "You won't be sorry—you'll see."

"I am already sorry," said the blue man miserably.

"I'd better hop down to the mess hall and tell—what was his name again?—anyway, I'd better tell him that the fight's on." The Dancer ruffled Tojo's straight black hair with his hand, then left the office.

"Tojo, please wait outside," said Mr. Ahasuerus.

The hunchback climbed down off the couch he was sitting on and walked out into the corridor.

"Mr. Flint, that was an underhanded and deceitful thing to do," said the blue man, his eyes blazing. "You knew what he was going to say."

"Yes, I did," admitted Flint. "Your job is money; mine is people."

"It was a terrible burden to place on his shoulders," continued the blue man, his fingertips pressed so hard against the top of his desk that the color all but vanished from them.

"He's tougher than you think," said Flint. "He can bear up under it."

"Someone will die because of what you forced him to do," persisted the blue man, his tones cold and emotionless.

"Someone would have died anyway. You don't seriously doubt that Kargennian would have gone straight to the Dancer if we'd turned him down, do you?"

"I do not know," said Mr. Ahasuerus, his fury reflected in his lean, angular face. "All I know is that you have manipulated me into a position that is all but untenable, and it will be a long time before I can forgive you for it."

"I had no choice," replied Flint seriously. "The fight was going to take place with or without our blessing, and I knew that *I* was never going to persuade you to change your mind." He paused. "You know, I've seen five men killed in boxing rings back on Earth. It was tragic, and nobody wanted it to happen, but it didn't stop prizefights from taking place, and it didn't stop people from wanting to see them."

"Including you?" asked the blue man ironically.

"Including me."

Mike Resnick

"Am I to understand that you will actually *enjoy* watching this exercise in barbarism?"

"I'd never admit it to the Dancer," said Flint, "but yes, I would. Haven't you ever wondered if he's as quick as we think he is?"

Mr. Ahasuerus stared at him for a long moment. "Mr. Flint, we have worked together so closely and for so long that I occasionally forget just how alien we are from one another. I have nothing further to say to you today." He pressed a button, and the door opened. Flint shrugged and stepped into the corridor, and the door immediately slid shut behind him.

"Are you still here?" asked Flint, as he almost bumped into Tojo, who was leaning against one of the smooth, polished walls.

"I just wanted you to know that I figured it out," said the little hunchback.

"I don't know what you're talking about."

"I'm not deaf, and I'm not stupid, Thaddeus. You told me to *bring* the Dancer, not *send* him. My guess is that you must have been arguing with Mr. Ahasuerus and couldn't persuade him to let the fight go on. Grilling the Dancer like that was just camouflage."

"You always *were* a bright little bastard," said Flint. He sighed. "It was the only way. *You* know he's got to go through with it."

"Yes," answered Tojo. "I wish it wasn't so, but it is. I have just one question."

"Shoot."

"Why did you choose *me?*"

"I'm sorry I had to put you through it," said Flint sincerely. "We've got maybe a hundred people on the ship who would have voted for the fight, but you're the only one I could trust to convince the skeleton that you wanted it for the right reason, and the only one whose opinion I could ever get him to buy." He paused. "It was a shitty thing to do to both of you." He looked as if he wanted to say something more, then seemed to think better of it.

"You didn't use to feel bad about doing things like this when I first met you," remarked Tojo, shuffling his feet against the matted floor of the narrow passageway.

"Maybe I'm getting older," said Flint. "We've come a long way since you and I first hooked up." He began walking down the corridor, heading to the bank of elevators at the end of it. "Try not to be too mad, Tojo," he said when they were about halfway there.

"I'm not mad, Thaddeus. I'm sorry it had to be such an unpleasant scene, but I'm flattered that of all the people on the ship, you felt I had the best chance of convincing Mr. Ahasuerus." He paused and looked up at Flint. "There was a time, not so many years ago, when I would have deeply resented being used like this, even though it was something that had to be done. I guess we've both gotten older."

"I guess." Flint increased his pace, quickly reached the elevators, and pressed a glowing red-gold button to summon one.

"Anyway, it's been a long time since you've done anything to make me mad," concluded Tojo, catching up with him. "You're my oldest friend," he added, "and you and the carny are the only family I've got."

"Thank you," said Flint. "I suppose when you get right down to cases, you're the only friend *I've* got, too."

Tojo smiled. "What about Mr. Ahasuerus, and all the girls who keep finding their way to your room?"

"Girls come and go; *you* stay," said Flint. "As for Mr. Ahasuerus, I think the only killing he'd approve of right about now is mine." Suddenly he gave Tojo a friendly slap on the shoulder. "Come on down to the mess hall and I'll buy you a beer."

"I'd like that, Thaddeus," said the little hunchback. "I really would."

"You've got a funny expression on your face," noted Flint, as the elevator door slid open. "How come?"

"In the twelve years I've known you, that was the first time you've ever apologized to me for anything."

For just a moment Flint looked his surprised. "Well," he said at last, with an awkward attempt at flippancy, "stick with me for another twelve years, kid, and it just might happen again."

"Yes, Thaddeus," said Tojo, forcing a resigned smile to his homely face as he followed Flint into the elevator.

10.

One by one, the Dancer called them out,
One by one, the Dancer mowed them down.
One by one, the Dancer won each bout,
One by one, the Dancer kept his crown.
With guns or knives
He'd end their lives.
One by one, he faced each roustabout,
One by one, he terrorized each town.
One by one, the Dancer called them out,
One by one, the Dancer mowed them down.

—from "The Ballad of Billybuck Dancer"

"It sort of reminds you of a hockey stadium, doesn't it?" remarked Flint as he looked around the huge arena.

"It's certainly impressive," agreed Tojo.

They walked the circumference of the ring area, getting the feel of the place, as Kargennian, who had flown in for the event, was going over camera placements with the native Darbeenan crew.

"Must be thirty thousand seats," said Flint. He waved to a number of early arrivals, who simply stared at him. "They tell me that a couple of thousand hard-core bloodbath fans have been waiting in line since yesterday afternoon."

"I can't imagine why," said Tojo.

"Same reason they go to the Indy 500," said Flint with a smile, "only here they don't pretend it's a sporting event."

A Darbeenan—short, lithe, red-skinned, and humanoid—approached them and barked something in its native language.

Flint pointed to his ear and shook his head, to indicate that he didn't understand, and the Darbeenan activated its translating device.

"You are Mr. Flint?" it asked.

"Right."

"Haven't you been supplied with a translator?"

"Yeah, someone gave me one a couple of hours ago," replied Flint. "I think I left it in the press box after I gave out a couple of interviews."

"You really should be more careful with your equipment."

"Is that what you've come over here to tell me?"

"No," said the Darbeenan. "Allow me to introduce myself. My name is Quanlichot, and I am the assistant manager of this stadium."

"Pleased to meet you," said Flint. "And this is Tojo. He's our announcer."

"Hello," said Quanlichot distractedly. He turned back to Flint. "I am afraid we have a problem in the making, Mr. Flint."

"Oh?"

The Darbeenan nodded. "When we agreed to let you set up your games and exhibits just outside the stadium, I'm afraid we didn't know quite what you had in mind." He paused. "Mr. Flint, some of those so-called games are out-and-out dishonest!"

"That's quite a serious allegation," said Flint calmly.

"It is the truth."

"Well, Quan—you don't mind if I call you Quan, do you?—if you can prove a game is rigged, I'll close it up. Otherwise, they stay open."

The Darbeenan shook his head vigorously. "That is out of the question," he said. "You've set up more than sixty game booths, and the crowds will be arriving in the next few minutes."

"Then perhaps you ought to just sit back and relax and let everyone have a good time," suggested Flint easily.

"The games must be shut down right now," said Quanlichot firmly.

"You're sure?"

"Absolutely."

"Well," said Flint with a shrug, "you're the boss. Do me a favor, though, will you?"

"What?"

"See that ugly little red butterball over there with your camera crews?"

"You mean Kargennian?"

"Right. Tell him we're leaving."

"We?" repeated Quanlichot. "You mean Tojo and yourself?"

"I mean me and the Dancer," said Flint. "My man doesn't set foot into this arena if you close up my games."

"But he's due to be on worldwide video in two hours! All the arrangements have been made!"

"That's hardly *my* concern."

"You're bluffing!"

"You're welcome to think so," replied Flint. He turned toward an exit. "Come on, Tojo."

They had walked about ten paces when the Darbeenan called after them, and Tojo saw the trace of a smile flash briefly across Flint's lips just before he stopped.

"Can't we discuss this?" asked Quanlichot.

"I'm always open to discussion," said Flint reasonably. "Tojo, take a walk."

The little hunchback nodded, and made another tour of the arena, stopping to watch the construction of the ring where Julius Squeezer would be wrestling the Darbeenan champion as a preliminary entertainment. When he returned a few moments later Quanlichot was gone and Flint was standing by himself.

"Well?" asked Tojo.

"He didn't seem to mind his people being fleeced so much after I slipped him a couple of thousand credits," remarked Flint wryly. "I guess death and taxes aren't the only constants in the universe."

"Do you think we should check on the Dancer?"

"I did that about half an hour ago," said Flint. "He's in his dressing room, telling Jiminy what it was like in Dodge City back in 1875."

"He didn't seem excited?" persisted Tojo.

"Not as far as I could tell," answered Flint. "Funny, isn't it? I thought he'd be psyching himself up like a football player on Super Bowl day."

Tojo smiled. "You still don't understand him, Thaddeus. Facing an armed opponent is a natural function to him, like breathing in and out. He psyches himself up to talk to people, or play cards with Diggs, or help set up a game booth."

"Then why did you think he'd be excited?"

"From eagerness. He's waited a long time for this day—ever since he had that gunfight in South America."

"Did *he* tell you he fought down there?" asked Flint, surprised.

"So did you," answered Tojo.

"Yeah, but I never believed it. It just made a nice story."

"It's true."

Flint shrugged. "So he's going for a second notch on his gun instead of a first."

"Let's hope he gets it," said Tojo devoutly. "Those are wicked-looking weapons the Darbeenans carry."

"Kargennian was telling me about them this afternoon," said Flint, as larger groups of Darbeenans began entering the arena. "As near as I can make out, they're like the ray guns we used to see on the covers of old pulp magazines."

"That might mean they don't have to be as accurate," said Tojo, frowning. "Just point toward an area and wiggle your hand."

"Pointing toward areas is easy. Pointing toward the Dancer when he's going for his gun is a little harder."

"I hope so."

They stood and watched the seats filling up for a few moments, and then Kargennian approached them.

"Everything seems to be going smoothly, Mr. Flint," said the rotund alien. "The stadium is sold out, we estimate that more than two hundred million Darbeenans will be watching via video, and I'm just on the verge of closing a deal to display holographic films of the event throughout five different planetary systems." He paused, looking quite pleased with himself. "Yes, everything is working out perfectly!"

"Let's just hope the right side wins," said Flint.

"Surely you're not worried, Mr. Flint!" said Kargennian. "Believe me, the Dancer is the best gunfighter I've ever seen."

"Have you seen the guy he's got to face?" asked Flint.

"No," admitted Kargennian. He turned away uncomfortably and pretended to count the house. "Has Mr. Ahasuerus changed his mind?" he asked at last.

"No. He's still in the ship, pouting."

Kargennian shook his head. "It's a pity he can't see the potential in this situation."

"I think he might say the same thing about us," replied Flint wryly.

"He's a competent administrator," said Kargennian, passing right over the remark, "but limited—very limited. He simply cannot see the Big Picture. I suppose that's why he hasn't risen higher up the Corporate ladder after all these years."

"I suppose," said Flint noncommittally.

The little alien pulled a notebook out of his colorful one-piece suit. "What else did I want to ask you?" he mumbled, thumbing through the pages. "Ah, yes—Max Bloom. Am I to understand he will not be performing tonight?"

"He's under the weather," replied Flint. "We left him with the ship."

"From what I have been able to determine from his work record, he seems to miss an inordinate number of performances."

"He's seventy-five years old," said Flint. "What the hell do you expect?"

"Nevertheless—"

"Now you listen to me, hotshot!" said Flint irritably. "Stogie came out here with us and he's worked his ass off for us, and until you build a retirement home for over-the-hill vaudeville comics from Earth, he'll stay with us and work when he can and stay in bed when he has to. You got that?"

"Certainly," said Kargennian, taken aback. "I only meant to say that—"

"I know what you meant to say," interrupted Flint. He took a deep breath and released it explosively. "Jesus! I liked it a hell of a lot better when you and I were enemies. Now why don't you go tend to your cameramen and leave me alone?"

Kargennian glared at Flint for a long moment, then turned on his heel and walked back to the cluster of Darbeenan video technicians who were gathered around the wrestling ring.

"He's not pouting," said Tojo.

"What?" asked Flint distractedly.

"Mr. Ahasuerus," replied Tojo. "He feels very deeply about what we're doing here."

"I know," said Flint. "I shouldn't have said what I did. But how the hell can you explain something like that to a clown like Kargennian?" He looked at the little alien, who had climbed into the wrestling ring to set up some camera angles, and smiled. "Maybe Julius and I could take on Kargennian and one of the local boys in a tag-team match. I'd sure love an excuse to get my hands around that little bastard's neck."

"I don't think Kargennian would approve of it," said Tojo, returning his smile.

"No," said Flint wistfully. "Probably not." He heard a loud grating sound and turned in the direction from which it had come. "What's going on?"

"Protective shielding for the audience," replied Tojo as one huge wall of a transparent, plastic-like substance after another was lowered into place around the arena. "Just in case some bullets go astray. I asked one of the Darbeenans about it a little while ago."

"Makes sense," acknowledged Flint. "I suppose if we had anyone except the Dancer working for us, we'd have killed a couple of dozen spectators by now." He stared at it, squinting. "That stuff's pretty thin. Will it really stop a bullet?"

"They say it will," answered Tojo. "I suppose they ought to know."

"Where are you going to be standing?" asked Flint.

"Once they disassemble the wrestling ring—I gather it breaks down in just a minute or so—the gunfighters will face off in the center of the arena, and I'll be over there"—he pointed—"by those box seats."

"Yeah?" said Flint, a note of concern creeping into his voice. "Well, if this guy the Dancer is facing looks like he might actually be able to wiggle his hand like you say, make sure you hit the deck."

"I will, Thaddeus."

"I'm not kidding."

"I know," said Tojo. "I appreciate your concern."

"I just don't want all that money we spent on that gold whistle to go down the drain," replied Flint gruffly. He turned as he saw Jiminy approaching. "Aren't you supposed to be selling Mystical Magical Rejuvenation Pills or something like that?" he asked, grateful for the interruption.

"I'm all sold out," replied Jiminy, looking inordinately pleased with himself. "Besides, I promised Billybuck I'd watch the contest."

"I saw you talking to him half an hour ago," said Flint. "Are you trying to tell me you sold out your whole stock since then?"

Jiminy grinned and pulled out a thick wad of bills. "I *told* you I was good at this kind of thing."

"We sure could have used you back in Vermont," said Tojo admiringly.

"Wish I'd been there," replied Jiminy pleasantly. "Well, where do we sit?"

"They gave me a box over there across from the wrestling ring," said Flint. He looked around and saw that the stands were almost full. "Come on. We might as well go there now." He turned to Tojo. "See you later."

"Okay," said the hunchback.

"And remember what I told you."

"I will, Thaddeus."

Flint and Jiminy walked across the floor of the arena, found an almost invisible door in the transparent barrier, and were sitting in the box a moment later.

"Sure is a nice crowd," said Jiminy. "There's got to be five times as many people here as we could squeeze into the tent."

"That's why we agreed to it," replied Flint. "How's the Rigger doing?"

"He says to tell you that it's like taking candy from babies."

"I hope he remembers that most of these babies wear guns," said Flint, looking at some of his neighbors.

"They seem like a pleasant enough batch of people," said Jiminy.

"Let's just hope they don't get ugly after Julius and the Dancer beat their heroes."

"You think they might?" asked Jiminy, alarmed.

"It's been known to happen," replied Flint. "I can remember hearing about some full-scale riots that started at South American soccer games." He smiled at Jiminy's sudden consternation. "Don't worry about it. You can always change into a Darbeenan if you have to."

"Change in front of them?" said Jiminy, genuinely shocked. He shook his head vigorously. "Believe me, they're much more likely to tear me limb from limb for being a Jimorian than an Earthman."

"The worst of two possible worlds," commented Flint ironically.

Suddenly the lights dimmed and an unseen band began playing very atonal music on instruments that Flint couldn't identify. Then a spotlight raced across the arena and came to rest on Tojo, who was standing behind a microphone. He blew his whistle twice, then activated his translating device and began speaking.

"Would you like me to translate for you?" asked Jiminy when he noticed that Flint had no device of his own.

"Not necessary," replied Flint. "I know what he's saying."

Tojo spoke for a few minutes, then paused as another spotlight hit Kargennian and the little alien stood up and took a long, lingering bow. The light then sought out his Darbeenan counterpart on the far side of the arena, the red-skinned humanoid bowed even lower and longer than Kargennian, and suddenly the building was dark again.

A moment later a cheer began building through the crowd, and Flint knew that the Darbeenan wrestler must be making his

way to the ring. The spotlight came on and found him when he
had completed half his journey and followed him the rest of the
way, as the screams built to an ear-shattering crescendo. Then
Julius Squeezer entered the arena, wrapped in a gold satin robe,
and approached the ring amid polite applause.

"What the hell is that on the back of his robe?" asked Flint.

"An ad for the pills we're selling," replied Jiminy with a
smile. "Billybuck told me that it's quite common on Earth."

"He's seen too many second-rate fighters and bad movies,"
commented Flint. Then he shrugged. "What the hell—if it'll sell
one extra bottle, why not?"

The two wrestlers removed their robes and moved to the
center of the ring, where a Darbeenan referee issued instructions,
first through a translator to Julius, then in his native tongue to
the huge green muscleman's opponent.

"Well," remarked Flint, "I'd say Julius has a good hundred
and fifty pounds on him."

"True," said Jiminy, as the wrestlers circled each other, then
reached out their hands tentatively. "But the Darbeenan looks
very quick."

"He'd better be," said Flint confidently. "A ring's a hell of a
hard place to hide."

Suddenly the Darbeenan grabbed Julius Squeezer's outstretched
hand, slipped under a brawny arm, and twisted sharply. The green
giant spun through the air and fell heavily to the canvas as the
crowd screamed its approval.

Julius was on his feet in an instant, but as he lunged for his
smaller opponent his incredibly powerful hands closed only on
empty air, and he received a swift kick in the stomach for his
trouble.

"It's gonna be a long night," muttered Flint.

"If Julius can just get hold of him!" said Jiminy plaintively.

"Not tonight," said Flint, as the Darbeenan ducked under
Julius again and brought him to the floor with a leg lock. "It's
like watching a rhinoceros trying to run down a sheepdog."

The spectacle continued for another five minutes, with Julius
receiving a kick or a chop every time he tried to enfold the
Darbeenan in his massive arms. His movements became slower
and slower, his chest rose and fell heavily, and finally his
opponent saw an opening, struck like a snake, and encircled the
huge green wrestler's head and neck in an intricate grip that had
him unconscious within ten seconds.

Flint opened the transparent door and walked quickly to the

ring as the Darbeenan's hand was being raised in victory to thunderous applause. He climbed up the steps and was at Julius Squeezer's side just as the green muscleman was regaining consciousness. The wrestler was disoriented for a moment, then realized what had happened.

"I'm sorry, Thaddeus," he said as Flint led him from the ring to some scattered applause. "I don't know what happened."

"It's okay," said Flint, escorting him to the door that led to the dressing rooms. "You'll get him next time."

"I doubt it," said the big alien with disarming honesty. "But if you want me to try, I will."

"Take a shower and get some rest," said Flint. "We'll talk about it later."

"I'm really sorry," said Julius Squeezer again. "I've lost before, but never like *that*."

"You just weren't ready for him," said Flint soothingly. "You're still the best goddamned wrestler I've ever seen."

"Do you mean it?"

"Would I lie to you?" said Flint. "Now get yourself fixed up. I've got to get back to my seat."

"Yes, you would," said Julius Squeezer.

"Yes I would *what?*"

"Yes, you would lie to me. And I thank you for it." The green alien turned and went into his dressing room.

By the time Flint had rejoined Jiminy in the box, the stadium crew had disassembled the ring, and now the crowd was stirring restlessly, anticipating the main event.

"How is he?" asked Jiminy.

"He'll be all right."

"He just wasn't fast enough."

"Let's hope it's not an omen of things to come," said Flint, fixing his eyes on the empty floor of the arena.

The tension built and finally an official-looking Darbeenan walked over to Tojo and said something. The little hunchback nodded, waited until the official had returned to the stands, and then blew his golden whistle once again.

The house lights, which had been turned up after the wrestling match, were once again dimmed, and Tojo began speaking into the microphone. He droned on for a few minutes, telling the audience the histories of the two participants, and of how Kargennian and his counterpart had put the contest together. Finally there was the Darbeenan equivalent of a drumroll from the hidden band, and Billybuck Dancer, dressed in his most worn-out faded denim pants and shirt, entered the arena from the north end of the building. There was no scattered applause this time, just silence as the crowd studied this innocuous-looking killer.

Then Tojo spoke again, and a Darbeenan, clad in silver and blue, entered from the south end. This time the ovation was so loud that the entire stadium literally shook from the vibrations.

"What's his name?" asked Flint, staring at the lithe, confident red gunfighter.

"I'm not quite sure," replied Jiminy, "the crowd was making so much noise. But it sounded like Dacklan." He turned and said something to the Darbeenan sitting next to him, thanked him politely for his answer, and turned back to Flint. "I was right: Dacklan."

Tojo said something else, and the two gunmen, who had been coached by Kargennian and his counterpart, approached each other. Dacklan held his arm out in a salute, and the Dancer touched the brim of his hat with his fingers. Then Tojo spoke once more, and the Dancer and Dacklan backed away from each other until the distance between them was about forty feet.

Tojo walked to the stands, opened a door, and was handed a small mechanism by one of the officials. He then returned to the microphone and said something further.

"It's a type of metronome," explained Jiminy. "They are to draw on the fifth note."

"I know," said Flint.

"I thought you couldn't speak—"

"It was my idea," interrupted Flint, staring intently at the two combatants.

Tojo held the metronome up and activated it, and a musical chime was heard throughout the suddenly silent arena. Another second, another chime, and the Dancer's fingers, long and lean, snaked down toward his holster, while Dacklan's small tense hand was poised over his intricate weapon.

Two more chimes.

Damn it! thought Flint. *He's too relaxed!*

Then came the fifth chime and the sudden explosion of a gunshot, and Dacklan flew backward and fell heavily to the ground, his hand still on his weapon, his weapon still in its holster.

The crowd, which had been silent with suspense, remained

silent with shock, while the Dancer twirled his pistol once and replaced it in his holster. He looked at Tojo expectantly, and suddenly the little hunchback came to life and began speaking again. Finally, after almost a full minute, perhaps two hundred of the thirty thousand Darbeenans in the stadium applauded. The Dancer, looking slightly morose, tipped his hat and walked to his dressing room.

"Well, that's it," said Flint, belatedly noticing that all of the carnival's human contingent except Monk had entered the building to watch the gunfight. "I sure as hell hope these jokers are good losers."

A team of eight Darbeenans, marching like an honor guard, walked onto the floor of the arena with a brass litter and began transferring Dacklan's body to it, while Tojo made some form of closing speech and turned off the microphone.

The crowd milled about, seemingly unsure of what to do next, but displaying no hostility toward the humans, and finally the band music was piped in again.

"Nobody seems to have figured out what to do after the finale," remarked Flint. "They need someone like Stogie."

"I think they were probably planning on carrying Dacklan around the ring on their shoulders just about now," answered Jiminy.

"Well," said Flint, getting to his feet, "I'm sure Kargennian's going to be collecting the money, so let's you and me go collect Tojo and the Dancer and head back to the ship. It's been a long day."

He walked to the transparent door, with Jiminy close behind him, strode onto the floor of the arena, called to Tojo, left through another door, and made his way down the long, winding corridor leading to the Dancer's dressing room. He slowed his pace enough for Tojo to join them before he got to the door, then knocked loudly.

There was no answer.

"He couldn't have gotten lost," muttered Flint, knocking again. When there was still no response, he opened the door and entered the room, followed by Tojo and Jiminy.

The Dancer was sitting on a table, staring at the dull-gray wall, tears running down his face.

"Look, Dancer," said Flint gently, "I know you feel bad about this, but it was a fair contest."

"It wasn't no contest at all," said the Dancer softly.

"What are you talking about?" demanded Flint.

The young sharpshooter turned his tortured eyes to Flint. "Next time I want to face four of 'em at once," he said, and his expression reminded Flint of nothing more than a child who has waited all year for Christmas and unwrapped a lump of coal.

11.

————◆————

"I've run through my competition,"
Said the Dancer, still feeling that yen.
"I'd much rather suffer perdition,
Than never hit leather again."

"So hunt up the best,
Put me to the test,
Let's have it out once and for all.
My hands they are steady,
I'm rarin' and ready,
I won't be the first one to fall."

—from "The Ballad of Billybuck Dancer"

Flint walked into the galley, took a large pot of coffee from one of the robots, and made his way through the crowded mess hall to his usual corner table, where he found Tojo, Diggs, and Jiminy already eating breakfast.

"I hope I'm not intruding," he said caustically.

"If you see another empty table, I'll take it," said Diggs, stuffing another forkful of artificial omelet into his mouth before looking up. "I guess everyone got hungry at the same time."

"I can't imagine why," said Flint, looking distastefully at Diggs' plate.

"You're in a great mood today, aren't you?" said Diggs. "I should think you'd be a little more cheerful on the day after your boy won his gunfight and made you ten million credits."

"Two million," Flint corrected him.

"What's all this I've been hearing about ten, then?" persisted Diggs, chewing noisily.

"Five for the Corporation, one for the Dancer, and four for the carny. Half of the four is mine."

"Would the Corporation have paid five million credits if the Dancer had lost?" asked Diggs.

"What do *you* think?" said Flint with an ironic smile.

"Me? I think that when Kargennian finally dies, you're going to need a crowbar to pry his fingers loose from the first penny he ever made." He pushed his plate away and cleaned his fingers fastidiously with a paper napkin. "He's still around, you know."

"Who?"

"Kargennian. I saw him going into your partner's office about an hour ago." An alien crew member walked by with a foul-smelling green-and-blue concoction, and Diggs wrinkled his nose.

"That'll just make Mr. Ahasuerus' day," commented Flint, an amused grin on his face. "The little bastard's probably setting up a distribution network for the films of the fight." He looked around the mess hall. "I see the Dancer hasn't come down yet."

"I hope he's all right," said Tojo, carefully spreading artificial margarine on an artificial roll.

"Why shouldn't he be?" asked Diggs. "He really looked sharp last night—kind of like John Wayne and Gary Cooper and Clint Eastwood all rolled into one."

"I stopped by his room this morning," volunteered Jiminy, who had not eaten any food, but seemed to have developed the same enthusiasm for orange juice that Mr. Ahasuerus had for coffee. "He's pretty much the same as usual."

"That means he's sitting in the dark, staring at a wall," chuckled Diggs.

"Exactly," replied Jiminy seriously.

Stogie, dressed in pajamas and a tattered terrycloth bathrobe, entered the mess hall just then, with his schnauzer tucked under his arm.

"Come on over and have a seat, Max," called Diggs, shouting to be heard above the din created by the untranslated alien voices, and the ancient comic made his way carefully to the table.

"I thought you were supposed to be in bed," said Flint.

"I had to walk Schnoozle," replied the ancient comic, as the little dog twisted in his grasp, eager to see what was on the table. "Besides, I get lonely staying in my room all day."

"You start disobeying Fuzzy-Wuzzy's orders and you're likely to spend even more time there," said Flint.

"He's a nice guy, Thaddeus," protested Stogie, accepting a piece of Tojo's roll and feeding it to Schnoozle, who gulped it down happily. "But what the hell does a big yellow caterpillar know about taking care of human beings?"

"He's the only doctor we've got," said Flint.

"He'd never seen a bone in his life until he came to work for us," chimed in Monk, who was sitting a few tables away with Batman. "He's the reason I walk with a limp."

"You're having breakfast with the reason you walk with a limp," said Flint. He looked at Monk and the Sabellian. "Is there some reason why you two are wearing yellow scarves around your necks, or am I going to wish I hadn't asked?"

"*You're* sitting with the reason for it," replied Monk.

"Oh? Who?"

"Him," said Monk, jerking a thumb in Jiminy's direction. "Every time he gets shook up he starts looking like Batman, so I told Batman to wear a scarf so I could tell them apart."

"And *you* think he looks like Monk?" asked Flint, turning to Batman.

"Occasionally," replied the Sabellian.

"A shrink could have a field day with those two," said Flint, turning back to his companions. "Seriously, Max—how *are* you feeling today?"

"Old," said Stogie. "Old and tired. I think Schnoozle and me are having a race to see who keels over first. He's thirteen, you know; not much time left for either of us." He petted the little dog's head. "I hope to God I outlast him. He wouldn't know what to do if he was still around here after I die. Would you, Schnoozle?" He smiled as the schnauzer licked his wrinkled face, then looked up. "You know, the poor little son of a bitch hasn't had a girlfriend in six or seven years."

"He's got a lot of company," said Diggs sardonically. "Thaddeus is a monopolist, in case you hadn't noticed." He looked at Flint and shook his head in puzzlement. "I can't imagine why. You ain't as ugly as Tojo, but you're no Errol Flynn, either."

"I think the current standard of comparison is Robert Redford," offered Tojo.

"What's your secret, Mr. Flint?" asked Jiminy with a smile.

"The two greatest aphrodisiacs in the universe," answered Flint easily. "Money and power." He paused. "A hell of a lot of rhinos could have kept their horns if people had just looked at things the way they are, instead of the way they'd like them to be."

"Money I'll grant you," admitted Diggs. "But what's this power crap? You're just a carny owner."

"I can fire you," said Flint. "Can *you* fire *me*?" He didn't wait for an answer. "On a carny ship, that's all the power there is."

"How about firing *me*?" said Stogie, only half jokingly. "Then Schnoozle and me can go home to die on a *real* world, one with only one moon, and people who don't look like nightmares, and air that doesn't tire you out just from breathing it."

"Don't be silly, Max," said Flint. "You're just feeling gloomy because you're sick."

"Or the other way around," said Stogie.

"I can't imagine why anyone would want to go back to Earth," said Diggs. "There's races we haven't even dreamed of up here, and each of 'em just waiting to be fleeced."

"Earth's my home," said Stogie stubbornly.

"It's mine, too," replied Diggs. "All the more reason never to see it again. Too many attachments back there, too many things to hold a man down. We're freaks, Max—you and me and Monk and the rest; that's why we're carnies in the first place." The amusement vanished from his face. "It's better to put temptation out of the way and just stay with the show."

"I wasn't always a carny," said Stogie.

"Don't tell us again how you appeared on the same bill with the Andrews Sisters," moaned Diggs in mock anguish.

"Well, I did," said the old comic defensively. "And Bert Lahr, too," he added. "And once I had a part in a Laurel and Hardy film. It wasn't just a walk-through, either."

"We've heard all that before," said Diggs.

"Well, fuck you, Rigger!" exploded Stogie. "I'm seventy-five years old and I'm dying and I haven't *got* any new stories to tell!"

Schnoozle, sensing his master's distress, bared his teeth and began growling at Diggs.

"Hey!" snapped Flint suddenly. "Let's everyone calm down, or I'm going to repossess my table. I came down here to relax."

"I'm sorry, Thaddeus," said Stogie, stroking Schoozle to calm him down. "Just tell him to stop picking on me."

"That's just the way he is, Max," said Flint. He turned and

stared directly into Diggs' eyes. "But if he does it again before I get up to leave, he's going to wish he hadn't." He paused. "Is that clear?"

Diggs nodded, looking like a schoolchild who had just been scolded by his teacher. As he did so, the Dancer entered the room. The alien games workers gave him a standing ovation as he walked over to Flint's table, and finally he tipped his hat in acknowledgment of their plaudits.

"Mind if I sit down?" he asked.

"Be my guest," said Flint. "You know, that was more applause than you got last night."

"That's 'cause they didn't see how easy it was," said the Dancer.

"I hear you whipped him good," said Stogie.

The Dancer looked at him expressionlessly, but made no reply.

"Talkative as ever," muttered the comic, and turned his attention to his schnauzer.

"I saw Julius in the gymnasium this morning," remarked Jiminy, trying to break the uncomfortable silence.

"Is he feeling any happier?" asked Flint.

"I think *determined* is more the word," said the Jimorian. "He had put away his weights, and was working on agility exercises. He looked pretty serious about it."

"The picture of an agile three-hundred-pound green lizard is a little more than my mind can take this early in the day," commented Flint.

"At least *his* opponent put up a fight," said the Dancer softly.

"He did more than put up a fight," said Flint, refilling his coffee cup. "He beat the shit out of him."

"Still . . ."

"Stop feeling so goddamned sorry for yourself. You're a hero."

"I don't feel like one."

"Just the same," continued Flint, not without a trace of resentment, "long after the rest of us are gone and forgotten, you'll still be a household name."

"You really think so, Thaddeus?" asked the Dancer.

Flint nodded. "They'll make up songs about you, and never get the facts quite right. Little six-armed alien kids will run home crying because their friends won't give them a turn at pretending to be Billybuck Dancer. Hell, they'll probably even build a statue to you somewhere. It won't look like you, but at least it'll be there. They're not going to build any statues of Thaddeus Flint.''

"I wish I could do something to deserve it," said the Dancer unhappily.

Flint threw up his hands in exasperation. "You're just not going to be happy until I hunt up someone who can kill you!"

"Ain't nobody who can," said the Dancer confidently.

"Then what's your problem?"

"You just ain't never gonna understand, Thaddeus." The Dancer sighed and stared off into space.

Flint looked at him for a moment, then sighed and shook his head. "You know, they *will* write a song about him someday." He paused. "What a waste."

"Well," said Diggs, rising to his feet, "I've got to get to work."

"What work?" said Flint. "We're taking off in four hours and the games are all loaded on the ship."

"That was a polite lie, Thaddeus," said Diggs sardonically. "The truth of the matter is that I'm getting a little sick and tired of listening to all these people talking about how they want to die."

"They're talking about death," stammered Tojo. "It's not the same thing."

"Yeah? Well, then it's just not different enough for my taste."

Diggs bussed his plate and walked out of the mess hall.

"I hope he's not too upset," said Tojo.

"He'll get over it as soon as he can't scare up a card game anywhere else," replied Flint. "Then he'll be back, all friendly and smiling."

"I think I'm getting ready to take a shot at playing him," said Jiminy.

"Watch yourself," said Flint. "Playing cards with Diggs isn't exactly the same as selling snake oil. In this case, the snake'll be dealing."

"Still, as long as I'm in the persona of a Western pitchman, I ought to see how I measure up across a gaming table."

Flint shrugged. "You're a grown-up. I'm not going to tell you how to run your life." He smiled. "And after he beats you, you can always change into something else. A bartender, maybe."

"I've been meaning to talk about that with you," said Jiminy.

"Changing the way you look?"

Mike Resnick

"In a manner of speaking," answered Jiminy uneasily. "I hate to complain . . ."

"So does everyone else around here," interrupted Flint wryly. "But they all do it. Why should you be any different?"

"Well, ever since you passed the word to the crew about what Mr. Ahasuerus calls my defense mechanism, people have been coming up and begging me to drop my guard, so to speak." Flint smiled in amusement. "It's not funny, Mr. Flint. It's something I have no control over. After I explained that to Lori, she threatened me with a steel pipe, just so she could have another look at some boy she left behind on Earth." He looked at Stogie. "Even Max . . ."

"Really?" asked Flint, interested. "Who do you see when you look at him, Max—Fanny Brice?"

"I see me," said Stogie defensively.

"You? You can see yourself in a mirror, you old narcissist."

"Not me like I am now," said the old comic, his eyes suddenly misty. "I see me like I was fifty years ago, tall and handsome and healthy, with my whole life ahead of me." He looked defiantly at Flint. *"That's* what I see."

"As I said," explained Jiminy, "it's not necessarily a loved one that one sees, but rather one's heart's desire."

"And everyone's been asking you?"

"Not Monk and Batman," replied Jiminy, as Tojo squirmed uncomfortably on his chair. "They ask me *not* to. And of course Billybuck never asks."

"Just as well," said Flint. "He'd probably kill you."

"I thought Doc Holliday was the fastest gun in the West," said Jiminy with a smile.

"What about Doc Holliday?" asked the Dancer, coming out of his trance at the mention of the name.

"Nothing," said Flint. "We were just talking about him."

"You know," said the Dancer, his face alight with interest, "they made a lot of movies about him, but none of 'em ever got it right. In *My Darling Clementine*, they even made out that he was a surgeon."

"Maybe it was because he was called Doc," suggested Jiminy.

"He was a dentist," replied the Dancer. "He became a gambler when he lost all his patients on account of his coughing."

"I've seen his photo in your room," said Jiminy. "He looks a lot more like a gambler than a dentist."

"The photo's wrong."

"He looked more like a dentist?" chuckled Flint. "What the hell does a dentist look like?"

The Dancer shook his head impatiently. "It's the only photo that was ever took of him, and the photographer kind of colored in all the light places. That's why everyone thinks he had black hair and dressed like he was going to a funeral. He was really blond, just like me, and he always wore gray."

"Why gray?" asked Flint, curious in spite of himself.

"Showed the dust less."

"How big was he?"

"Maybe five-ten, five-eleven. And skinny as a rail, 'cause of the consumption. But he was tough," continued the Dancer with a smile. "By the time he got out West he was too weak even to lift up a shotgun, and people thought they could pick on him because of how puny he looked." The Dancer shook his head at the foolishness of Holliday's foes. "Three of the first four men he killed, he killed with a knife. He kept it hanging around his neck, like Tojo's whistle."

"Interesting guy," commented Flint.

"I wish I'd have known him," said the Dancer.

"I can just see the two of you, fighting side by side at the O.K. Corral," said Flint. "You'd have wiped out the whole damned country."

"Uh-uh," said the Dancer. "I've have been on the Clantons' side."

"Weren't they the bad guys?" asked Tojo.

"Don't make no difference," explained the Dancer patiently. "A man's measured by his enemies, not his friends. I'd have been on whatever side Doc wasn't on."

"I thought Doc Holliday was your hero," said Flint.

"He is."

"And yet you'd want to shoot it out with him?"

"When you were a kid, Thaddeus," replied the Dancer, "didn't you want to strike out Mickey Mantle, or maybe hit a homer off of Sandy Koufax?"

"I never thought about it."

"How do you know how good you are, unless you go up against the best?"

He broke off speaking and suddenly resumed staring at the wall, locked in mortal combat with Doc Holliday in the landscape of his mind.

"*Could* he have beaten Doc Holliday?" asked Jiminy curiously.

"I don't know. Probably. Just be careful about letting him see you like that. Looking like Holliday is one thing; shooting like him is another.'' Suddenly Flint slammed a fist down on the table. *"Son of a bitch!"* he exclaimed, startling everyone in the mess hall except the Dancer, who continued to stare serenely into space.

"What is it?" asked Tojo.

"I've got it!"

"Got what?"

Flint grinned. "I've got the solution to all our problems: mine, the Dancer's, even the skeleton's."

"What are you talking about?"

"I've figured out who the Dancer's next opponent will be."

"Mr. Ahasuerus won't like it, no matter who it is," said Tojo.

"He won't have any objections to this one," said Flint confidently.

"Well?" stammered Tojo impatiently. "Who is it?"

"You wouldn't believe me if I told you," said Flint, getting up from the table and heading off to see his partner.

12.

The blue man looked up from his desk as the door slid back and a hand holding a white handkerchief was extended into the room.

"Come in, Mr. Flint," he said wearily.

Flint entered the room, a huge smile on his face, walked directly to his partner's refrigerator, took out a beer, and sat down on the least uncomfortable couch he could find. He looked around, saw a new painting that made even less sense to him than the rest of the blue man's artwork, and winced.

"Where did you pick *that* thing up?" he asked.

"Boriga II, if you must know," replied Mr. Ahasuerus.

"That was—what?—two years ago? I don't blame you for keeping it hidden until now."

"Have you come up here solely to criticize my taste in art?" asked Mr. Ahasuerus coldly.

"As a matter of fact," said Flint, still smiling, "I came up here to make peace with you."

"Oh?"

"And to hit you with a proposition."

"Oh."

"Aren't you even curious?"

"I am sure you will get around to telling me when you feel like it," said the blue man. "As for making peace, it will not bring the dead Darbeenan back to life."

"No—but my proposal will see to it that there aren't any more."

"We are leaving the planet this afternoon. There will not be any more."

Flint finished half his beer in a single long swallow. "Jesus! This stuff is worse than usual." He leaned forward in his chair. "I meant that there won't be any more *anywhere*."

"Has Billybuck agreed to stop fighting?"

"Don't be silly."

"Then I fail to see how you can make such a promise."

"That's why *I'm* coming to *you* with the idea, instead of the other way around." He paused. "But first I want to ask you a question."

"Go ahead," said the blue man, not quite able to mask his curiosity behind an indifferent expression.

"Why do the robots—the ones in the galley and the ones who set up the show—look the way they do?"

"I'm afraid I don't understand what you mean, Mr. Flint."

"They look like big, skinny, clanking metal monsters."

"Despite the fact that you do not approve of the way they manufacture beer and cigarettes, they are quite efficient," said Mr. Ahasuerus defensively.

"I'm not arguing that, much as I'd like to," said Flint. "But why do they look like machines?"

"They *are* machines."

"I know," said Flint, fighting to hold back his irritation with the blue man's literal-mindedness. "But why don't they look like people?"

"What purpose would be served?"

"Hah!" said Flint. "Then they *could* look like people."

"Of course," said Mr. Ahasuerus. "But the expense would be enormous."

"How much?" persisted Flint.

"For a ship's entire contingent of robots?" asked the blue man incredulously.

"No. For just one."

"To be virtually indistinguishable from a member of a sentient race?" mused Mr. Ahasuerus. "It would depend on the race, of course."

"Human beings."

The blue man shrugged. "I have no idea. Possibly as much as thirty or forty million credits."

"Good!" said Flint. "Then we're in business."

"I am afraid that none of this has made any sense to me," protested Mr. Ahasuerus.

Flint finished his beer and tossed the can into a trash atomizer at the far end of the room.

"We're going to build an opponent for the Dancer!" he said triumphantly.

"We are?"

Flint nodded. "We're going to make him the spitting image of Doc Holliday, and the Dancer will fight him all across the galaxy, twice a day and three times on Saturdays." He got up and began pacing around the office in his excitement. "It's perfect! We'll rig the robot to lose, which means no one will get killed, so you'll be satisfied. He'll look just like Doc Holliday, so that the Dancer will be satisfied. We won't have to keep hunting up new opponents, so Kargennian will be satisfied. And I'll get everyone off my back, so I'll be the most satisfied of all."

He looked at his partner expectantly as the blue man considered the suggestion.

"We can only have one fight per planet," said Mr. Ahasuerus at last. "If Billybuck outshoots the robot fifteen times a week the duel will lose all of its excitement. After all, it happens very fast, and no one can see the bullets flying through the air, so we will have to build up suspense and have the gunfight on getaway day."

"Then you like it?"

The blue man nodded his head. "No one else will die. And considering how much money we made last night, I doubt that Kargennian would be amenable to doing away with gunfights entirely. This compromise should satisfy everybody involved."

"And we're friends again?" asked Flint.

"We were never enemies, Mr. Flint," said Mr. Ahasuerus. "We just have very different values. I am still quite upset about last night, and especially about how it came to be, but I am willing to let bygones be bygones provided that such a thing never happens again." He paused. "How is Billybuck today?" he asked, his voice filled with concern.

"As unhappy about the gunfight as you are," said Flint.

"I knew it!" exclaimed the blue man. "Surely now he understands the grievous cost, not just to the vanquished but to the victor as well, of taking a life."

"He's unhappy because he won too easily."

Mr. Ahasuerus slumped back in his chair, defeated. "I have been abroad in the galaxy for almost forty years, Mr. Flint," he said softly. "And in all that time, I have never met anyone even remotely like you and your associates." He began his litany of incomprehension. "Gloria underwent surgical alteration and left the show, Monk spent a full year trying to kill Batman in the ring, Diggs would probably die of a broken heart if he couldn't swindle at least one person a day, and Billybuck . . .'' He shook his head.

"The Dancer's a little strange even for a carny," Flint admitted. "Still, this ought to keep him happy. I suppose we'd better send for Kargennian and see how much financing we can wring out of the little red bastard."

The blue man nodded, activated his intercom, requested Kargennian's presence in his office, and made himself a cup of artificial Colombian coffee while Flint popped open a beer.

The rotund red alien entered the office a moment later.

"Good morning, Mr. Flint," he said, mildly surprised to see the blue man's partner in attendance. He turned to Mr. Ahasuerus. "You wished to speak with me?"

"Sit down, Kargennian," said Flint. "We're all friends again today, distasteful as the prospect may be." The little alien sat down on a metal chair while Flint made some headway on his beer.

"Well?" said Kargennian at last.

"Right," said Flint, wiping his mouth on his shirtsleeve. "We've got a little deal for you."

"I hope it doesn't concern Billybuck Dancer," said Kargennian apprehensively.

"Oh? Why not?"

"Because he's a far less viable commodity this morning than he was last night."

"Yeah? What's changed?" asked Flint.

"I have been making certain inquiries on the ship's radio," explained the alien, "trying to line up future matches for him— and it turns out that news of last night's performance has already spread throughout most of our Community of Worlds."

"Then they ought to be dying to see him," said Flint.

"Oh, they are," agreed Kargennian. "But I have only found three worlds that are willing to pit their champions against him, and none of the three would post more than half a million credits. I have a terrible feeling that wherever he goes from now on, his reputation will precede him."

"Then sit back and listen," said Flint with a smile, "because you're gonna love what I have to say."

"That would be a pleasant change," commented Kargennian. "Have you discussed whatever this scheme is with Mr. Ahasuerus?"

"Yes," interjected the blue man. "And I am in total agreement."

"All right," said Kargennian, turning back to Flint. "Let's hear your proposition."

"What would you think of building a robot—" began Flint.

"This ship has more robots than it needs," interrupted Kargennian.

"Not the kind *I'm* talking about," said Flint. "This one will be identical to a human being in every way. He'll look like one, walk like one, maybe even talk like one. And more to the point, he'll shoot like one."

"For what reason?"

"So he can go up against the Dancer."

"I *like* it!" said Kargennian, a look of enthusiasm spreading across his pudgy face.

"We won't have to hunt up any more opponents," Flint continued. "It'll just be the Dancer and Doc Holliday—that's what we're calling him—man to man, or man to robot as the case may be."

"Excellent!" exclaimed Kargennian. He got up and began walking excitedly around and around his chair. "Of course, the robot will need a few preliminary fights, but that can be arranged. After all, I have three worlds on tap already."

"*Preliminary* fights?" repeated Flint. "What the hell are you talking about?"

"Before the big one," said Kargennian.

"What big one?" asked Mr. Ahasuerus.

"Why, his duel to the death with Billybuck Dancer!" said Kargennian, as if speaking to an uncomprehending child. "We've got to build his reputation, so the fight won't seem one-sided. This will be a one-time-only chance to cash in big, so we have to cover every angle. The pre-fight publicity may take as much as a year, but when it's done, I'll have all three thousand Community planets subscribing to a live transmission of the fight." He slapped his hands together. "Better still—the carnival will book bets on the fight! Even if we return ninety percent of the money wagered, we could clear close to a billion credits!"

"Don't go understanding me so goddamned fast, Kargennian," said Flint. "This isn't what we had in mind."

"Of course not," said Kargennian smugly. "That's why the Corporation has given me freedom of action in respect to its entertainment division—because I see opportunities that others miss." He continued his frenzied pacing. "I know just the person to create the robot. I've seen his work, and it's excellent. He won't be cheap, but he'll be worth what we pay him."

"*Kargennian!*" cried Mr. Ahasuerus. "Will you be quiet and listen for a moment?"

"No," said the little alien. "*You* listen! This is a chance for the carnival to show a profit such as never before seemed possible, and I'm not going to let Mr. Flint's pigheadedness and your moral fastidiousness stand in the way of it. There's money in this for everyone, and a promotion for me, and I won't have you interfering. I'll be happy to have your help, but if you try to dissuade me, I'll simply put the matter up to Billybuck Dancer, and we all know who's side he'll be on." He slapped his little hands together again. "I must talk to Diggs! He'll have suggestions on setting up a wagering network."

He walked to the door and left without another word.

The blue man sat in his chair, staring silently at his interlaced fingers for more than a minute. Finally he looked up.

"I realize that this isn't exactly your fault, Mr. Flint," he began. "But the next time you have an idea . . ." He let the sentence dangle, unfinished.

"I think I'll go down and wring that little bastard's neck," said Flint grimly.

"Just once," said the blue man, "why don't you try to deal with a problem in a manner that doesn't involve anyone's being killed?"

"It's getting harder than you might think," replied Flint with more than a touch of irony in his voice.

13.

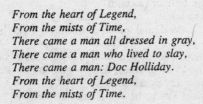

From the heart of Legend,
From the mists of Time,
There came a man all dressed in gray,
There came a man who lived to slay,
There came a man: Doc Holliday.
From the heart of Legend,
From the mists of Time.

From the wealth of Fable,
From the fruit of Lore,
The Dancer cast a nameless spell,
The Dancer chimed a mystic bell,
The Dancer called him up from Hell.
From the wealth of Fable,
From the fruit of Lore.

—from "The Ballad of Billybuck Dancer"

"No," said the Dancer, standing back and looking at his companion. "A little thinner."

"Thinner *still*?" asked Jiminy, adjusting his appearance to the Dancer's directions. "I wonder what kept him alive."

"Not much besides guts."

The two of them were standing in the middle of the Dancer's poster-laden room, while a small red alien of Kargennian's race watched them.

"There!" exclaimed the Dancer. "Now you've got it!"

"You're sure?" asked Borilliot, the robotics expert who had arrived earlier that day. He was sitting on the Dancer's bed, taking copious notes on a pocket computer.

"Yeah, that's the height and weight, more or less," said the Dancer, stepping back with his hands on his hips and staring at Jiminy. "I still ain't happy with the face, though. Try making it a little sharper around the cheekbones."

Jiminy altered his image again, and the Dancer looked from him to the photograph of Doc Holliday that he held in his hand, and then back again.

"A little thicker mustache," he suggested at last.

"Thicker?" repeated Jiminy, puzzled.

"More hair. But not bushier. Keep it neat."

Jiminy did as he was told.

The Dancer stared, nodded, and turned to Borilliot. "That's as close as we're gonna get."

The rotund red alien, who looked as if he could have been Kargennian's twin, nodded, grunted, and began taking holographs of Jiminy from every possible angle.

"We're going to want this to be as accurate as possible," he announced at last, "so let me ask you some further questions."

"Shoot," said the Dancer, leaning up against a wall next to photos of Cole Younger and Bat Masterson, both of them dressed formally and posed very self-consciously.

"Did Doc Holliday always wear gray? Having seen your pictures of famed desperadoes, I think he'd look much more striking in black, which seems to have been almost a tribal color."

"Gray," said the Dancer firmly.

"You're sure?" asked Borilliot. The Dancer nodded, and the little alien sighed. "All right. Gray it is. What about a hat?"

"What about one?"

"Did he wear one, and if so, what type?" persisted the alien. "I notice that most of the men in your photographs are wearing hats, and that the styles differ markedly."

The Dancer glanced up and down his wall, found a hat that he liked, and pointed to it. "Make it like this one."

"Gray, too?"

"Yep."

"Now, this knife hanging down from his neck," continued Borilliot, pointing toward Jiminy. "Are you absolutely sure that you want it? After all, he won't be using it in your contest."

"He wore it."

"I'm sure he did, but—"

"He *wore* it," repeated the Dancer.

Borilliot sighed again, made a note on his computer, and looked up. "Was he right-handed or left-handed?"

"How should I know?" responded the Dancer.

"Right-handed, I think," offered Jiminy. "Most of the humans on the ship favor their right hands, so you might as well have the robot do the same."

"All right," agreed the alien. "How about scars?"

"I don't think he had any," replied the Dancer. "At least, he wasn't never wounded."

"Not once in all those gunfights?" asked Jiminy in disbelief.

The Dancer shook his head. "Closest he ever came was at the O.K. Corral—a bullet bounced off his belt buckle."

"He must have been a formidable figure," remarked Borilliot. "I wish he didn't look so infirm."

"He was dying."

"Ah, yes—the tuberculosis. Shall I give him a cough? I could make it absolutely spontaneous." The little red alien smiled. "It might even save your life, if it should occur during the battle."

"I don't need no edge," said the Dancer.

Borilliot stared at him for a moment, then shrugged. "Did he have any other physical deficiencies I should know about?" he asked at last. "Nearsightedness, perhaps?"

"No. Just the consumption," said the Dancer. "It was ailment enough for any man." He turned to Jiminy. "You know, he was so weak from it that he had to use a cane to walk to the O.K. Corral." He smiled, as if remembering the event personally. "But once he got there, he killed both McLowry brothers."

"Needs a cane to locomote," muttered Borilliot to himself as he made an entry on his computer.

"Not this time around, he don't," said the Dancer.

"But—"

"I don't care how puny he looks," said the Dancer. "This time he fights healthy."

"It's your funeral," said the alien with a shrug. He shifted his weight on the bed. "Now, the robot will have to participate in numerous interviews as part of the pre-fight publicity, so I will have to know what the real Doc Holliday's voice was like."

"You mean high or low or like that?" asked the Dancer.

Borilliot nodded.

"I don't know. He came from Georgia, though, so I guess he talked with a Southern accent. Does that help?"

"Not unless you can tell me what a Southern accent sounds like."

"Jenny's from one of the Carolinas," said the Dancer. "Listen to her."

"Who is Jenny, and what is a Carolina?" asked the alien.

"Carolina's a place," answered Jiminy. "Two of them, actually. As for Jenny, I'll point her out to you."

"How did you know about the Carolinas?" asked the Dancer curiously.

Jiminy smiled. "You think *you're* the only one I talk to on this ship?" He paused. "By the way, can I change back now?"

"You need any more pictures?" the Dancer asked the little alien.

"I guess not," answered Borilliot.

"Thank you," said Jiminy, instantly changing to his usual persona.

"That's quite an ability you have there," remarked Borilliot. "I've never seen a Jimorian before."

"I wouldn't bet every last credit I owned on that," said Jiminy.

The alien looked startled for a moment, then emitted a low chuckle. "Probably you're right." He stared at Jiminy. "Tell me, is it difficult to establish an identity?"

"Only at first, like when I was being Doc Holliday," replied Jiminy. "After I've maintained an identity for a few days, it becomes almost second nature to me."

"I could certainly use you in my business."

"No, thanks," said Jiminy. "I'm happy right where I am."

"You're sure?" Jiminy nodded. "Well, if you ever change your mind, Mr. Ahasuerus knows how to get in contact with me. There could be a lot of money in it for both of us." He waited for a reaction, didn't receive one, and turned back to the Dancer. "I'll need a few details for the robot's first couple of interviews."

"For instance?"

"How long did Doc Holliday live, and how many men did he kill?"

"He died when he was thirty-five," answered the Dancer. "As for how many men he killed, no one's real sure. Anywhere from twenty to sixty."

"That's a pretty big range," noted Borilliot. "Don't they keep records on your planet?"

"Well," replied the Dancer with a smile, "it wasn't the kind of thing that the folks involved was real eager to see go into the record books, if you catch my drift."

"All right," said Borilliot, concentrating on his computer's tiny keyboard. "If Doc Holliday were to brag about the biggest odds he ever faced, what would he say?"

"He wouldn't," said the Dancer. "Old Doc, he never bragged about what he done."

"You don't understand," explained Borilliot. "I need this information to program the robot."

"If the robot's gonna be like Doc, he shouldn't brag neither," said the Dancer firmly.

"I *must* have some details!" said Borilliot irritably. "The Corporation is putting a lot of time and money into this, and I can't just give them a robot that blushes and sucks his finger and says that he's too modest to discuss his accomplishments!"

"All Kargennian cares about is that the fight comes off," said the Dancer.

"Wrong," said the alien. "The fight has to come off before a paying audience—and we can't draw a paying audience unless you cooperate with me."

The Dancer lowered his head in thought for a long moment, then looked up. "All right—but I ain't making nothing up."

"You won't have to," interjected Jiminy. "That's why we're doing a Doc Holliday robot in the first place."

"I repeat," said Borilliot, "what were the biggest odds he ever faced?"

"Once, in Dodge, he faced twenty-five or thirty men who were ganging up on Wyatt Earp. Pat Garrett was one of 'em—that was back before he turned lawman and gunned down Billy the Kid—and old Doc, he made the whole lot of 'em back off."

"How many of them did he kill?" asked Borilliot.

"None."

"But I thought you said—"

"You asked me the biggest odds he ever faced. I told you."

"What was the largest number he ever faced in a fight?"

"By himself?" asked the Dancer. "They say he killed eight Mexicans in a fight over a card game south of the border."

"Eight men," repeated Borilliot, entering it in his computer.

"Most people don't believe it, though," added the Dancer. "Doc got blamed for lots of stuff once he got a reputation."

Borilliot looked across the small room at the Dancer. "Did he actually kill *anyone*?"

"Yep."

"You are doing everything you can to hinder my compilation of the data I need," complained Borilliot. "I cannot work under these conditions."

"You ain't asking nothing important," said the Dancer.

"And what would *you* consider an important question?" said the alien sarcastically.

"If it was me making a gunfighter, I'd want to know how good he was with a gun."

"All right. How good was he?"

"The best," replied the Dancer.

"Then tell me why you think so!" demanded Borilliot hotly.

"I really think you should, Billybuck," added Jiminy. "After all, he can't build the robot without this information, so the sooner you tell him all the things you've told me, the sooner he can go to work."

"Okay," said the Dancer grudgingly. "But Doc can't sound like he's bragging."

"He won't—I promise."

The Dancer spent the next hour telling the little alien about Holliday's days in Dodge City and Tombstone, Denver, and Las Vegas, his life as a dentist in Dallas and as a gambler in Leadville. When he had finally finished his litany of death, Borilliot turned off the computer and shook his head.

"An amazingly primitive planet," he remarked in wonderment. "But then," he added thoughtfully, "if it wasn't, it wouldn't have produced people like you and Doc Holliday, would it?"

"Actually," said Jiminy defensively, "they're a fascinating race. Very few of them go around shooting each other."

"Only because of a lack of weapons, I'm sure," replied Borilliot. "It is common knowledge within the Corporation that this entire enterprise began because Mr. Flint kidnapped twelve tourists, and certainly the biggest money-maker the carnival has had besides Billybuck Dancer was Jupiter Monk during the period when he and Batman of Sabellius III waged what amounted to a war in the ring."

"Well, now," said Jiminy, "I never said they were comprehensible—but they *are* fascinating."

"Actually," said a wry voice from the doorway, "I only kidnapped *eleven* tourists. Mr. Ahasuerus was their guide."

"Hi, Thaddeus," said the Dancer, as Flint entered the small compartment.

"Just seeing how things are coming along," said Flint. He gestured to the refrigerator. "Got anything in there besides milk and Coke?"

"Icewater," was the reply.

Flint made a face. "I think I'll pass." He turned to Borilliot. "Jesus, but you're the spitting image of Kargennian!"

"I'll assume that's a compliment," replied the alien.

"Assume any damned thing you want," said Flint. He looked in the refrigerator, just to make sure the Dancer hadn't forgotten to mention a six-pack of beer. Finally he straightened up. "How long is it going to take to build this damned robot?"

"Fifteen to twenty days," answered Borilliot. "Kargennian told me that this was to be a rush job."

"I suppose it is," replied Flint without enthusiasm.

"I will charge accordingly."

"Somehow I'm not surprised," said Flint. He paused. "Just how good is this machine going to be?"

"It will be indistinguishable from the real Doc Holliday, as least insofar as Billybuck Dancer's information is accurate. You may rest assured that it will appear human in every respect."

Flint shook his head impatiently. "That's not what I meant. How good is it going to be with a gun?"

"It will be the fastest, most accurate gunfighter ever seen," said Borilliot confidently.

"We'll just have to see about that," drawled the Dancer, the trace of a smile playing about his lips.

"Can you really make it as fast as the Dancer?" persisted Flint.

"I've never seen Billybuck in action, of course—but I think I can promise that this robot will be as efficient as any human being can be."

"I was afraid you were going to say that."

"Thaddeus?" said a voice from the corridor.

"In here," called Flint.

"I *thought* I heard your voice," said Tojo, entering the compartment.

"What's up?"

"I just thought you should know that we had to break up another fistfight between Monk and Batman." He smiled. "Actually, Julius broke it up. I just kind of directed him."

Jiminy made his way to the door. "These rooms weren't made for so many people," he announced. "I think I'd better leave."

"Stick around," said Flint. "I've got something to say that concerns you."

"Me?" repeated Jiminy.

"Right," said Flint. "Tojo, say hello to—damn! I've already forgotten your name."

"Borilliot," said the rotund alien.

"You mean you're not Kargennian?" asked Tojo, startled.

"Absolutely not."

"Boy!" exclaimed the little hunchback. "You could sure have fooled me! Are you joining the show?"

"No."

"Borilliot's job is manufacturing absolutely lifelike robots," explained Flint. "We seem," he added ironically, "to have commissioned him to build a Doc Holliday model."

"For display?"

"For gunfighting."

"Is that possible?" asked Tojo dubiously.

"Of course," said Borilliot. "That's why I'm here."

"But I thought a robot couldn't harm a human being."

"Who the hell told you that?" demanded Flint.

"I read it somewhere," replied Tojo.

"Science fiction?" asked Flint sardonically. He shook his head. "You read enough of that shit and your brain'll start seeping out through your ears. This robot will do anything we tell it to do, and we're telling it to shoot as well as the guy it's patterned after."

"Better," added Borilliot.

"And the Dancer is going to fight it?" asked Tojo.

"Not right away," said Flint. "As things stand now, the Dancer's reputation is too big for him to attract the kind of crowd we want, unless people think the guy he's facing has got a chance to beat him. And since having him go into the tank for a couple of fights is just a little impractical, what we've got to do is build up his opponent instead."

"How do we do that?"

"That's where you and Jiminy come in. The robot will be ready in less than a month, and Kargennian is supposedly lining up four fights for him; I think he's trying to hold the last one back on Darbeena." He paused. "Anyway, we can't afford to divert the whole show for four penny-ante warm-up fights, so we're going to send you two out with him. Tojo, you'll do the barking, just like you always do—and Jiminy, you're a smooth-talking bastard who's good at picking up languages, so you'll be the carny's representative once you land. You can fill an encyclopedia with what Kargennian doesn't know about booking an event or greasing the right palms, so we're going to count on you to see that everything comes off without too many hitches."

"What if the robot loses?" asked Tojo.

"He won't," said Borilliot.

"But *if* he does," persisted the hunchback.

"He will have human physiological responses," said the alien. "A wound, or a fatal bullet, will affect him exactly as it would affect a human being. However," he added confidently, "it's not going to happen."

"Okay," said Flint, trying to ignore Borilliot's remark. "I'll be letting you two know when and where you're going as soon as Kargennian lets *me* know. Any other questions?"

"No," said Tojo reluctantly. "But . . ."

"But what?" asked Flint.

"I've got a bad feeling about this, Thaddeus," said the hunchback.

"Welcome to the club," replied Flint.

14.

On Molluteipanth VII, the Doc Holliday robot made his debut. He strode into the center of the huge stadium, waited calmly for his rangy Mollutei opponent to make the first move, and just as calmly put five bullet holes through the Mollutei's chest before his opponent's gun ever cleared its holster.

On Selba IV, the robot decided to try out his left-handed reflexes, and won just as easily.

By the time he reached Alpha Ceti II, his reputation had preceded him, and the fight was postponed for two days, until the largest arena on the planet became available. The robot faced two members of the dominant race of pink-skinned marsupials, and in a maneuver his namesake would have been proud of, killed the first, flipped his gun to his other hand, and neatly drilled a bullet right between the eyes of the second.

They were waiting for him on Darbeena, and he drew an even bigger crowd than had watched the Dancer. The Darbeenans gave him a cordial welcome, then sent out their five best remaining gunfighters to face him. This time the robot was all business, using both guns to dispatch all five opponents in the twinkling of an eye.

Where the Dancer had drawn only a smattering of grudgingly given applause, the Doc Holliday robot was given a standing ovation despite the crowd's partisanship, and a statue of him was already on the drawing board before he, Tojo, and Jiminy left Darbeena and returned, at long and bloody last, to the carnival.

15.

"Thaddeus? Are you in here?"

Flint growled an obscenity and put a pillow over his head. A moment later a hand reached out and shook him gently by the shoulder.

"Thaddeus?" repeated the voice.

"Go away, you goddamned dwarf!" muttered Flint.

Tojo turned the lights on, breathed a sigh of relief to find that Flint had no bedmate, and closed the door behind him.

"Wake up, Thaddeus," stammered the little hunchback. "It's important."

"Why aren't you on Darbeena?" growled Flint, his head still buried under his pillow.

"The three of us just got back from there," said Tojo. "I came right to your room."

"How thoughtful of you. What time is it?"

"Two in the afternoon, ship's time."

Flint tossed the pillow on the floor and slowly sat up. "Coffee!" he rasped.

"You don't have any made," replied Tojo.

"Shit!" muttered Flint. He stood up, turned toward the bathroom, and almost knocked the little hunchback over as he made his way to the shower stall. He turned on the cold water, bellowed another curse, and stepped out a moment later.

"All right," he said, wrapping a towel around his waist and drying his head and shoulders with another one. "What's so damned important?"

"Do you get up like this every day?" asked Tojo, momentarily distracted from his purpose.

"You lived in the same goddamned trailer with me for seven years," said Flint.

131

"I remember you demanding black coffee," said Tojo, "but screaming in the shower is new to me."

"It was freezing," said Flint. "I could yodel, if it'll make you feel any better about it." He tossed both towels aside and began climbing into his clothes. "How did things go?"

"We've got a problem," stammered Tojo.

"Big?"

"Very."

"Is the robot on the fritz?" asked Flint. He walked to a small mirror that hung on the bathroom door and began combing his hair.

"No," said Tojo, looking at the barren walls of the compartment and wondering, as he always did, why only Flint of all the crew refused to hang any posters or other mementos of home. "The robot is working just fine."

"Then what is it?"

"Thaddeus, I don't think the Dancer can beat him."

Flint turned to face him. "What are you talking about?"

"I'm talking about the Doc Holliday robot," said Tojo patiently. "He faced five Darbeenans and killed them all."

"So could the Dancer," said Flint.

"Maybe," admitted Tojo. "But I've been in the ring with both of them, and I've had a chance to watch them both in action, and I think the robot's going to win."

"Horseshit!" snorted Flint, putting his comb back in his pocket. "Nothing can beat the Dancer."

"The robot's awfully good, Thaddeus."

"You're *sure* he can win?"

"No, I'm not *sure* about anything," said Tojo. "But he doesn't look or act like any other robot I've ever seen."

"For what he cost, he'd better not," interjected Flint.

"He's smooth, and he's graceful, and he never misses."

"The Dancer's smooth and graceful, and *he* never misses either."

"Thaddeus, don't you understand what I'm trying to say to you?" demanded Tojo in exasperation. "I was there. I *saw* him!"

Flint sat down on a lounge chair and stared at an empty wall. "How badly did he beat the Darbeenans?" he asked in a thoughtful voice.

"Only one of them even got his gun out, and he was dead before he could fire it."

"That's pretty fast," admitted Flint softly.

"There's more," said Tojo. "The local video stations were showing replays all night long, and one of them ran the robot and the Dancer side by side, with a timer on them."

"And the robot won?"

Tojo nodded.

"By how much?"

"A couple hundredths of a second."

"That's nothing," said Flint.

"That's *enough*," replied the hunchback.

"The Dancer was only facing one guy," said Flint. "Maybe he could draw faster if he had to."

"Maybe," agreed Tojo reluctantly.

"But you don't believe it."

"No."

Flint sighed. "All right," he said, getting to his feet. "Thanks for coming to me first with it."

"What are you going to do?" asked Tojo.

"I'll think of something." He walked to the door. "Get some sleep."

"If I can be of any help . . . ." offered Tojo.

"If you can, I'll let you know. And in the meantime, don't tell anyone else what you told me—and especially not the Dancer. He's likely to shoot it out right inside the ship if he thinks he can find such hot competition."

They left the room and parted at the elevator bank, and a moment later Flint entered his partner's office.

"Lock the door," he said.

"I beg your pardon?" replied the blue man.

"We've got some serious talking to do, and we don't want to be disturbed."

Mr. Ahasuerus shrugged and pressed a button on his desk console. "It is locked," he announced.

"Good," said Flint. "Now pull out the bottle of Pinch that you've been keeping locked up in your desk since Mr. Romany's last shipment from Earth. I need a drink."

"I am sure I don't know what you are talking about," said Mr. Ahasuerus austerely.

"You want me to walk over and pick the lock myself?" asked Flint irritably.

"But I've been saving it for a special occasion," protested the blue man.

"This is as special as they get," said Flint.

Mr. Ahasuerus sighed and opened his desk drawer, while Flint looked at his newest piece of artwork, which was hanging just to the right of the door.

"What do you do?" he asked, indicating the painting. "Go around to all the loony bins in the galaxy and pick up their used Rorschach tests?"

"That was created by a poet and philosopher of Korindus XVI," said the blue man, pulling out the bottle of Scotch from his bottom drawer.

"It sure as hell wasn't done by an artist, that's for certain," remarked Flint. He walked over to Mr. Ahasuerus and took the bottle from him.

"Don't you want a glass?" asked the blue man as Flint unscrewed the cap and took a long swallow.

"Are you joining me?"

"Certainly not."

"Then this'll do fine," said Flint, taking another, smaller mouthful, and sitting down on an oddly shaped chair.

"Perhaps now you'd like to tell me what this is all about."

"You want it straight from the shoulder, or do you want the kind of ten-minute lead-in that you'd give me?" asked Flint.

"Straight from the shoulder will be satisfactory," replied Mr. Ahasuerus.

"You know that Tojo and Jiminy are back?"

"I know," said the blue man grimly. "I understand that the robot killed nine sentient beings."

"Yeah. Well, Tojo think's he's going to kill a tenth when he goes up against the Dancer," said Flint.

Mr. Ahasuerus muttered something in his native tongue, the first time in Flint's experience that he had done so. Finally he looked up at Flint. "We must cancel the fight," he said in English.

"Out of the question," replied Flint. "For one thing, the Dancer'll never stand for it."

"But if he can't win . . ."

"I didn't say he couldn't win. I said Tojo *thinks* he can't win."

"And what do you think, Mr. Flint?"

Flint shrugged. "I don't know."

"But you think he may be right?" persisted Mr. Ahasuerus.

"It's a strong possibility. Tojo says they compared tapes they made of the Dancer and the robot, and the robot is faster."

"But this is terrible!" exclaimed the blue man. "If we allow

Billybuck to go through with this, it will be nothing short of murder!''

"Maybe," said Flint. "What you've got to consider is that the robot is a machine; he's always going to draw at the same speed. The Dancer's a man; he might be able to draw faster if he knows he's got to."

"And he might not," said Mr. Ahasuerus.

"And he might not," agreed Flint.

"Then what are we to do?" asked the blue man desperately.

Flint took another swig of Scotch. "There's an alternative," he said at last.

"To call off the fight," said the blue man firmly.

"Stop talking nonsense," said Flint irritably. "Even if you and I and the Dancer agreed to call it off, the Corporation would never let us get away with it. They've invested too much money."

"Then what is your suggestion?"

"You ain't going to like it."

"Let *me* be the judge of that, Mr. Flint."

"We get hold of Borilliot, have him build a robot the Dancer can beat, pay him twice what it's worth, and promise to slit his fat little neck if he ever tells anyone what he did." He fumbled for a cigarette, found that he hadn't brought any with him, and settled for another swallow from the Pinch bottle. "It'll probably cost us every penny we've made, but at least we'll keep the Dancer alive, and we can put the new robot in the show like we originally planned to do."

The blue man shook his head. "It is too late," he said unhappily.

"What are you talking about?" scoffed Flint. "Borilliot can make one up in two weeks, and the fight is four months off."

"That is not what I meant," explained the blue man. "Kargennian was in touch with me this morning. Evidently more than half a billion credits have already been wagered. If we rig the fight, we'll be perpetrating the biggest fraud in the Community's history."

"Half a billion?" asked Flint, curious in spite of himself. "Who's the favorite?"

"What difference does it make?" exploded Mr. Ahasuerus, pounding the polished desk with his fist. "We *must* see to it that the fight does not take place!"

"Mr. Ahasuerus," said Flint, "will you please try to get it through your thick blue skull that Kargennian isn't about to return half a billion credits?"

"But he must!"

"Why? So you won't have to make a decision?" said Flint sardonically. "Why don't you just admit to yourself that there's going to be a gunfight, and start figuring out just what kind of a gunfight we ought to have. And calm down—you look like you're going to have a stroke."

"How can I be calm, when you have presented me with two untenable positions?" said the blue man, his eyes mirroring his distress. "All my life I have lived by a strict moral code. I have tried to uphold the values with which I was raised. Now I am presented with a situation not of my own making, in which, if I act, I will become a swindler on a galactic scale, and if I do not act, I will be an accomplice to murder. There is no easy way out of this predicament."

"What ever made you think there would be?" said Flint. "We're not living in one of Tojo's books, where being strong or having good intentions automatically makes you a winner. This is the *real* world."

"But what am I to do?" persisted the blue man. "Both courses of action are morally repugnant to me."

"Then you decide which one is worse and you choose the other," said Flint firmly. "And never forget: there's always a chance that the Dancer might win."

"If you thought so, you wouldn't be here."

"True," admitted Flint. "But as hard as this may be for you to believe, I've been wrong before."

"But if there is even a *chance* that the robot could win—"

"If there wasn't a chance, we wouldn't have been able to put this fight together in the first place. What we're concerned with now is whether or not the *Dancer* has a chance."

"You make it all sound so simple," said the blue man, staring blankly at the holograph just above Flint's head.

"It is," replied Flint. "There's a big difference between being easy and being simple. This is a simple situation to define; it's not an easy one to solve."

"You have usurped my authority so many times in the past, why did you not simply do it again in this case?" asked Mr. Ahasuerus bitterly.

"Because we've got to be united on this one," said Flint. "If we don't get another robot and the Dancer dies, I don't want you blaming me for the next twenty years. And if we do get another robot and someone finds out about it after the fight is over, we're going to be in one hell of a lot of hot water; I don't want you accusing me of putting you there against your will."

The blue man stood up and walked over to an abstract construction that sat on a small table. He picked it up and began examining it absently.

"If I weren't here, what would you do?" he asked suddenly.

"But you *are* here," Flint pointed out. "You may wish you weren't, but you wanted to run a business, and being here goes with the territory." Flint paused and leaned back in his chair, idly playing with the Pinch bottle. "Besides, did it ever occur to you that maybe I'm getting sick and tired of being responsible for everyone else?" he said. "That I am goddamned fed up with being the only one who can decide how to make Gloria happy, and when to make Monk and Batman stop fighting, and whether to let Diggs fleece the other crew members, and whether Stogie will kill himself if he keeps working, and whether to let the Dancer face the robot or not?"

"*Are* you tired of it?" asked Mr. Ahasuerus dubiously, as he put the artifact back down and returned to his chair.

"I'm getting there," said Flint. "Mostly, though, I'm tired of watching you dither. We've got a problem, and we've got two solutions, and neither of them is very pleasant, and all the fence-straddling in the world isn't going to make the problem go away."

"It is not that simple, and all the verbal games you can play will not make it that simple!" said the blue man desperately. "I am being forced to make a decision that every fiber of my being tells me not to make—except that by not making it, I am *still* influencing what happens."

"Hobson's choice," remarked Flint wryly.

"I do not know anyone named Hobson. I only know that I cannot take on this responsibility alone. I must discuss it, and there is no one with whom I can discuss it with except you."

Flint stared at him for a long moment, then screwed the cap back on the Pinch bottle and set it down on the floor beside his chair. "You don't happen to have any cigarettes or cigars hidden away in here, do you?"

"No."

"You're sure?"

"I am sure."

"Too bad." He took a deep breath and released it slowly. "All right. I say we buy another robot. If we work it right, we'll not only be able to use it in the Dancer's act for the next few years, but we can amortize a goodly part of the cost by betting a few million credits on the Dancer. I'm sure Borilliot will loan us the money at forty or fifty percent interest, once he knows it's going on a sure thing.''

"That is out of the question!" exclaimed the blue man, horrified. "If we agree to buy the robot, we will *not* use our special knowledge of the fight's outcome to place wagers on it!"

Flint smiled. "Will the fight be any less crooked if we don't bet on it?"

Mr. Ahasuerus closed his eyes and held very still for a long minute. Finally he looked at Flint and spoke.

"I know that you are an essentially decent man, Mr. Flint, and that you are more compassionate than you want people to believe." He sighed heavily. "But you are also a morass of moral ambiguities, and I simply cannot judge the rightness or wrongness of a course of action by using your values."

"What is *that* supposed to mean?" asked Flint.

The blue man stared intently at him. "That under no circumstances will we wager on the outcome of a gunfight when that outcome has been predetermined. If I agree to commit an act of fraud, I will not make a personal profit from it."

"Even if it means that we'll be broke when the dust clears?" asked Flint.

"Even so."

"All right," said Flint. "Then let's get back to the problem at hand: do you want to buy the robot or not?"

"I just don't know," replied the blue man. "Are you *sure* that Billybuck will lose?"

"No."

The blue man uttered something in his native tongue again. "If I just knew for certain . . ."

"There's only one way to find out," said Flint.

"I know. But if he *could* win, then——"

"Wishing isn't going to help," interrupted Flint. "If I was as sure of the Dancer today as I was yesterday, we wouldn't be sitting here talking about it."

"I know," murmured the blue man. He sat perfectly motionless, staring at his interlaced fingers.

"Well?" said Flint after a few minutes had passed.

"I cannot make the decision," said Mr. Ahasuerus, his face agonized, his long fingers turning pale from the pressure he had put on them.

"Okay," said Flint. "There's a third alternative."

"What?" asked the blue man.

"Cut and run."

"I'm not sure I understand you."

"We tell Kargennian and the Corporation to go fuck themselves, and we leave. It's as simple as that."

"Just the two of us?"

"And Tojo," added Flint. "We can take the money we were going to spend on the second robot and start a new show. We'll take any of the crew who want to come along, and we won't be beholden to the Corporation ever again."

"We'd go broke within a month," said Mr. Ahasuerus. "Do you realize the start-up costs of such an undertaking? Just the cost of a ship alone is—"

"We'll owe so much money our creditors won't dare let us go broke," said Flint decisively.

"We can't."

"Why not?" asked Flint. "To be perfectly honest, I enjoyed *getting* to the top a hell of a lot better than *staying* there. Maybe a new challenge is just what we need."

The blue man shook his head sadly. "Mr. Flint, you are an entrepreneur, and it is perfectly natural for you to look for new worlds to conquer. It is your nature always to be dissatisfied with your situation, and continually to seek out new challenges." A note of regret crept into his voice. "But I am a company man. I have devoted forty years of my life to the Corporation. I am not unhappy with the shape my life has taken—or at least, I haven't been until recently."

"It wasn't much of a life from what I could see," replied Flint. "You were just a two-bit tour guide when I met you. That's not much to show for your first thirty-five years."

"I was a tour guide by choice," Mr. Ahasuerus pointed out gently. "You are a climber by nature; I am a wanderer. I have always wanted to see new worlds and exchange ideas with new species."

"Then leave with me and do it to your heart's content," urged Flint.

"I can't. There is more separating us than our natures, Mr. Flint. My life expectancy is far longer than yours."

"Then you'll own everything after I die."

The blue man shook his head. "What would I do with it? Let us not kid ourselves, Mr. Flint. I may handle the money and the paperwork and the various details that annoy or do not interest you, but you have been the driving force behind the carnival from the day we established our partnership. Besides," he added softly, "sooner or later you would tire of the carnival, and you would leave."

"*Me* leave the carnival?" scoffed Flint. "Not a chance!"

"You would," repeated Mr. Ahasuerus. "You left your home planet, and you left the woman you were living with, and you left the show that you owned. As soon as something threatens to form any kind of bond with you, whether it is a world or a person or a business, you leave. It is the way you are, so you have no need to feel ashamed, but neither is there any reason to deny the fact of it." He sighed. "And if I were to go with you now, there would come a day, probably sooner than you think, when you would leave, and I would not be able to return to the Corporation that has nurtured and cared for me. I cannot take such a step, Mr. Flint." He tried to contort his lips into his version of a smile, and failed miserably. "I wish I were like you, but I am not. I cannot leave."

Flint got to his feet and stretched. "I'm going to do you a favor, Mr. Ahasuerus," he announced at last.

"And what is that, Mr. Flint?"

"I'm not going to bully and badger you into leaving." He smiled suddenly. "I *could*, you know."

"Probably," agreed the blue man.

"You're making a big mistake."

"Then I shall have to learn to live with it."

Flint shook his head. "I feel sorry for you."

"The feeling is mutual, Mr. Flint."

"Yeah?"

"I have always been content with my lot in life. You probably never will be."

"I've always wanted what people told me I couldn't have," responded Flint. "You've never wanted all that much of anything. Which do you suppose is worse?"

"Right at this moment, all I truly want is peace of mind," said the blue man. "It seems as if that is something *I* cannot have."

"One thing you can have is a little less self-pity," said Flint sharply. "Whether we decide to let the Dancer go up against the robot or we toss in a ringer, either way you'll live with the decision. After all, I offered you a way out of it, and you turned me down."

"That is not fair, Mr. Flint."

"Where did you get the idea that life was fair, Mr. Ahasuerus?"

replied Flint dryly. "Now get on the phone, or the radio, or however you do it, and tell Borilliot to make a beeline for the ship and to keep his goddamned mouth shut."

"We are going to commission a second robot?"

"Unless you'd rather see the Dancer take his chances with the first one."

"Not if it means his death."

"I'm kind of fond of him myself, God knows why," admitted Flint. "And anyone who bets more than they can afford is fair game for a carny, anyway." He paused. "Yeah, get Borilliot here on the double, and make sure he builds us a robot we can use ten or fifteen times a week for the next few years."

"All right," said the blue man, grateful that his partner had once again lifted the burden of responsibility from his shoulders.

"You know," mused Flint, picking the Scotch up from the floor and taking another swallow, "if the Dancer ever finds out what we've done, he's going to hunt up the original robot and have it out with him." He smiled ironically. "Wouldn't it be funny if he won?"

16.

"Mr. Flint, you must speak with Billybuck," said Kargennian.

"You got any particular subject in mind?" asked Flint, standing a little way from the Bozo cage and watching Batman taking an occasional pot shot at Monk during the lull in the late-afternoon business.

Three months had passed since the Doc Holliday robot had returned from Darbeena, and the carnival was in the middle of a very profitable three-week stand on Philobis VI, a cool, temperate world with four tiny moons that raced continually across the cloudless sky. Borilliot had delivered the second robot, which was safely locked away in one of the ship's storerooms, and Kargennian had enlisted the full force of the Corporation's massive advertising arm in his efforts to publicize the upcoming gunfight.

"The robot was frightfully dull during his first two interviews," complained Kargennian.

"Well, gunfighters were never expected to be real exciting public speakers," replied Flint, wincing as Monk once again fell into the chilly vat of water and slowly pulled himself back up to his unsteady perch.

"Mr. Flint, this is a multibillion-credit promotion. We simply *must* make Doc Holliday more colorful."

"Paint him green."

"This is not a joking matter!" snapped the rotund little alien.

"Why are you talking to *me* about it?" demanded Flint irritably. "If you need information from the Dancer, go talk to *him*."

"Have you ever *tried* to speak to Billybuck when he's being reticent?"

"I imagine it's not a hell of a lot harder than squeezing blood from a turnip," replied Flint wryly. He slapped at his neck,

142

peeled an orange-and-blue insect off his hand, and turned to Kargennian. "Okay, I'll talk to him."

"Good! I'll have Borilliot meet you there."

"Borilliot?" said Flint, frowning. "Is *he* here?"

"He arrived yesterday, to get more data for the robot. Billybuck has been most uncooperative."

"How's everything else going?" asked Flint, starting to walk down the long line of games and exhibits that formed the Midway's main corridor.

"It looks as if the betting pool will total almost five billion credits," replied Kargennian.

"Yeah? What's the morning line?"

"Diggs tells me it's called a future book," Kargennian corrected him. "And Doc Holliday is the early seven-to-five favorite."

"That's because he's killed more people," said Flint. "I'll make you a little side bet, if you're interested."

"You wa. t Billybuck?"

Flint nodded. "A thousand credits?"

"Done!" Kargennian agreed. "But this is an even-money bet. You could do better betting through our network."

"I promised Mr. Ahasuerus I wouldn't," said Flint. He flashed the little alien a smile. "But I'm sure he wouldn't mind my making a friendly little wager with you."

They stopped by Julius Squeezer's wrestling ring, and Flint, noticing that part of the mat was coming loose from the flooring, directed one of games workers to get a robot to fix it before the green muscleman went to work that evening.

"By the way, Mr. Flint," said Kargennian, when Flint had finished inspecting the rest of the ring, "we've finally found a world."

"I didn't know one was missing," remarked Flint.

"I meant for the gunfight. It's a dusty, barren little planet which very much resembles your Old West as Billybuck has described it. It was used as a military outpost for a number of years, until most of the beings stationed there were destroyed by a truly repugnant form of chemical warfare. Since their home planet was also destroyed, the handful of survivors have remained there. A pretty sad-looking lot, I must say; most of them are quite incapacitated by the effects of the chemical agents that were used."

"Is it safe?" asked Flint.

"Oh, yes. We've run numerous tests on the atmosphere and

water, and we'll be building the town in a totally uninhabited section of the planet.''

"The town?" repeated Flint. "What town?"

"We have decided to faithfully construct a Western town—or as faithfully as we can, anyway. There will be no audience, no arena or grandstand, just a few camera technicians and reporters and the two participants squaring off in the middle of the street.''

"What are my people going to do for customers?" demanded Flint.

"Your employees can take a few days off,'' answered Kargennian. "Believe me, Mr. Flint, there's enough money involved in this promotion so that you'll never miss the few paltry credits they might have added to our anticipated revenues.''

"Maybe,'' said Flint. "But let's raise our bet to two thousand credits, just to make me feel better.''

"Fine,'' agreed Kargennian. He smiled. "You haven't asked me the name of the world yet.''

"You noticed,'' said Flint.

"I think you'll approve of it,'' persisted the little alien.

"I'm all ears.''

"Tombstone!" said Kargennian triumphantly.

"It's not bad, at that,'' admitted Flint grudgingly.

They came to the end of the Midway, and Flint turned back to the ship.

"You're going to speak to Billybuck now?" asked Kargennian.

"Yeah, unless you nag me so much that I change my mind,'' said Flint.

Flint left Kargennian where he was and began walking back to the ship through the Midway's maze of games. He stopped by Barbara's booth to tell her when he thought he'd be through with the day's chores, gave some free tickets for the Null-Gravity Ferris Wheel to a group of Philobin children, and finally reached the ship. He went to the Dancer's room, where he found the sharpshooter sitting on his bed, staring off into space, as usual. He lit a cigarette, then activated the intercom system and summoned Borilliot.

"Hi, Thaddeus,'' said the Dancer, snapping out of his trance. "What's up?''

"Kargennian tells me you've been a bad boy,'' replied Flint with a smile.

"They want to turn Doc into a comic-book character,'' said the Dancer fiercely. "I'm not gonna let 'em do it!''

"Was Doc Holliday a stupid man?" asked Flint.

"Of course not. He was a dentist, wasn't he?"

"You never heard of a stupid dentist?"

"He was smart," repeated the Dancer.

"Well, he doesn't *sound* smart when they interview him," responded Flint. "He sounds dull and stupid. Now, if you want him to keep sounding like that, fine . . . but, if you want him to sound smart and interesting, you're going to have to give Borilliot some stories he can use." He paused and studied the sharpshooter. "Otherwise, people are going to think you're going up against a retard who can barely buckle his gunbelt."

"You really think so, Thaddeus?" asked the Dancer, his brow furrowed in thought.

"It's a possibility."

"All right," said the Dancer at last. "But I ain't gonna tell him nothing that might make people laugh at the Doc."

"Fair enough," said Flint. "He'll be here in a minute or two. You want me to stick around and referee?"

"That'd be nice."

"I almost hate to ask, but what have you got in your refrigerator today?"

"Milk," said the Dancer. "Well, not really. I tried to tell the galley robots what buttermilk was like, and what I got is what they came up with." He sighed. "It ain't real good, but I suppose it's healthy enough. Looks pretty awful, though."

"I think I'll take a raincheck," said Flint, turning one of the Dancer's plain wooden chairs around and sitting down with the back pressed against his chest.

Borilliot entered the compartment a moment later.

"Ah, Mr. Flint!" said the alien. "How delightful to see you again."

"I kind of hoped I wouldn't be seeing *you* again," replied Flint. "At least, not until after the gunfight."

"Never fear," said Borilliot. "My lips are sealed."

"Well, I suppose sealed lips are a lot better than a slit throat," said Flint, his face pleasant but his tone ominous.

"Believe me, you have nothing to worry about," Borilliot assured him.

"That's not quite true," said Flint. "But just keep telling yourself that if anything goes wrong, I've got a lot less to worry about than you do."

"What are you guys talking about?" asked the Dancer.

"Oh, just a couple of bets we made," said Flint. He turned to the Dancer. "Now let's get down to business."

"I need colorful stories and anecdotes about Doc Holliday," explained Borilliot, "and thus far Billybuck has been most reluctant to give them to me."

"You promise you won't make him sound like some kind of clown?" demanded the Dancer.

"On my honor."

"Okay," said the Dancer with a sigh. He got up, walked over to his photo of Holliday, and stared at it. "Once, when he was in Dallas, some guy who thought he was cheating at cards wanted to shoot it out with him. Old Doc had already had a couple of run-ins with the Texas law, and he wasn't hot for no more go-rounds, so he kept putting it off. Finally this guy started getting real pushy, and Doc agreed to meet him the next day. But that night the guy had a toothache, and since Doc was the only dentist in town he had to go to him. And old Doc, he put him under laughing gas and pulled every tooth in his head, and then set off for Kansas before the guy woke up."

"Excellent!" said Borilliot, making notes with his pocket computer. "That's just the kind of material I need."

"Good," said the Dancer.

"Tell me some more."

"There ain't no more. Doc didn't spend much time as a dentist after that."

"The stories needn't be about dentistry," said Borilliot, trying to keep his frustration in check. "*Any* colorful incident will suffice."

"He wasn't a colorful kind of guy," said the Dancer. "He was a dying man, trying his best to find someone fast enough to put him out of his misery."

"His foes, then," suggested Borilliot. "Surely *they* must have been a colorful lot."

"They had colorful names, but they weren't much to write home about," said the Dancer. "Except maybe for Johhny Ringo."

"Tell me about *him*, then."

"Ain't much to tell. He was a hired killer."

"What made him different from the rest?" persisted Borilliot.

"He was probably the only gunman in the West who'd gone to college," replied the Dancer. "Even Doc didn't, you know. Anyway, Ringo used to read poems and stuff like that in Greek, in between shooting people."

"Fascinating!" remarked the alien.

"You think so?"

"Absolutely. Do go on."

"I've *went* on. That's all there is that's interesting about him."

"How did Doc Holliday kill him?"

"Nobody's real sure about that. Once, he called Doc out in Tombstone. He was wearing this bandanna, and he wanted each of 'em to hold one end of it in their teeth and draw while they were like that. Doc was willing, but Wyatt Earp, he was having his troubles running the town and thought it would be bad for business, so he broke it up. Then Doc decided to go out hunting for Ringo after the gunfight at the O.K. Corral. They found Ringo a couple of weeks later, sitting propped up against a tree with a book of poems in his hand and a bullet hole smack dab between his eyes."

"You see?" said Borilliot happily. "It *was* interesting."

"And that's the kind of stuff you need for these here interviews?" asked the Dancer. He shook his head. "They're gonna be dull as dishwater. The people ought to know about how fast he was. They don't care about Johnny Ringo, or what he did to some guy with a toothache in Dallas."

"Why don't you let *me* be the judge of that?" replied Borilliot.

The Dancer shrugged, but made no reply.

"Maybe I can help," suggested Flint, who had been listening silently.

"I would certainly appreciate it," said the alien.

"Dancer, I want you to tell him about every gunfight Doc Holliday was in, and I want you to name the men he killed. Can you do that?"

"I guess so."

"And he ought to know about—what the hell was her name? You know, the whore he hung out with."

"No."

"She broke him out of jail once. Don't you think people ought to know about it?"

"They'll think the wrong things," said the Dancer. "He never cared for her. He just let her hang around 'cause she'd saved his life, and when she tried to turn him in a few years later he kicked her out."

"Tell him anyway. What was her name?"

"Big Nose Kate Elder," said the Dancer reluctantly.

"Very picturesque," remarked Borilliot.

"Well, I ain't gonna talk about her."

"I thought you were going to be helpful," Flint reminded him.

"Telling people that he lived with a whore ain't being helpful to *Doc*," said the Dancer.

Flint sighed. "Well," he said, turning to Borilliot, "I guess you're not going to hear about his love life. What else do you need?"

"A description of Tombstone would be helpful."

"He wasn't there all that long," said the Dancer.

"It doesn't matter," replied the alien. "You're going to face the robot in a town built to resemble the Old West, and it might as well be Tombstone as any other."

"Really?" said the Dancer, his face brightening perceptibly. "You mean we ain't fighting in a stadium?"

"That's right."

"Well," said the Dancer, suddenly enthused, "the O.K. Corral was on Fourth Street, right between Fly's Photo Studio and a mineral assay office. Then, to the north . . ."

He went on and on, rapturously detailing the street where he would face the robot, and Flint, after seeing that the verbal reconstruction of Tombstone was likely to continue for an hour or so, quietly got to his feet and walked out into the corridor.

He went down to the mess hall, which was deserted except for a pair of Korbussian games workers, huge furry beings who looked as if they ate humans for appetizers but were actually vegetarians, got himself a beer and a rare steak, cursed at the galley robots for changing the color of the artificial meat from blue to yellow, and sat down at his usual corner table.

Kargennian entered a few minutes later and walked over to Flint's table, taking a winding path through the room to keep as much distance between himself and the Korbussians as possible.

"May I speak to you for a moment, Mr. Flint?"

"Shoot."

"Galaheen IX has offered us three million credits if Billybuck and the robot will appear on the same bill for a single performance. I thought I would check with you first and make sure we can fit it into our schedule before I agree to it."

"Out of the question," replied Flint, washing down the last of his steak with the remainder of his beer.

"But we have four empty dates between Ruthven II and Beta Delta IV. Surely we could divert to the Galaheen system for a day!"

"First of all," said Flint, "I don't know where the hell any of these worlds are. Second, I don't remember when *I* became *we*.

And third, you can't put the Dancer and the robot on the same bill.''

—''Why not?''

''Because if the Dancer sees him in action, nothing in the world can make him wait for Tombstone. He'll call him out then and there.''

''Would he really do that?'' asked Kargennian skeptically.

''I already told you he would,'' said Flint. ''But if you don't believe me, go ahead and accept the date. I mean, hell, it's only money.''

''No,'' said Kargennian uneasily. ''I think I shall defer to your judgment in this matter. We can't chance Billybuck's getting injured.'' He paused, lost in thought for a moment, and then looked up. ''In fact, I think it might be best if he were not to perform any dangerous tricks in the ring for the next month.''

''It's nice to know that you care about him so much,'' remarked Flint with a smile.

''I care about *all* sentient beings,'' answered the rotund little alien. ''And of course, we don't want to do anything to jeopardize the promotion.''

''You're real people, Kargennian,'' said Flint.

''Why, thank you, Mr. Flint,'' replied Kargennian. ''And just to show you there's no hard feelings about turning down the Galaheen playdate, why don't we up our bet to five thousand credits?''

''That's awfully rich for my blood,'' said Flint. ''Are you sure you're not trying to flim-flam me?''

''Absolutely not,'' said Kargennian with a predatory smile.

''Well, then,'' grinned Flint, ''in the name of friendship, I guess you've got yourself a bet.''

17.

A world born in sickness and shame: Tombstone.
A world that lived up to its name: Tombstone.
A world that deserved no acclaim: Tombstone.
A world for the halt and the lame: Tombstone.
A world even God would disclaim: Tombstone.
A world that events overcame: Tombstone.
A world where the Fates fanned a flame: Tombstone.
A world that would soon live in fame—Tombstone!

—from "The Ballad of Billybuck Dancer"

"You know, it really *does* look like something right out of a John Wayne movie," remarked Flint as he and Tojo walked down the dusty frontier street. "I wonder how the hell they made the sagebrush."

"The Dancer must have given them a very thorough description," agreed the little hunchback. "Look! They even have a watering trough for the horses."

"You don't suppose that little red bastard blew a couple of million credits on a robot horse, do you?" Flint said suddenly.

"I haven't seen one," said Tojo.

They walked a bit farther, past the general store and the editorial offices of the Tombstone *Epitaph* and the Tombstone *Nugget*, and stopped again in front of the jail.

"If I didn't know better, I'd swear the Earp brothers were inside there, sitting around playing poker," remarked Flint as he stood back and looked at the stone structure.

"The Dancer says that their headquarters were outside the city," responded Tojo. "He says that their battle was against the local sheriff and a bunch of hoodlums he was associated with."

"For ten years nobody could get a word out of him," said Flint irritably. "Now all of a sudden he's a professor of history." He wiped his forehead off with the sleeve of his shirt. "Damn! As long as they were starting from scratch, they could have picked a cooler planet."

"Kargennian was very pleased with this one," said Tojo. "It has a G-type sun and only one moon, just like Earth, and the climate is very similar to Arizona's."

"Save it for the press," muttered Flint. "It's hot and it's uncomfortable." He flicked his hand at a couple of buzzing insects. "Now I remember why I never took the show to Phoenix when we were back on Earth." He shrugged. "Oh, well. At least we're only here for two days." He looked down at the little hunchback. "Have you figured out what you're going to wear tomorrow?"

"I haven't even thought about it," admitted Tojo.

"Well, you'd better. You're going to be appearing in front of something like eighty billion viewers."

"That many?" asked Tojo, suddenly looking very nervous.

Flint smiled. "Would you feel better if I told you it was only fifty billion?"

"I'm sorry," apologized the hunchback. "I just hadn't thought of it in those terms before." He paused. "I suppose I'll wear my carnival uniform. After all, that's what I am—a carny barker."

"You'll be the flashiest guy there," remarked Flint. "The robot wears gray, and I just know the Dancer is gonna wear those faded jeans of his."

"Speaking of tomorrow . . ." began Tojo hesitantly.

"It's taken care of," said Flint, leaning against a wooden hitching post.

"Can I ask how?"

"As long as you keep your mouth shut," said Flint.

"I will," promised Tojo.

"We're running a ringer."

"A second robot?" asked the hunchback.

Flint nodded. "I'll make the switch tonight."

"Isn't that cutting it awfully close?"

"Not really," replied Flint, lighting up a cigarette. "Besides, this way we don't have to program it to go through all those damned interviews. Kargennian's got this place as busy as Super Bowl week." He mimicked the reporters' voices. "What does

Billybuck eat for breakfast? How many teeth did Doc Holliday pull in his career? Why doesn't the Dancer ever practice? Why didn't we give the robot tuberculosis? Jesus—if they could, they'd go to Earth and ask the Dancer's parents where they bought him his first cap pistol!''

"They *do* ask some pretty silly questions, don't they?" said Tojo with a smile.

"That's the problem with a gunfight or a boxing match or anything else like that. They can find out everything they need to know in five minutes, and then they've got to start interviewing third cousins and family doctors to justify the money their publishers and networks are spending on them."

"Getting back to the robot," said Tojo, "do you know how to activate it?"

"Yeah. Borilliot showed me how. You use six words in combination, just like with the other robot."

"How will you know you're activating the right one?" persisted Tojo.

"Different code words." He rattled them off, and Tojo nodded.

"They're different from the ones Jiminy and I used," said the hunchback. "I just hope it works."

Flint looked up the street and saw the Dancer walking toward them. "Isn't he supposed to be doing a last set of interviews?" he asked.

"I thought so," agreed Tojo.

"Hey, Thaddeus!" called the Dancer when he was about fifty yards away.

"Yeah. What is it?"

"We got a real serious problem," said the sharpshooter, covering the last few steps on the run.

"Oh?"

"You just walked down Fourth Street," said the Dancer, obviously agitated. "Didn't you see it?"

"See what?" asked Flint.

"Come on," said the Dancer, heading back up the street. "I'll show you."

Flint ground his cigarette out on the dirt, then fell into step behind the Dancer and Tojo. They walked for perhaps two hundred yards and stopped in front of a colorful barroom.

"There it is," said the Dancer.

"Looks like a tavern to me," said Flint impassively. "It probably has a few gambling tables, and rents the upstairs rooms by the hour. So what?"

"So what?" repeated the Dancer. "It's the Long Branch Saloon!"

"Okay," said Flint. "It's the Long Branch Saloon. I still don't see the problem."

"It belongs in Dodge City!" exclaimed the Dancer, looking as if he might burst into tears any second.

"You're sure?" said Flint. "I mean, they wouldn't have put it here if you hadn't told Borilliot about it."

"I told him about it when I was telling him about when Doc and Wyatt Earp were just starting out. It doesn't belong here."

Flint grimaced. "I don't know how to tell you this, Dancer," he said, "but this place isn't really Tombstone and this world isn't really Earth. So what the hell difference does it make if a bar from Kansas wandered over to Arizona? I won't tell anyone if you won't."

"But they were supposed to do it the way I told them!" complained the Dancer. "It's just *wrong!*"

"It's a little late to tear it down and build a new one," said Flint. "Why don't you just learn to live with it?"

"Can't we even change the sign?"

Flint shook his head. "All the construction people are gone."

"Well," muttered the Dancer, "I don't like it, and *Doc* won't like it neither."

"I'll make you a deal," said Flint. "If *he* complains too, I'll change the damned sign myself."

"You mean it?"

Flint nodded.

"Thanks, Thaddeus," said the Dancer, heading off for his interview.

"He's a little crazier than usual these days, isn't he?" remarked Flint, watching the sharpshooter's slender figure kicking up clouds of dust as he turned east toward the video studio on Third Street.

"He'll be all right after he fights the robot," said Tojo.

"I sure as hell hope so," replied Flint. "If he comes up to me tomorrow afternoon and tells me he still wants hotter competition, I just might take him on myself."

"A lot of people would pay to see that."

"You think so?"

Tojo smiled. "Most of them work for you."

Flint returned his smile. "You'd probably bark that one for free, wouldn't you, you ugly little dwarf?"

Tojo shook his head. "I've learned a lot from you, Thaddeus. I don't do anything for free anymore."

Flint chuckled and began retracing his steps. "Has Kargennian told you where you're going to be tomorrow?" he asked as they passed between the bank and the feed store.

"Yes," said the hunchback. "I'll be sitting on the chair right outside the sheriff's office. I guess the Dancer will start from the O.K. Corral, and the robot will come out of one of the saloons. The video technicians will be hidden all over the place so they can shoot the fight from every possible angle, and the members of the carny crew who want to watch will be in the Long Branch. I guess that's why they put so many windows into it."

Flint looked up and down the street. "I think I'll watch from the general store. It looks like it'll have a better view."

"It all depends where they finally stop," said Tojo. "But I think they're going to have a cameraman in the store."

"Then he'll have some company," said Flint firmly. "By the way, what are those white blocks leaning against the side of the livery stable?"

"I don't know," replied the hunchback, looking where Flint indicated. "I didn't see them before."

Flint walked over to the stable, followed by Tojo, and soon stood in front of a pair of granite tombstones.

"I guess we're prepared for all eventualities," he said dryly.

"*Billybuck Dancer, born 1958, died 1987,*" read Tojo.

"Read the other one," said Flint in an amused tone.

"*Doc Holliday, born 1852, died 1887. Born again, 1987, died 1987.*" Tojo looked up. "It sounds eerie."

"Think of what some exploration team from Earth will think when they stumble across it a few thousand years from now," replied Flint with a smile.

Tojo stared at the headstones for another minute, then turned to Flint.

"I'm going to go back to the ship," he announced. "I don't know why, but these things make me nervous."

Flint gave them one last glance. "I'll come with you. It's too goddamned hot to be walking around in the sun. I don't know how Arizonans get through the day."

They turned back onto Fourth Street and started walking toward the ship, which was about half a mile distant.

"Hold on a minute," said Flint, ducking into the general store and emerging a moment later with a piece of licorice. He tore it in half and held out a piece for Tojo. "Want some?"

"No, thank you."

He shrugged, put it into his pocket, and bit into the other piece.

"Shit!" he muttered, spitting it out onto the dirt.

"What's the matter?" asked the hunchback.

"Wax," he said. "Or something like it." He shrugged. "It's my own damned fault for thinking Kargennian was a classy guy. I should have known he'd cut every corner he could. I can't wait to take that bastard's money tomorrow."

"Thaddeus . . ."

"Yeah?"

"What are you going to do with the *real* robot?" asked Tojo. "What if somebody finds it?"

Flint grinned. "We've got to bury *something* in the Holliday grave, don't we?" He paused. "Borilliot will announce that he's got to remove some valuable parts from the robot's brain or innards or somewhere before we bury him, and he'll make the switch; it was included in his fee. Then, a month or so from now, after he's had a chance to patch the ringer up and make it a little more durable, we'll announce that we've bought a new Doc Holliday from him, and that'll be that."

"It sounds simple," agreed Tojo.

"It is," he replied. "Now let's go tell the press what a close contest it's going to be, and hope nobody sees that we've got our fingers crossed."

18.

‹•••——◆——•••›

The Dancer he growled,
The Dancer he glared,
The Dancer he spoke,
And his soul he bared.

"Now, Doc," said the Dancer,
"You should understand, sir,
I must have the answer
Before I can rest.

"And so I demand, sir,"
Said Billybuck Dancer,
"You ready your hand, sir,
To see who's the best.

"You haven't a chance, sir,"
Said Billybuck Dancer.
"Now heed my command, sir,
And on with the test!"

And the Doc he smiled,
And the Doc he grinned,
And the Doc he roared
Like a howling wind.

"All right, fill your hand, sir,
Young Billybuck Dancer,
If you think you can, sir:
I've just acquiesced.

"To tell you my plan, sir,
I aim to remand, sir,

To Billybuck Dancer
A hole in his chest.

"My gun I will fan, sir,
And Billybuck Dancer
Will make his last stand, sir,
And soon lie at rest."

—from "The Ballad of Billybuck Dancer"

"What was that?" shrieked Jenny, pulling the covers up over her breasts.

"Alarm clock," muttered Flint, swinging his feet over the side of the bed and rubbing his face and scalp briskly.

"But you don't *have* an alarm clock!" said Jenny, blinking very rapidly and trying to clear her mind.

"Same thing," said Flint, feeling around on the floor for his pants and starting to slip them on. "I told the ship's computer to buzz me on the intercom at four o'clock."

"What in the world is so important that you have to do it at four in the morning, Thaddeus?" she asked.

"A couple of last-minute arrangements for the fight," he answered, putting on his shirt and hunting around the darkened compartment for his shoes and socks. He stubbed a toe, bellowed an obscenity, and continued searching more delicately.

"I'll be glad when that damned gunfight is finally over," said Jenny, lying back down on the bed.

"You and me both," agreed Flint. "Where the hell are my shoes?"

"I don't know," she said sleepily. "Come back to bed and forget about your shoes."

"Not just now," he replied. After another minute of futile fumbling, he turned on the light. "Son of a bitch!" he murmured. "How the hell did they get on my desk?"

"Turn it off!" moaned Jenny, rolling onto her stomach and sticking a pillow over her head while Flint donned his footware.

He walked over to the bed, lifted the covers, took a long, approving look at what lay beneath them, gave Jenny a fond pat on her buttocks, and walked out the door of his compartment, switching off the light as he went. He strode the length of the empty corridor to the elevator bank, summoned one that took him down to the bowels of the ship, and emerged a moment later. The storage area was silent and deserted, a huge maze of rooms filled to overflowing with crates and boxes, some of which had not been opened since Flint had joined the Corporation. He was aware of the hollow echo of his footsteps as he walked across the highly polished floor, and the grotesque shape of his shadow in the dim light. Finally he found the room he sought, opened the door, tried unsuccessfully to find the light switch, and finally decided to make do with the diffused light that trickled in from the corridor.

There were numerous boxes stacked neatly around the compartment, and he began opening the larger ones at random. The first contained two of Gloria Stunkel's breakaway evening gowns, the second held an aluminum stool for Monk's long-departed animals, and the third housed a trio of plastic dummies from the time when Stogie was thinking about becoming a ventriloquist.

"Looking for something, Thaddeus?" drawled a soft, amused voice.

Flint stood erect and wheeled around, peering into the shadows at the back of the room.

"Maybe I can help you," said the Dancer, stepping out from behind a pair of upright crates. "Catch."

A small round object flew out of the darkness toward Flint in a gentle arc. Flint caught it, held it up, and stared at it.

"What the hell have you done?" he demanded.

"Maybe I should ask you the same thing," replied the Dancer pleasantly.

"You're going to look pretty goddamned silly fighting a headless robot," said Flint.

"It ain't from *my* robot, Thaddeus," said the Dancer. "It's from yours."

"What are you talking about?"

The Dancer stepped forward so that Flint could make out some of his features instead of just his outline. "I come down here every night to talk to the Doc," explained the sharpshooter patiently. "Of course," he added with a smile, "since he's turned off he don't say nothing back, but he's a real good listener. Anyhow," he continued, "one day a couple of months back there was a new box in the room, and I got a little curious about it, so during a lull in the conversation I moseyed over to see what was in it."

Suddenly his smile vanished, to be replaced by a look of *hurt*. "You didn't have no right to make another one, Thaddeus."

"Then you knew about it all along?" demanded Flint.

The Dancer nodded.

"Yep. But I figured if I ripped it up too soon, you might get another, so I waited for tonight." He walked to one of the upright crates and opened it to reveal what very little remained of the second Holliday robot.

"You asshole!" exploded Flint. "Do you know how much that machine cost me?"

"You shouldn't of done it," said the Dancer placidly.

"You just tore thirty-five million credits to shreds!" ranted Flint. "Plus ten million more to keep that ugly little red bastard quiet! Do you know how much money that is?"

"Don't make no difference. You done wrong."

"Shut up!" Flint tried to pull a cigarette out of his pocket, inadvertently broke it in half, and hurled the rest of the pack against a wall. The robot's head followed a second later, bouncing off the wall with a sickening thud. "Do you know how long I had to work for that fucking money?" He began pacing back and forth down the length of the room. "Do you have any goddamned idea what you just did? I spent damned near every penny I had just to save your stupid fucking life, and you tear the goddamned robot apart!"

"What are you talking about?" asked the Dancer, frowning. "I'm gonna win."

"You're going to lose!" snapped Flint. He made a conscious effort to control his temper and lower his voice. "They ran a tape of you and the robot back on Darbeena, and he's faster."

The Dancer stared at him, puzzled.

"You mean your robot was *slower*?" he asked at last.

"Of course it was slower. What the hell did you think it was?"

"I just figured it was a robot that could get back up and fight me every time we hit a new planet," said the Dancer sincerely. "I figured you didn't want a fight to the death like everyone's talking about."

Flint shook his head. "I don't *care* if you kill the robot," he said slowly, articulating each word as if speaking to a child. "I just wanted to make sure he didn't kill *you*."

"You really think I'll lose?" asked the Dancer, his voice curious but unperturbed.

"Yes," answered Flint reluctantly, squinting into the darkness and trying unsuccessfully to see the expression on the sharpshooter's face. "Yes, I do."

"And they really clocked him out faster'n me?"

Flint nodded.

"Well," said the Dancer, turning his head just enough for Flint to see his satisfied smile, "it ought to be an interesting fight."

"Don't you understand what I'm telling you?" persisted Flint.

"Uh-huh," said the Dancer, moving to the middle of the room and sitting down atop a large box. "You're telling me that I'm finally gonna face someone who's got a chance."

"He's got more than a chance, Dancer," said Flint, walking over to his cigarettes and picking them up off the floor. "Don't you understand? They ran the two of you side by side, and he's faster. Not by much, but faster."

"I wouldn't want him any other way," said the Dancer, his face mirroring his happiness. "He's the best opponent a man could have."

"You just don't understand!"

The Dancer chuckled softly. "Sure I do, Thaddeus," he replied with an amiable smile. "But no one would remember the O.K. Corral if Doc and the Earps had faced a bunch of kids or cripples, and ain't no one gonna remember me for killing that Darbeenan feller." He looked into Flint's eyes. "You measure a man by what he beats, Thaddeus—not by what he avoids."

"And what if *he* beats *you*?" asked Flint, lighting up a cigarette.

"If it's in the cards, then that's the way it'll be," answered the Dancer with a shrug.

"You still think you can win!" exclaimed Flint in disbelief.

"Old Doc ain't never going to get no faster," said the Dancer, "Me, I plan to."

"You mean you can draw faster than you did on Darbeena?"

The Dancer shrugged again. "Who knows? I guess we'll all find out tomorrow."

"You act like this is some kind of game," said Flint. "Well, let me tell you—it isn't." He paused. "And stop calling him Doc."

"That's his name."

"But he's a robot, not Doc Holliday. Try to get that through your head. He's not going to wake up coughing, because he doesn't have any lungs. If it's windy or raining, he's got twenty trillion circuits that will take it into account and allow for it in less time than you can measure. If he stands facing the sun, he'll adjust the prismatic lenses in his eyes so he can still see you.

He'll never need a cane, or have a muscle cramp, or an upset stomach, or a headache, or a hangover." Flint paused for breath. "He's *not* Doc Holliday. He's a goddamned killing machine!"

"If he's faster than the Doc, so much the better," said the Dancer after seeming to consider what he'd heard.

"You *mean* that!" said Flint in wonderment. "You really mean it!"

"That's the way I want it," said the Dancer. "Just once, I got to face someone good."

"Even if he kills you?"

The Dancer nodded. "Even so. Ain't nobody I know of ever avoided dying, Thaddeus. The best a man can do is choose when and how . . . and I can't think of no better way than facing Doc Holliday on the streets of Tombstone."

Flint ground his cigarette out on the floor and immediately lit another. "Look," he said, starting to pace again. "We can call the fight off—postpone it for a month. I can get Fuzzy-Wuzzy to testify that you've sprained your gun hand or something like that. Then, during the interim, I'll have Borilliot make the robot exactly the same speed as you. Hell," he added, "we might even make enough extra money with another four weeks of betting to pay for the one you destroyed. What do you say to that?"

"I say no."

"But, damn it, Dancer. I thought you wanted a fair contest!" yelled Flint. "This one is rigged for the robot!"

"He don't care if he wins or loses," said the Dancer gently. "I do. That evens up the odds."

"By the same token, he also won't care if we rig him to draw two hundredths of a second slower."

"Probably not," agreed the Dancer. "But *I* will. This is the fight you set up; this is the fight that's gonna take place."

"Damn it, Dancer!" said Flint, unable to decide whether he was sad or furious. "All of the talking in the world isn't going to make him any slower, and it's not going to make you any faster."

"Then I guess we're all through talking," said the Dancer with a shrug.

"No!" Flint slammed the flat of his hand into a bulkhead. "I'm not sending you out to get killed, and that's that!"

"You ain't sending me nowhere," said the Dancer serenely. "I'm going because I want to."

"But you just don't understand . . ."

"You're worried about me, and I appreciate it, Thaddeus. I truly do. But I've been waiting for something like this since I was seventeen, and I can't let you take it away from me. I know you don't believe it, but I'd rather be shot down by someone faster than me than spend the rest of my life never knowing if I was the best or not."

"A fat lot of good it'll do you," muttered Flint.

"Dying ain't the worst thing that can happen to a man, Thaddeus," said the Dancer. "Sometimes living's worse, if he don't know what he's living for. And besides," he added with a smile, "I don't aim to lose."

"He's faster," replied Flint wearily.

"Sometimes being faster ain't enough. Maybe I'll crouch down when I draw, like the Sundance Kid used to do."

Flint shook his head sadly. "He'll adjust. He can think faster than you can."

"And maybe I'll just beat him because I want it more than he does."

"I can't let you face him, Dancer," said Flint.

"You ought to be just about the last guy in the world to stop someone from doing what he wants, Thaddeus," replied the Dancer.

"What makes you think so?"

" 'Cause nobody ever stopped *you*," answered the Dancer with a gentle smile. "Remember when you kidnapped Mr. Ahasuerus and all the other aliens? We all told you not to, but you did it anyway."

"We were starving," said Flint. "And besides, it all worked out in the end."

"It worked out when *you* wanted it to," the Dancer reminded him. "You kept 'em like animals. Everyone bitched about it, but you did what you thought you had to do—and when you thought you had to turn 'em loose, you did that, too." Flint stared at him, but said nothing. "And even before that, no one could ever tell you what to do. If you wanted to go north and we all wanted to play Florida, we went north. If you wanted the girls to work strong and they didn't want to, they worked strong. When Jupiter wanted more animals and you didn't see any need for 'em, he didn't get 'em."

"There were decisions to be made," said Flint. "Someone had to make them."

The Dancer shook his head. "Not *someone*, Thaddeus—*you*. That's the way you are. Like when you decided Monk and

Batman had fought long enough, you saw to it that they never went into the ring again.''

"I had nothing to do with that," said Flint defensively.

"Come on, Thaddeus—I was *there*. Those two guys didn't have no problem that wasn't of their own making until the night you got sick and tired of what they were doing." He paused and smiled again. "I ain't saying that what you done is good or bad, Thaddeus. I'm saying that it was what you wanted to do—and now I'm asking you to let me do what I want to do."

"I never wanted to kill myself."

"Neither do I. But I seen you take on a hell of a lot of rubes and cops and unhappy husbands who were bigger and stronger than you, and you never let nobody tell you not to. So why are you telling me what *I* got to do?"

"It's not the same thing," said Flint uneasily. "You're . . . well . . ."

"A little bit crazy?" asked the Dancer. He chuckled. "Don't look so upset. I heard you say it often enough. Well, maybe I am." The smile vanished. "But maybe I looked at things only I could see, and now, tomorrow, everyone's gonna get a chance to see 'em—so maybe I ain't so crazy after all. Maybe Jiminy was like kind of a sign, the way he turned into Doc Holliday that first day he was on the ship. If you want something as bad as I want this gunfight, if you wish for it as hard and as long as I been wishing for this, then maybe it's just got to come true." He paused. "It's gonna take place in seven or eight more hours, Thaddeus. Don't make it not come true."

"Even knowing the odds, you want it that bad?" asked Flint.

"I do."

"I've got to think it over," said Flint slowly.

"No you don't, Thaddeus," replied the Dancer. "You just got to step aside and let it come to pass." He stood up. "Besides, we ain't got around to the nitty-gritty of it yet."

"And what's that?"

"That if it comes down to cases, you can't stop me."

Suddenly Flint was staring down the barrel of the Dancer's six-shooter.

"Who the hell do you think you're kidding?" asked Flint, smiling and pushing the pistol gently aside with his hand. "You're not going to shoot me."

"I know," said the Dancer, returning his smile. "But I know the words to make Doc come alive, and if I got to, I'll say 'em here and now. It's up to you whether we fight on the street tomorrow, or in this room right now, but you can't stop it from happening one place or the other.''

Flint stared at the Dancer for a long minute. Finally he sighed. "Okay, Dancer. You've got what you want.''

"Thank you, Thaddeus—and I'm sorry I cost you all that money over the robot. You can have what I got coming to me if it'll help.''

Flint shook his head. "I'll think of some way to make it back. Besides, what the hell is there to spend it on up here?''

"You're sure?''

Flint shrugged. "It's only money.''

"Now *that's* a line I never thought I'd hear from you.''

"Sometimes I even surprise myself,'' said Flint wryly. He paused. "Despite what I've told you, you know I hope you win, don't you?''

"Sure I do, Thaddeus. We're carnies, ain't we? And a carny never pulls against his own.'' He stood up, and his face was lost in shadow again. "But just in case I lose, I want you to see that Tojo gets all my pictures. He's a friendly little feller, and he's always seemed kind of interested in them.'' He paused thoughtfully. "At least, he asks questions about who they were and what they did, which is a whole lot more than anyone else does.''

"I'll see to it,'' said Flint softly.

"And you can keep my money. I figure I owe it to you for busting up the robot.''

"I told you: don't worry about the money.''

"I ain't worried about it,'' said the Dancer patiently. "But a man ought to put his affairs in order before he goes up against Doc Holliday.'' He paused, and Flint thought he heard a small sigh. "I wish there was some way to get word to my mother about what I done, but I guess there ain't.''

"No, there isn't,'' said Flint.

"Besides, for all I know, she's dead now. I hope not, though.''

"Maybe you'd better go upstairs and get some sleep now,'' suggested Flint gently. "I'll walk you to your room.''

"Thanks, Thaddeus,'' said the Dancer, walking farther into the darkness. "But I reckon I'd better stay down here with the Doc.''

"I won't sneak back down here,'' Flint assured him.

"I know you won't,'' said the Dancer, his voice somber. "But I just feel more comfortable with him.''

"Have it your way," said Flint with a shrug. He walked to the door.

"Thaddeus?" the Dancer called after him.

Flint turned and peered back into the shadows. "Yeah?"

"Will they really write a song about me?" asked the Dancer with disarming boyish charm.

19.

❖

The Dancer and the Doc,
The Dancer and the Doc.
The fastest man and the fastest machine,
The most glorious gunfight ever seen.
The Dancer and the Doc.

—from "The Ballad of Billybuck Dancer"

The late-morning sun beat down on the back of Flint's neck as
he made his way from the carnival ship to the streets of Tombstone.
When he had covered half the distance he came upon the two
headstones again, this time laid out on the ground next to a
freshly dug grave that would be filled in later in the day. Flint
stopped for a moment to look into the rectangular hole, and idly
wondered if they might be burying not one but two gunslingers
before the day was out. Finally he shrugged and continued
walking toward the makeshift cowtown.

Tojo, decked out in his candy-striped jacket and straw boater,
was sitting outside the sheriff's office with Jiminy, while a
couple of sound technicians were checking his miniaturized
microphone, and another was carefully hiding an amplifier behind a watering trough.

"Good morning, Mr. Flint," said Jiminy. "Lovely day for a
killing, isn't it?"

Flint glared at him silently.

"It's all right, Thaddeus," said Tojo. "He knows." He smiled
apologetically. "He was so worried about the Dancer that I told
him. I hope you don't mind."

Flint turned to the technicians. "Scram," he said.

"But—" one of them tried to protest.

"You heard me," said Flint ominously.

The three technicians walked away, muttering to each other.

"What's the matter, Mr. Flint?" asked the Jimorian.

"Tojo lied to you," said Flint.

"I don't understand," said Tojo.

Flint turned to the little hunchback. "It wasn't a lie when you said it, but it is now. The Dancer found the ringer and busted it up."

"You mean he's going to face the *real* Doc Holliday?"

"Jesus!" snapped Flint. "You sound just like him. He's going to face the original robot."

"But he can't!" stammered Tojo. "It'll kill him!"

"It's a possibility," said Flint grimly. He paused. "This is the way he wants it. That's why he wrecked the ringer."

"But that's because he thinks he can win. *You* know he can't!"

"I *suspect* that he can't," said Flint. "I don't *know* anything. Neither do you, and neither does the Dancer. All we can do is hope he's right."

"He isn't," said Jiminy. "I was there when the robot killed those five Darbeenans. Nothing can beat it."

"Can't you call it off?" asked Tojo.

"You don't understand," said Flint patiently. "He knows about the replay you two saw, and he doesn't care. He's spent his whole life hunting for someone who could push him to his limits." Flint smiled bitterly. "Now he's found him."

"Does Mr. Ahasuerus know yet?" asked Tojo.

Flint shook his head. "I'm going to tell him as soon as I see him."

"Maybe *he* can find some way to call it off," said Jiminy hopefully.

"You don't listen real well, do you?" said Flint irritably. "The Dancer doesn't *want* it called off." He looked around distractedly. "What the hell time is it, anyway?"

"Almost eleven-thirty," said Tojo, pointing toward a large clock in the church steeple a furlong away. He turned back to Flint. "My God, Thaddeus—what are we going to do?"

"We're going to let him face the robot and hope he's as good as he thinks he is."

Suddenly Flint saw Mr. Ahasuerus walking out of the barber shop, followed by a pair of video technicians, and he called the blue man over.

"Everything seems in order, Mr. Flint," said Mr. Ahasuerus. "Billybuck stopped by my office before I left the ship this morning and told me that he'd show up at about eleven-forty."

"Everything's *not* in order," said Flint.

"Oh?"

"I haven't got time to lay it on you gently, so I'm going to tell it to you straight. The Dancer's fighting the original robot."

"But how can this be?" asked the blue man, shocked.

"He discovered the ringer and destroyed it." Flint spat on the wooden sidewalk. "It's too late to stop it."

"It's my fault," murmured the blue man miserably. "I should never have listened to you."

"Knock it off!" snapped Flint. "You did everything you could to make sure he didn't get killed, and now you won't even be cheating the audience. It's nobody's fault."

"It is mine," repeated the blue man. "I compromised my principles, and this is the result." He looked off toward the O.K. Corral. "Mr. Flint, we've got to call it off."

Flint shook his head. "Not a chance. I think he'd kill anyone who tried."

"But he doesn't know what they discovered on Darbeena!"

"He knows."

"And he *still* wants the fight to proceed?" said the blue man incredulously.

"He thinks he can win," said Flint.

"But that's insane! We must order him not to fight!"

"He'll fight no matter what you order him to do," said Flint. "He's not here for the money, and he's not here for the audience. He was all set to shoot it out with the robot in the storage room last night. He'd have done it, too, if I hadn't promised him that we wouldn't cancel the fight."

"None of your other promises ever meant anything to you," said Mr. Ahasuerus bitterly. "Why should this one?"

"It doesn't," replied Flint. "But since nothing's going to stop him from facing the robot, he might as well do it here and now."

"I'll talk to Kargennian!" said the blue man suddenly. "Surely *he* will see the need to put a halt to this contest!"

"That little moneygrubber?" snorted Flint. "He's got a couple of years' pay riding on the robot. How hard do you think he's going to try to stop it once he knows the score?"

"But I can't just stand by and do nothing!"

"You can stand by and hope to hell that he wins, just like the rest of us will be doing," said Flint. "And that's *all* you can do."

"Has he any chance at all?" asked Mr. Ahasuerus.

Flint shrugged. "We'll know in less than half an hour."

"This is terrible!" whispered the blue man. "There must be *something* we are overlooking. Does anyone have any suggestions? Tojo? Jiminy?" He looked around and discovered that the Jimorian was no longer to be seen. "Where did Jiminy go?"

"I don't know," said Flint. "He was here just a minute ago."

"I think he went into the *Epitaph* office," volunteered Tojo.

"This is a hell of a time to be reading a newspaper," remarked Flint disgustedly. He turned back to his partner. "You and the rest of the carnies are going to be in the Long Branch, right?"

"Yes," said Mr. Ahasuerus.

"Make sure they stay inside until it's all over," continued Flint. "I know the robot is only programmed to go for the Dancer, but who the hell knows what he'll do if he catches a flash of motion out of the corner of his eye?"

"I will attend to it," said the blue man. "Will *you* try one last time to dissuade Billybuck from his course of action?"

"It won't do any good."

"But will you *try*?" persisted Mr. Ahasuerus.

"Yeah, I'll try," said Flint.

"Maybe this time he will listen to reason."

"Don't hold your breath."

The blue man stared coldly at him, then turned on his heel and walked off toward the Long Branch Saloon.

"I can't believe this is happening, and that we're powerless to do anything about it," remarked Tojo unhappily.

"You know," said Flint wearily, "I listen to you and Jiminy, and I think about those tapes on Darbeena, and I know he can't win. And then I remember seeing him in action, and I can't imagine anything in the universe whipping him." He sighed. "I have a feeling that this goddamned fight just may live up to its billing."

"Mr. Flint," said one of the technicians, approaching the sheriff's office, "I absolutely *must* make a final check of your announcer's equipment. We're transmitting in five more minutes."

Flint nodded and stepped aside, and almost bumped into the Dancer. The young sharpshooter had cast aside his denims, and was wearing a straight-brimmed black hat, a handsomely tailored black frock coat over a white formal shirt, a black string tie, and black pants with thin, wide-set pinstripes on them.

" 'Morning, Thaddeus," he said pleasantly, no trace of tension about him.

"Where'd you get that outfit?" asked Flint, curious in spite of himself.

"Had it made up ten or twelve years back. I been saving it for today."

"You didn't know you'd be facing Doc Holliday on an alien world ten years ago."

The Dancer smiled. "I knew that I'd be facing someone, somewhere, who was worth facing in these duds."

"I assume you haven't changed your mind?"

"Nope."

"There's nothing I can do to make you postpone it?"

The Dancer shook his head.

Flint extended his hand. "Then I wish you good luck, Dancer."

"He's going to need it," said a low voice from behind them.

Both men turned and found themselves facing Doc Holliday.

"No!" cried one of the technicians, rushing out across the street. "We're not ready for this yet!"

Doc Holliday turned his head toward the technician. "You in that much of a hurry to die, son?" he asked.

The alien stopped dead in his tracks, and the gray-clad gunfighter turned back to the Dancer.

"I'm ready when you are, Billybuck Dancer," said Doc Holliday.

The Dancer moved two steps away from Flint, then pulled his frock coat back to expose his holster. Doc Holliday did the same—

—And suddenly he wasn't Doc Holliday any longer.

"What are you doing, Jiminy?" said the Dancer. "I could of killed you."

Flint saw an apelike alien standing where Holliday had been.

"I tried!" murmured Jiminy. "I tried my best! I was in control until it looked like he was going to draw . . ."

It took him a full minute to regain his composure, while the carnival crew stared at him curiously, and the technicians, who had never experienced a Jimorian before, gaped at him in shock. Finally he tensed, and was once again an aging Western snake-oil salesman.

"Jiminy, what the hell is going on?" said Flint at last.

"I'm sorry, Mr. Flint," said Jiminy unhappily. "I thought I could do it."

"But *why*? He would have shot you in another second."

"Better than the robot killing *him*," said Jiminy, still badly shaken. "He's my *friend*, Mr. Flint."

"That was stupid," muttered Flint with a sigh. "It's not as if you would have been sacrificing your life to save his. Two seconds after he fired everyone would have known you weren't the robot."

"I didn't think of that," said the Jimorian, startled. "It was a spur-of-the-moment thing. I knew you couldn't talk him out of it, so I decided to see if I could trick him into fighting with me instead."

"I thank you for the thought, Jiminy," said the Dancer slowly, "but there ain't no one forcing me to go up against the Doc." He smiled. "Most of 'em are trying to do just the opposite."

"Then listen to them," pleaded Jiminy. "They've got your interests at heart."

The Dancer shook his head sadly. "There ain't a one of 'em even knows what my interests *are*, except maybe Thaddeus." He paused and sighed. "You better get off the street now."

"Go on over to the general store," said Flint, not without compassion. "We'll watch it together."

Jiminy nodded and slowly trudged down the street.

"You'd better leave too, Thaddeus," said the Dancer. "It's getting near time."

"In a minute," said Flint. "But first I've got to ask you a question."

"Go ahead."

"How did you know it was Jiminy? I thought he looked like Doc Holliday to you when he let his guard down."

"I got a *real* Doc Holliday now," said the Dancer. "I don't have to wish for him no more."

"Then what *did* he look like?" persisted Flint.

"That's hard to say," replied the Dancer wistfully. "Like a real skinny old man. He was decked out in black, and he was all kind of hunched over."

"Do you know anyone like that?" asked Flint.

The Dancer shrugged. "Not as I can recall." He paused. "Funny, ain't it?"

A sudden gust of wind whipped the artificial sagebrush down the street and stirred up a cloud of dust.

The Dancer looked off toward the church clock. "I got to go to the O.K. Corral now, Thaddeus. It's ten minutes to noon."

"Take care of yourself, Dancer," said Flint softly.

"I will," said the Dancer. "You do the same."

Then he turned and headed south down the middle of Fourth Street. Flint watched his tall, lean figure for a moment, then checked the clock once more and walked to the general store.

"I thought your people were supposed to be in the saloon," said a bored, three-legged camerman into his translating device as Flint walked through the door. "What are you two doing here?"

"Same as you," replied Flint. "Waiting for a gunfight."

The camerman rippled his flesh, which Flint assumed was the equivalent of a shrug. "Well, just don't step in front of the camera, and remember to duck if they start running all over the street."

"They won't run all over the street," said Flint emotionlessly.

"Well, they're your performers," said the alien, rippling his skin again. "But if they even look in this direction, I'm switching on the tracking mechanism and getting behind a counter."

"Suit yourself," said Flint.

"Mr. Flint," said Jiminy, approaching him. "There is something I have to know."

"Yeah? What?"

"After I lost control of the image, I know what I looked like to you and Tojo and the others, but I should still have seemed like Doc Holliday to Billybuck. How did he know it was me?"

"He's got a new heart's desire," said Flint. "This time you looked like Death to him."

Jiminy closed his eyes. "That poor boy!"

"Cheer up," said Flint grimly. "Maybe it was Holliday's death."

"We're on," commented the cameraman. He tapped his earphone twice. "Has that announcer of yours got some kind of speech impediment?" he asked. "I'm getting his untranslated voice, and he sure sounds different from you two."

"Shut up," said Flint. He stepped up to the window and looked up and down the empty street. "They ought to be showing up pretty soon," he said to the Jimorian.

"The Long Branch!" whispered Jiminy, and Flint, peering out through the glass, saw the incredibly thin, gray-clad figure of Doc Holliday step out through the swinging doors of the saloon. He turned to his right and began walking south on the raised wooden sidewalk, his eyes scanning all the stores and alleyways of Fourth Street, but always coming back to the O.K. Corral.

When he reached the sheriff's office he stopped for a moment and stared coldly at Tojo, who was sitting in a wooden rocking chair, speaking softly into a hidden microphone. Then he looked back toward the corral, stepped down onto the dusty street, walked another few yards, and came to a stop.

Flint turned his head and looked toward the O.K. Corral. For a moment there was no sign of motion, but then the Dancer emerged and began walking slowly up the street.

"It looks like I'm going to be behind the robot," said the cameraman into a small transistorized communicator. "I think your best shot at it will be cameras two and seven, and maybe the one on the roof of the gunsmith shop." Then he was silent again, training his camera on the tall blond sharpshooter as he continued approaching Doc Holliday.

Finally the Dancer, too, came to a halt, perhaps forty feet from his foe, and stood just as motionless as the robot.

Doc Holliday pulled a gold watch out of his vest pocket, looked at it, then met the Dancer's eyes.

"I've been waiting for you for five minutes," he said with a markedly Southern accent.

The Dancer smiled. "I been waiting for you all my life," he replied.

"The clock'll be striking high noon in another minute," said Holliday, placing his left hand behind his back and gathering his coat into it. "Is that acceptable to you?"

The Dancer nodded. "On the twelfth chime," he said.

"Then there's nothing left to say, is there?"

"Not a thing," agreed the Dancer, pulling back his coat to expose his holster.

The two gunfighters stood and stared at each other, calm and motionless, as the clock ticked inexorably toward the moment each had been created for.

"Remember to crouch!" muttered Flint, a strange hollowness in the pit of his stomach.

"That announcer sounds pretty nervous," remarked the cameraman, tapping his earphone again. "Oh, well, it'll never show up once they translate his voice."

Flint looked up the street, and saw a blue face at one of the windows of the Long Branch, flanked by Diggs and Priscilla. The other three girls and Swede, the huge roughie, were at the next window, and Stogie, holding his schnauzer tightly to his chest, was at a third. Only Monk, of the carny's human contingent, was not to be seen.

Suddenly the stillness of the moment was broken by a loud chime.

Flint looked quickly to the Dancer: his fingers had crept down to a position just above the handle of his gun, but otherwise he could have been asleep, so relaxed did he seem.

Another chime.

A tiny sneer curled over Doc Holliday's lips as he glared at the Dancer.

Four more chimes, and the Dancer's fingers dropped another centimeter.

"He looks every inch a killer," whispered Jiminy, staring at the robot in awe.

Flint glanced quickly toward Doc Holliday on the seventh chime, then brought his gaze back to the Dancer between the eighth and the ninth.

"Remember!" he whispered, but as he looked at the Dancer's long lean frame still standing erect, he knew that the sharp-shooter had no intention of crouching, that he planned to face this foe as he had faced every other.

The clock chimed once more.

"Is that ten or eleven?" whispered Jiminy anxiously.

"Ten," said Flint, just before the clock chimed again.

"Draw now, damn it!" murmured Jiminy, but the Dancer remained still as a statue.

And then the clock struck twelve. Faster than the eye could follow, both of them went for their guns; so swiftly that even the freeze-frame holographs would be blurred, they pulled them out and pointed them; so closely together that two shots sounded like one, they fired.

The Dancer flew backward as if he had been hit in the chest with a sledgehammer, spun once around, then fell to the ground and lay still. Doc Holliday stared at him for a moment, then twirled his gun, replaced it in its holster, and began walking back to the Long Branch.

"Something's wrong with the sound transmission," complained the cameraman into his communicator. He seemed to listen for a few seconds. "Well, don't they have a back-up announcer?"

"Mr. Flint!" cried Jiminy, peering through the window. "Tojo's been hit!"

Flint raced to the door.

"Don't go out there!" cried Jiminy. "He may shoot you too!"

But Flint was in the street and running toward the sheriff's office before the words were out of the Jimorian's mouth. The robot, hearing the sound, turned and stared at Flint, but made no motion toward his weapon.

Flint reached Tojo just as the little hunchback was trying to pull himself back onto the rocking chair. There was a growing red stain on his right side, and a trickle of blood ran down from his mouth.

"He lost," he stammered unbelievingly. "He really lost!"

"Be quiet," said Flint, gently laying Tojo down on the wooden sidewalk. "Try to save your strength. We'll have the doctor here in a minute."

"I'm sorry, Thaddeus," said the hunchback, coughing up still more blood. "I know I should have ducked . . ." he added groggily. Then his homely face clouded over with puzzlement again. "But he never missed before!"

Tojo coughed again and lost consciousness, and Flint was suddenly aware of a rush of bodies in his direction.

"Where the hell is Fuzzy-Wuzzy?" he yelled as he spotted Mr. Ahasuerus struggling to make his way through the crowd.

"Here!" cried a being who resembled nothing more than a huge yellow caterpillar.

"He's been shot," said Flint as the ship's doctor reached his side.

"I know," replied Fuzzy-Wuzzy, bending almost in half and starting to unbutton Tojo's shirt. "We're going to have to stop this bleeding," he muttered.

Flint slipped off his own shirt and, balling it up, pressed it against the little hunchback's ribcage just below the bullet hole.

"That won't help, Thaddeus," said Fuzzy-Wuzzy. "We'll have to get him to the infirmary. I'll send for a stretcher."

"He can't wait!" snapped Flint. *"Julius!"*

"Yes?" said the huge green wrestler, shouldering his way through the crowd.

"Rip the door off the jail!"

"You mean you want me to—"

"You heard me!" snarled Flint.

The reptilian muscleman shoved a couple of Diggs' alien games workers aside, gripped the door in his massive hands, planted his feet, and grunted as he pulled against the hinges. For a moment nothing happened, and then the door came away with a loud cracking noise.

"There's your stretcher," said Flint to the doctor. "Now get him to the infirmary and go to work."

Mr. Ahasuerus helped Flint transfer the hunchback's body onto the large wooden door, then gingerly lifted one end of it as Diggs stepped forward and took the other.

Flint fell into step behind them, but was stopped by the video team's director.

"What about the body, Mr. Flint?" asked the tripodal alien.

"What?" said Flint uncomprehendingly.

"Billybuck Dancer," repeated the director patiently. "Have you any particular ritual that you perform, or shall we simply move our cameras to the gravesite?"

Flint glanced anxiously toward the makeshift stretcher as Diggs and the blue man continued walking carefully toward the ship.

"It's all right, Thaddeus," said Fuzzy-Wuzzy. "There's nothing more you can do for the next few minutes."

Flint watched them for another moment. Then he shook his head vigorously, as if to clear it, and turned his attention back to the director.

"Now what's this all about?" he said.

"Billybuck Dancer," said the director. "Do you want us to dispose of him for you?"

"We take care of our own," said Flint.

"You *will* be burying him, though?" persisted the alien.

"Sooner or later."

"When?"

"We'll let you know."

"I don't wish to seem insensitive," apologized the alien, "but it *is* in our contract with you: full coverage, from start to finish." He paused, barely able to contain his excitement. "Billybuck Dancer has nothing to be ashamed of. It was a fabulous gunfight, wasn't it?"

"I suppose, as gunfights go."

"It will live as long as tales of courage and competition are told!"

"Too bad the same can't be said for the competitor," said Flint bitterly. He saw a pair of aliens approaching the Dancer's body. "Hey! Get the hell away from him!"

They jumped back, startled, and Flint called Julius Squeezer over.

"I've got to get back to Tojo," he said when the reptilian wrestler arrived. "Can you take care of the Dancer?"

"Take care of him?" repeated Julius, puzzled.

"Carry him over to the undertaker's," explained Flint. "There's a coffin waiting for him. Put him in it and see that it gets back to the ship."

"Sure, Thaddeus," said the muscleman. He paused uneasily. "Will Tojo be all right?"

"I don't know."

They walked over to the Dancer's body.

"He looks different dressed in black, doesn't he?" said Julius softly. "I think I'll always remember him in those faded denims he wore."

Flint nodded. "Don't forget to pick up his gun and put it back in its holster."

"I won't forget, Thaddeus."

"And brush the dirt off his clothes before you lay him out in his coffin."

Julius Squeezer nodded his massive head, then looked down at the Dancer. "That's strange," he remarked after a moment.

"What is?"

"He's almost got a smile on his face," said the green muscleman.

"Almost," agreed Flint.

"He looks happy."

"No," said Flint softly, taking a last glance at the Dancer before heading off to the ship. "He looks content."

20.

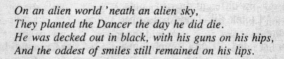

On an alien world 'neath an alien sky,
They planted the Dancer the day he did die.
He was decked out in black, with his guns on his hips,
And the oddest of smiles still remained on his lips.

Billybuck Dancer, Billybuck Dancer,
The fastest gun, so they tell.
Ran plumb out of foes,
Or so legend goes—
Now he's gunning for old Satan down in Hell!

—from "The Ballad of Billybuck Dancer"

"Well?" said Flint.

"It's a very serious wound," replied Fuzzy-Wuzzy. "The bullet went through his lung, spleen, and another organ that my anatomy tapes don't even identify, and it's currently lodged just below his heart."

Flint and the caterpillar-like medic were standing just inside the doorway of the ship's infirmary. There were six beds, each designed for a different class of life form, and on the smallest of these lay Tojo, two very thin tubes attached to his left arm and another disappearing into his nose. The little hunchback was unconscious, his breathing loud and labored. Mr. Ahasuerus, his lean blue face filled with concern, sat next to the bed, staring silently at the undersized patient.

"What are you going to do?" asked Flint.

Fuzzy-Wuzzy sighed. "By rights, I should operate immediately and remove the bullet."

"Then get on with it."

"Thaddeus, I've never operated on a human being before."

"How about all those times you patched Monk up after he and Batman had been in the ring?"

"Superficial wounds, nothing more," said the medic. "I don't even know what kind of anesthetic works on your system."

Flint turned and glared at Mr. Ahasuerus. "I *told* that son of a bitch I didn't want a doctor who didn't have any bones in his body!" he muttered.

"I resent that, Thaddeus," said Fuzzy-Wuzzy.

"Resent it all you want!" snapped Flint. "Tojo's dying, and you don't know what to do about it!"

"We have two options," said the medic. "I can try to get the bullet out myself, or we can go to the nearest vertebrate world of the Community, Ragobar III, which is about two days from here, and hope that I can keep him alive until then. I've pumped him full of antibiotics and cleaned the entry wound as best I can, and I've got him on oxygen; there's a chance he can last that long."

"How about the inhabitants of *this* planet?" asked Flint. "Aren't there supposed to be a batch of them a few hundred miles south of here?"

"They're nonvertebrate."

"Do they have a hospital?" persisted Flint.

"Thaddeus, they've never seen anything even remotely resembling a man before. Believe me, they're not a viable alternative." He paused uncomfortably. "I need a decision from you."

Flint turned to look at the unconscious hunchback and exhaled deeply. "What are his chances of making it to Ragobar?"

"Not very good."

"Fifty-fifty?" asked Flint.

"Thaddeus, I really don't know," said Fuzzy-Wuzzy helplessly.

"Mr. Ahasuerus," said Flint, raising his voice.

"Yes?" said the blue man, looking up.

"How soon can we get this ship packed up and ready to leave for the Ragobar system?"

"Perhaps an hour."

"Then do it, and radio ahead to let their biggest hospital know when we'll be arriving."

The blue man got to his feet and hastened from the infirmary without a word.

Fuzzy-Wuzzy emitted a sigh, an act that sent little shudders throughout the length of his yellow body. "I'll do everything I can to keep him alive until we get there, Thaddeus."

"You'll do more than that," said Flint. "Get ready to cut him open."

"But I thought—"

"We can't afford to wait," said Flint grimly. "Maybe they can still save him if you botch it." He paused. "Do you need any help—nurses, blood donors, anything like that?"

"I still have some plasma that I kept on hand for Jupiter," replied the medic. "But that was two years ago, and I don't know how long it keeps, even in a frozen state. Perhaps it would be best to get a new donor for a transfusion." He paused for a moment. "Anyone but Stogie. His health has been deteriorating for a long time now; I don't think he can spare it. No—wait!" he said suddenly. "Humans have different types of blood, don't they? I'll have to check my records and see who matches the type Tojo has."

"Is there any chance of him waking up before you start?"

"No," replied Fuzzy-Wuzzy. "He's in shock, and I've sedated him pretty heavily. Also, I won't start until we lift off."

"Good. Then I've got some business to take care of."

"I thought you'd want to stay here," said the medic. "I know how close you and Tojo have been."

"I'll be back," said Flint, walking to the doorway. "But we're taking off in an hour, and I've got a gunfighter to bury."

He turned to look at the little hunchback again. "Be careful with him," he said softly.

"I'll do my best, Thaddeus," said Fuzzy-Wuzzy gently.

"You damned well better," replied Flint. Then he was walking down the long corridor, and a moment later he had taken the elevator down to the main exit port.

Julius Squeezer was waiting for him there with the coffin.

"Where do you want him, Thaddeus?" asked the wrestler.

"Change of plans," said Flint. "We're going to have to bury him right now." He opened the lid and looked down at the Dancer's body. "Pass the word. If anyone's got any last respects to pay, they've got twenty minutes to get over to the grave. Then get someone to help you take him back out there."

"How's Tojo?" asked Julius.

"Still alive," replied Flint. "Get cracking now."

"Right," said Julius, heading off toward the main intercom system just outside the mess hall.

Flint walked once around the coffin, staring at the Dancer's unmarked, boyish face.

"I sure as hell hope it was worth it to you," he said softly.

Then he lowered the lid once again, and walked slowly out toward the gravesite. The carny crew started arriving in twos and threes, and by the time Julius and a pair of the burlier games workers had returned with the coffin, all of them were there except for Monk, Batman, and Priscilla. The video crew were also there, standing a little distance away and going about their work quietly and efficiently.

A rotund red alien sidled over to Flint as he supervised the lowering of the casket.

"We have to have a little chat, Mr. Flint," he said.

"Which one are you?"

"I wagered ten million credits on Billybuck Dancer," continued the alien. "I want to know what happened."

"Oh—you're Borilliot."

"You haven't answered my question."

"This isn't the time or the place for it," said Flint softly. "In case it's escaped your notice, you're attending a funeral."

"I lost a considerable sum of money, and now I want an explanation," whispered Borilliot. "Nobody plays me for a dupe!"

Flint reached out, grabbed the little alien by his single garment, and pulled him forward toward the grave. "Take a look!" he growled. "Do you think *he* played you for a dupe?" He released his grip. "Now get out of here before I toss you in after him."

Borilliot smoothed his garment and backed away, aware of the attention that had been suddenly focused upon him.

"This isn't the end of it!" he promised, turning and heading back toward the ship.

"Want me to send someone after him to rough him up a little?" asked Diggs, who had been standing next to Flint.

"No," said Flint, his gaze returning to the casket. "Leave him alone."

"I lost a bundle myself," said Diggs. He shook his head and sighed heavily. "I still can't believe he lost." He pulled out a cigar and stuck it into his mouth without lighting it. "It's a funny thing to say about a guy who spent all his time staring at walls, but I'm really going to miss him."

Mr. Ahasuerus walked over and laid a hand on Flint's shoulder.

"I understand that it is customary for someone to say a prayer before the grave is filled in," he said gently.

"I don't know any prayers," said Flint.

"Then if you have no objection, I should like to recite one in my native tongue."

Flint nodded, and the blue man stepped up to the edge of the grave and uttered a few brief lines in a language that sounded as if it was composed entirely of growls and moans.

When he was finished Diggs stepped forward.

"For the past forty years the only things I've prayed for were racehorses and dice," he announced. "I never even thought of praying for the Dancer, because I never thought anything could beat him." He paused. "So now I want to say a prayer. It's a silly prayer, but it's been a long time since I talked to the Lord about anything but gambling, and this is the only one I remember." He turned to Flint. "It's for Tojo too, Thaddeus."

"Go ahead," said Flint softly.

Diggs cleared his throat, and spoke:

> *"Now I lay me down to sleep,*
> *And pray the Lord my soul to keep.*
> *If I should die before I wake,*
> *I pray the Lord my soul to take."*

When he was finished Diggs looked at the crew defiantly, as if expecting snickering or laughter. There was none.

"Thank you, Rigger," said Flint.

"For what it's worth, it came from the heart," said Diggs awkwardly. "I hope the little dwarf pulls through."

"I had not heard that before," offered Mr. Ahasuerus. "It was very beautiful."

"It's just a kid's prayer," said Diggs, suddenly uncomfortable.

Flint waited until he was sure no one else wanted to speak, then signaled Julius to start shoveling dirt back into the grave. Then he returned to the ship and took an elevator up to the infirmary.

Priscilla was sitting on a chair, and Fuzzy-Wuzzy was in the process of withdrawing some blood from her arm as Flint entered the room.

"Hello, Thaddeus," she said, wiping some tears from her cheek with a tissue. "Fuzzy tells me I'm the only other person on board with Type A. I hope it does some good."

"You and me both," said Flint. He turned to the medic. "How soon will you be starting?"

"Twenty minutes, perhaps thirty," replied Fuzzy-Wuzzy. "It depends on how long it takes me to hit upon the right anesthetic."

"How about ether?" said Flint. "I seem to remember reading that they used to use it."

"It's not just the compound, but the dosage," said the yellow medic. "Too much could kill him, too little could be ineffective." He turned to Priscilla. "I'm through with you now. Lie down on one of the beds for a few minutes, and then you can leave."

"I feel fine right now," she replied.

"That's because you're still seated. I took quite a lot of blood from you. If you start moving around, you will experience considerable dizziness."

"Dizzy or not, I'm saying goodbye to the Dancer," she announced, getting to her feet and walking to the door. She wobbled for just an instant as she turned into the corridor, leaned against a wall for support, and then continued walking toward the elevators.

Flint went over to Tojo's bed and smoothed the little hunchback's rumpled hair. Then he glanced down at the wound and noticed that the blood was starting to seep through the dressing again.

"Thaddeus?" said Fuzzy-Wuzzy gently.

"Yeah?"

"I don't know how to put this delicately . . ." he began, "but you're only going to be in the way if you remain in here during the operation."

"I won't say anything," replied Flint. "I'll just sit in the corner while you work."

"The only purpose you will serve is to make me even more nervous than I already am." He paused for a moment. "Why don't you go get something to eat? I've got to run some tests on him before the ship lifts off, and I can't see the operation taking less than two hours."

"All right," said Flint reluctantly. He stepped back from the bed. "You'll page me the minute it's over?"

"I promise."

"Or if he . . . if anything happens during the surgery?"

"Yes."

Flint seemed about to say something else, thought better of it, and headed off toward the mess hall. Upon arriving, he ordered a cup of coffee and an artificial sweet roll, and took them over to his corner table, where he sipped at the coffee and stared at the roll without touching it. He was vaguely aware of people entering and leaving the mess hall during the next few minutes, but paid them no attention until Monk walked over and sat down next to him.

"What the hell are *you* doing here?" asked Flint irritably.

"I heard what happened," replied Monk. "I just wanted to tell you that I'm sorry about Tojo."

"He's not dead yet," remarked Flint dryly.

"He will be soon, if the caterpillar's working on him. He never could fix me up right, and *I* wasn't shot in the chest."

"Thanks for those words of comfort."

"Well, I know how close you are to him," said Monk, ignoring the sarcasm in Flint's voice. He paused for a moment. "By the way, did the Dancer come close?"

"Weren't you there?"

Monk shrugged. "What for?"

"I thought he was supposed to be your friend."

"I only got one friend," said Monk. "I was in the ship with him."

Flint shook his head. "Jupiter, I can remember you when you were a pretty decent human being."

Monk got to his feet. "Yeah?" he said pugnaciously. "Well, I can remember this show when you didn't need to read a fucking scorecard every night to see who'd gotten killed."

"That's funny," said Flint, with infinite weariness. "*I* can't."

21.

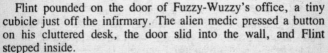

Flint pounded on the door of Fuzzy-Wuzzy's office, a tiny cubicle just off the infirmary. The alien medic pressed a button on his cluttered desk, the door slid into the wall, and Flint stepped inside.

"I keep calling you on the intercom and you keep telling me not to come up yet!" he snapped. "It's been six hours now, and I want to know what the hell is going on."

"Have a seat, Thaddeus," said the alien medic, indicating a chair that was covered by a pile of computer disks and cartridges.

Flint swept them onto the floor with a single motion of his arm. "All right," he said, sitting down. "Now suppose you tell me why you've been putting me off."

"I haven't exactly been hiding, Thaddeus," said Fuzzy-Wuzzy. "I haven't left the infirmary since they brought him in."

"Did you get the bullet out?"

"I didn't even try."

"Why the hell not?" demanded Flint.

"When I opened him up, I found that the bullet had chewed up his insides worse than I had imagined. Perhaps it's because he's a hunchback to begin with, perhaps it was just the way he was sitting, but whatever the reason, it did a lot of damage to a lot of organs before it got to where it is."

"What does that have to do with not removing the bullet?"

"Thaddeus, the only damage the bullet can do now is cause infection. And," said the medic grimly, "if the hospital on Ragobar doesn't have someone who knows human internal organs better than I do, he's going to be dead long before infection becomes a problem."

"Will he make it to Ragobar?" asked Flint.

"I hope so."

"You *hope* so?" repeated Flint.

Fuzzy-Wuzzy nodded. "His condition is grave."

"Is he in pain?"

"Some," replied the medic. "I've got him sedated, but he's been awake for a few minutes now."

"How long has he got?" asked Flint. "I want the truth."

Fuzzy-Wuzzy shrugged, a gesture that sent hundreds of little ripples down the length of his yellow, boneless frame. "I really can't say. Possibly a few hours, possibly he'll make it to Ragobar."

"Jesus!" muttered Flint. "It's not fair."

"Life seldom is," said the medic. "Neither, for that matter, is death."

"Can I talk to him? Will he understand me?"

"He certainly ought to," replied Fuzzy-Wuzzy. "Unless I guessed wrong about the dosage. Don't be alarmed if he's even harder to understand than usual, though. He's very weak."

"Right," said Flint, getting to his feet.

"Thaddeus?" said Fuzzy-Wuzzy.

"Yeah?"

"I did my best."

"I know," said Flint, leaving the office and walking over to Tojo's bed as the door slid shut behind him.

The little hunchback lay on his left side, his eyes half open. Four more tubes had joined the original three leading into his body, and his torso was swathed in carefully applied pressure bandages.

"Hi, Thaddeus," he stammered weakly.

"You should have ducked," said Flint, forcing a smile to his lips.

"I know."

"You'll do better next time."

Tojo coughed, and Flint thought he could see blood in the hunchback's mouth.

"There's not going to be a next time," he said, laboring over each syllable.

"That's right," said Flint. "I forgot about the Dancer."

"I'm not talking about the Dancer," replied Tojo, grimacing.

"Don't be silly. We'll have you back to work inside of three weeks."

Tojo tried to shake his head, then winced. "Just this once, don't lie to me, Thaddeus."

Flint sighed. "All right," he said at last. "I won't lie to you anymore."

The hunchback smiled gratefully.

"Is there anything I can do for you?" asked Flint.

"Try not to look so unhappy," whispered Tojo, his speech almost unintelligible now. "People die all the time." His body jerked spasmodically as he coughed again, and Flint wondered if he should call for Fuzzy-Wuzzy. "You'll replace the Dancer," continued Tojo painfully, and suddenly Flint realized that the little hunchback was trying to comfort *him*.

"Don't worry about the Dancer," he said. "You're worth ten of him. Now save your strength and try not to talk so much."

"I thought you were all through lying," murmured Tojo, trying to smile but wincing instead.

"I am. The Dancer died doing what he wanted to do, at the peak of his powers, in front of a huge audience. Very few people get to do that. Most of us die alone and unnoticed."

Tojo gripped Flint's hand as a wave of pain swept over him. "I know," he said, coughing again. "Thank you for being here, Thaddeus."

"It's just not fair!" Flint muttered.

"I've . . ." began Tojo. He had to pause to catch his breath before continuing. "I've been very lucky."

Flint snorted derisively.

"I have friends—you, and Diggs, and . . ." He was wracked by a paroxysm of coughing before he could enumerate the remainder of his tawdry band of friends. When it was finished he lay back until his breathing became regular, then moved his fingers to the golden whistle that Fuzzy-Wuzzy had replaced around his neck. "And I've been a carny barker," he concluded proudly.

"The best."

Tojo slowly, painfully, lifted the whistle an inch or two off his chest. "This is my most precious possession," he said, getting the entire sentence out with a burst of strength that seemed to weaken him further. "I want you to have it."

"You're sure?"

Tojo nodded feebly.

"Then I'm honored," said Flint, slipping it up over the hunchback's head and hanging it around his own neck.

"So you won't forget me."

"I wasn't going to forget you, you ugly little dwarf," replied Flint tenderly.

"You're a good person, Thaddeus," said Tojo. He stared at the ceiling and waited until he had enough strength to continue speaking. "You weren't always, you know."

"I know," said Flint, suddenly aware of the emptiness of the large room, the sterility of the clean white beds that surrounded him.

They fell silent for a few moments, each lost in his own private thoughts. The little hunchback's breathing became somewhat more labored, but his eyes remained open.

"I promised my books to Jupiter," Tojo said suddenly, and the sound of his hoarse, almost unrecognizable voice startled Flint. "But he doesn't read anymore."

"I'll give them to someone who does," said Flint.

"Thank you."

Tojo drifted off into a half-conscious state, and Flint sat back and stared at him, wondering about the technology that could send a ship through the endless void of space at faster-than-light speeds but couldn't cure one of its passengers. He felt chilly, walked over to the thermostat, found that the temperature of the infirmary was in fact quite warm, and returned to his chair. He pulled out a cigarette, stared thoughtfully at Tojo, and then replaced it in his pocket.

Tojo awoke a half hour later, and seemed surprised to see Flint still sitting at his bedside.

"Thaddeus . . ." he whispered.

"Welcome back," said Flint, not even trying to force a smile to his face this time.

"Tell me about the Dancer's grave."

"It's going to become a goddamned shrine," replied Flint. "People from all over the galaxy will come to look at it, and lay a wreath or two up against the headstone." He paused. "He belongs to *them* now. He's a hero."

Tojo turned painfully toward Flint. "I don't want to be left out here, where only strangers will pass by my grave."

"Name your place."

"I want to be buried at home," said Tojo, just before his body was racked by another coughing fit.

"You mean on Earth?"

Tojo nodded feebly. "With my parents. I know it's a lot to ask, but—"

"I'll take care of it."

"Really?"

"That's a promise."

A look of gratitude spread across the little hunchback's homely face. "Thank you, Thaddeus."

"Now try to relax, and maybe we won't have to worry about it," said Flint.

Tojo lay back and closed his eyes again, and Flint remained motionless, wishing that there were a clock ticking somewhere so that he wouldn't feel so helplessly suspended in time and space.

Suddenly a groan escaped the hunchback's lips, and his face contorted in pain.

"What is it?" asked Flint, quickly leaning over the bed.

"I don't know," mumbled Tojo.

"I'll get Fuzzy!"

"Please don't leave me, Thaddeus!" rasped Tojo. "I'm scared!"

Flint looked helplessly at the medic's closed door, then sat back down in his chair and held onto Tojo's clawlike hand.

"Thank you, Thaddeus," wheezed the hunchback, his body starting to relax. "You've always been my friend."

Suddenly he went limp, and Flint raced to Fuzzy-Wuzzy's cubicle and pounded on the door.

"What is it?" asked the medic, emerging and hastening to Tojo's bed.

"I don't know. He seemed to be in pain, and then he collapsed." Flint walked around the bed as the medic checked the little hunchback's pulse and respiration. "What happened to him?"

"He's merely unconscious," said Fuzzy-Wuzzy. "Probably from the pain. It's just as well; his breathing is less labored this way." He turned to Flint. "He'll probably sleep for a few hours. Why don't you try to get a little rest, too? It's been a long day for everyone. I'll have you paged when he wakes up."

Flint looked at the little hunchback's twisted frame, stroked his sweating head and straightened the pillow under it, and then nodded.

"All right," he sighed.

"Where will you be?" asked Fuzzy-Wuzzy, accompanying him to the door of the infirmary.

"I don't know," said Flint. "The mess hall first. Then probably my room." He looked at the yellow medic. "If I don't hear from you in a couple of hours I'll come back up here."

Fuzzy-Wuzzy nodded, and Flint wandered distractedly down the long matted corridor to the elevator. Then, because he felt restless, he continued walking to the small, spiral stairwell and climbed down the four levels to the mess hall, which was deserted except for Monk and Batman, who were sitting and eating quietly at the far end of the room.

Flint considered ordering coffee or a beer, decided he didn't want either, and sat down at his own table. He sighed, lit a cigarette, and stared at the ashtray.

After a few minutes he got up and poured himself some coffee, then returned and began sipping it thoughtfully. The artificial cigarette burned down to its artificial filter, and he lit another.

He was on his third cup of coffee and his eighth cigarette when Mr. Ahasuerus entered the mess hall and walked slowly over to Flint's table.

"Mr. Flint . . ." he began uneasily.

"Yeah?"

"I have just . . . I mean to say . . ."

"He's dead, isn't he?" said Flint bitterly.

"I am sorry."

Flint stared at the cigarette that was glowing in the ashtray.

"Had he any requests for the disposition of the body?" asked the blue man gently.

"Yeah," said Flint. Suddenly he sat up straight. "Shit!" he muttered.

"What is it?"

"I *can't* bury him with his parents," said Flint, looking up at his partner with tortured eyes. "I don't even know what his name was."

"It wasn't Tojo?" asked Mr. Ahasuerus.

"That's the name *I* gave him the first time I saw him."

"Perhaps it is just as well," said the blue man soothingly. "As I told you some time back, Earth has been closed to members of the Community."

"Not this time," said Flint.

"But—"

"I gave him my word. Promises aren't my strong point," he added wryly, "but I intend to keep this one." He lowered his head in thought for a moment. "I'll bury him next to my mother," he said at last.

"I thought you did not get along well with your mother."

"He wanted a family," said Flint softly. "I've got one to spare."

"I do not know if Kargennian will approve," said Mr. Ahasuerus.

"That implies he's got a choice. He hasn't."

"But what shall I tell him?"

"Tell him that Thaddeus Flint is taking his friend home," said

Flint, rising from the table and heading off toward the infirmary to say a private farewell to the hunchback. As he rode the elevator up to the fourth level he searched his memory for childhood prayers, and discovered to his surprise that he knew one less than Diggs.

22.

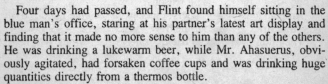

Four days had passed, and Flint found himself sitting in the blue man's office, staring at his partner's latest art display and finding that it made no more sense to him than any of the others. He was drinking a lukewarm beer, while Mr. Ahasuerus, obviously agitated, had forsaken coffee cups and was drinking huge quantities directly from a thermos bottle.

"But *why*?" he persisted. "Surely we can simply ship the body there on one of our cargo ships."

"And let one of the Corporation's six-legged four-eyed polka-dot employees cart it off to a cemetery in Trenton, New Jersey?" replied Flint with a tired smile. "Don't you think he might appear just a little bit conspicuous?" The smile vanished. "Besides, the only way I'm going to know that Tojo actually winds up on Earth is to go with him. I trust the Corporation just about as far as I can spit with my mouth closed."

"Kargennian will never permit it."

"You leave Kargennian to me," replied Flint.

The blue man drummed his fingers nervously on his desk. "I just cannot help feeling that you have not thought this through. Believe me, I *know* Kargennian. He has been looking for an opportunity to get rid of you for years. If you leave the show against his wishes, he will never allow you to come back."

"What makes you think I'm coming back?" said Flint.

"I *knew* it!" muttered the blue man. The drumming of his fingers became faster and louder until he finally balled them into a fist and slammed his hand onto the desk.

"Take it easy," said Flint. "I've never seen a blue skeleton have a stroke before, and I've got a feeling I wouldn't know what to do."

Mr. Ahasuerus took a long swallow from his thermos bottle, then looked intently at Flint.

"Are you so unhappy here?" he asked at last.

"Happiness isn't in the cards for everyone," replied Flint. "Let's just say that I'm tired. I came out here with a dozen misfits and no money, and in five years I built the biggest show in the galaxy. That ought to be enough."

"But why leave, now that the groundwork is done?"

"Because I'm just as broke as when I started," said Flint. "Because Tojo and the Dancer are dead, and Gloria and Fast Johnny Carp have become creatures that I used to have nightmares about. Because Monk is out-and-out crazy, and Stogie is dying. Aren't those enough reasons?"

"And what about the others?" persisted the blue man. "If we let you return, what about them?"

"They don't want to go back," said Flint. "Monk will never go anywhere without Batman. The only thing Diggs lives for is fleecing marks, and he's got more of 'em up here than he ever had on Earth. Stogie, for all his talk about going home to die, is never going to leave the one place that will let him work. Barbara's got three or four prison raps hanging over her head. The others have other reasons."

"Don't you think you owe it to them to discuss your decision with them?"

"I already have. Besides, the only person I really owe anything to is you. That's why I'm here now—and that's why you're going to keep quiet when the hotshot shows up."

The intercom beeped, and a translated voice told Mr. Ahasuerus that Kargennian had arrived.

"Send him up," said the blue man.

The two partners waited in silence until the rotund red alien entered the room.

"Good day, Mr. Ahasuerus," said Kargennian. He turned to Flint. "What is this I hear about your taking a leave of absence, Mr. Flint?"

"I'm taking Tojo back to Earth," said Flint. "Now sit down and tell me how you think you're going to stop me."

Kargennian seemed taken aback for just a moment, then quickly recovered his composure and sat down on a small metal chair. "And just how do you think you're going to get him there, Mr. Flint?"

Flint shrugged. "We've got a shuttlecraft and two small ships. Take your choice."

The little alien shook his head. "Those are company property, Mr. Flint. I'm afraid I can't let you use them."

"We both know you're going to let me take one of them,"
said Flint with a smile, "so why not cut through all the bullshit
and name your price on the front end—remembering, of course,
that I'm no longer a wealthy man."

"It really is out of the question. Earth is off-limits to Community members."

"I'm not a Community member," said Flint.

"Nevertheless."

"Kargennian, I'm going whether you want me to or not.
Now, as I see it, you've got four alternatives. You can be a nice
guy about it and wish me Godspeed, you can be your usual self
and squeeze every last cent you can out of the situation, or you
can be an asshole and send a couple of regiments of aliens out
hunting for me on a world that's not supposed to know you even
exist."

"That's only three," said Kargennian. "What is the fourth?"

"You can make me mad, in which case I'll have to dig two
graves when I get there."

"Are you threatening me, Mr. Flint?" asked Kargennian with
a smile.

"Absolutely," said Flint so coldly that all trace of amusement
vanished from the rotund alien's face.

"How do I know you won't immediately go to the authorities
and tell them about us?" demanded Kargennian.

"Because I don't plan to spend the rest of my life locked away
in a padded cell."

Kargennian stared at Flint for a long moment. "If I agree to
let you go to Earth, you know that we will never take you
back?"

"I know."

"I'll be very blunt with you, Mr. Flint," said Kargennian. "It
has been my conviction for quite some time now that, while your
entrepreneurial skills were probably necessary at the inception of
this project, you really should have been replaced by someone
with more managerial experience and a greater sense of Corporate teamwork two or three years ago."

"Someone like you, perhaps?" asked Flint dryly.

"As a matter of fact, yes."

Flint grinned. "I didn't know your circus was doing that
badly."

"That is neither here nor there," said the little alien, obviously flustered. "The fact remains that while I personally have

no objection to finally seeing the last of you, it is Corporate policy that no one may set foot on Earth.''

"Kargennian,'' said Flint, "I'm in a hurry. Get to the point and let's get this over with.''

"The point is that even if I were to convince the Corporation to make an exception in your case, you still have no means of transportation. It is, after all, a very expensive trip.''

"And you want to know how I'm going to pay for it?''

"Precisely.''

"I'd have thought the answer to that would be obvious,'' said Flint. "*You're* paying for it.''

"I beg your pardon?''

"Look,'' said Flint, lighting a cigarette and using one of the blue man's artifacts for an ashtray, "you plan to make a zillion credits replaying the gunfight throughout the Community of Worlds, don't you?''

"Of course,'' said Kargennian. "But what has that got to do with—?''

"*The Ahasuerus and Flint Traveling Carnival and Sideshow* had Billybuck Dancer under contract at the time of his death. What makes you think we're going to give you permission to play the fight?''

"What are you talking about?'' said Kargennian. "You are a wholly owned subsidiary. You may have owned the Dancer, but *we* own *you*.''

"You know it, and I know it, but I've seen the way your bureaucracy works,'' said Flint with a smile. "How long do you think it'll take you to prove it in court? How many contracts will you have to cancel in the process, and what kind of demand will there be for your holographs twenty years up the road when you finally win?''

"This is blackmail, Mr. Flint!''

"It certainly is,'' agreed Flint amiably. "If, however, you will agree not to hinder me and will pick up the tab for my trip, I'll sign over my rights to the Dancer here and now.'' He paused. "We were going to get a quarter of the take anyway, so this will put my twelve and a half percent right in your pocket.''

"Are you serious, Mr. Flint?'' said Kargennian, his face a mask of undiluted greed.

"Absolutely.''

"Done!'' he cried. "And good riddance to you! I'll draw up the papers myself, and send them up for your signature within twenty minutes.''

"Just a moment," said Mr. Ahasuerus, who had been a silent spectator throughout their conversation.

"Yes? What is it?" said Kargennian.

"If he is to leave, and it appears inevitable, we cannot let him leave destitute after all he has done for us. Surely we have an obligation to supply him with some currency."

"Speaking of currency, you still owe me five thousand credits from our wager, Mr. Flint," said Kargennian.

"True enough," agreed Flint. "I won't ask you for a five-thousand-credit grubstake and we'll call it square."

"Fine," said the rotund alien, leaving the office and scurrying away to draw up the necessary papers.

"This is unacceptable!" said the blue man hotly. "I will speak to him again about the money."

"Don't worry about it."

"But he is profiteering from your situation!"

"Poor little bloodsucker," said Flint with an amused smile. "He's the kind of guy who always shells out fifty bucks for a fancy new toy and then forgets to spend six bits on the battery."

"I am afraid I do not follow you, Mr. Flint," said the blue man, refilling his thermos with a fresh pot of coffee.

Flint walked to the desk, found a blank piece of computer readout paper, and scribbled a pair of brief sentences on it, signing his name with a flourish.

"Here," he said, handing the paper to his partner. "We didn't just have the Dancer under contract—we also own all the rights to the Doc Holliday robot. I just signed my share of them over to you, so now you'll have my percent from it."

"This really isn't necessary, Mr. Flint."

"You don't understand. If worst comes to worst, you'll still get as much out of this as you originally planned—but in the meantime, I'd strongly advise you to bleed that little bastard dry. He can't put his show on without the rights to *both* participants."

"I never thought of that," said Mr. Ahasuerus, flashing his teeth in his equivalent of a smile.

"Well, you're going to have to start thinking of things like that from now on," said Flint seriously.

"To borrow from your vernacular, I will screw things up terribly," said the blue man wryly.

"You'll do just fine," replied Flint. "If you run into trouble, ask Diggs for help. He's a devious son of a bitch if there ever was one."

"And you? What will you do with no money?"

"The same thing I always did," said Flint with a smile. "I'll get by."

"I suppose you will, at that," agreed the blue man. He paused. "You will not reconsider?"

Flint shook his head.

"But there are so many worlds you have yet to see!"

"One world's pretty much like the next."

"Think of the races you will never meet," urged Mr. Ahasuerus.

Flint smiled. "They're even more alike than the worlds. Put a blue sharkskin suit on Kargennian and you'd never know the difference." He paused. "Stick the dwarf in a healthy body and he'd have still been Tojo."

They sat and discussed the past five years for a few minutes, the high points and the low, the triumphs and the failures, and then one of the games workers entered with the papers from Kargennian. Flint glanced over them, signed them, and got to his feet as the worker left.

"I'll be taking one of the little ships, I think," he said. "No sense wasting something as big as the shuttlecraft for one passenger and a wooden box. I'd appreciate it if you'd have the ship's computer program one of the robot pilots while I'm collecting my gear."

Mr. Ahasuerus looked at him desperately. "Mr. Flint, won't you please stay on as a personal favor to *me*?"

Flint sighed. "I'm already doing a personal favor for someone else who asked first."

The blue man stared at him. "I shall miss you, Mr. Flint," he said at last.

"I'll miss you too," replied Flint sincerely.

Mr. Ahasuerus lowered his head and gazed at his long, interlaced fingers. "I always knew that you would leave someday. I just did not realize that it would be so soon."

He looked up to say something else, and found that he was alone in the room.

23.

"I still can't believe he's gone," said Diggs.

"It sure ain't gonna be the same without him," agreed Stogie.

The two men were sitting with Julius Squeezer, Jiminy Cricket and Mr. Ahasuerus at the corner table that had been Flint's for more than five years. The blue man was drinking coffee, Diggs and Jiminy had mugs of lukewarm beer before them, Julius had a foul-smelling fruit concoction, and Stogie was sharing a glass of artificial milk with his squirming little schnauzer.

Diggs shook his head. "He had it all—money, women, everything—and he just walked away. I don't understand it."

"Perhaps he did not view things in precisely the same way that you do," suggested Mr. Ahasuerus softly.

"He's a carny," said Diggs. "He's got no more interest in going out and associating with normal people than I do. Once he takes care of business, he's just going to hunt up another carnival to work for; it's the only thing he knows. So why leave at all, when he owned the biggest?"

"Possibly he did not wish to own the biggest carnival any longer," said the blue man.

"Horseshit!" said Diggs. "You know Thaddeus—the only way he ever measured anything was in terms of money."

"Maybe he found a better way," said Mr. Ahasuerus.

"There ain't none," said Diggs decisively.

"I'm certainly going to miss him," said Julius. "No matter what happened, he always seemed in control of things. If there was a problem, somehow you always knew that he could fix it."

"Or bribe it, or flim-flam it," added Stogie.

"I just don't know who's going to take charge now that he's gone," continued the huge green wrestler. He turned suddenly to the blue man. "Excuse me, Mr. Ahasuerus," he added quickly. "I didn't mean . . ."

"I agree with you," replied the blue man simply. "There is no need to apologize for stating the truth."

"I'll miss him too," said Jiminy, "but surely the carnival will continue to function without him."

"Of course it will," said Stogie. "But it won't be the same." He turned to the Jimorian. "Who's the strongest man you know?"

"Julius," replied Jiminy without hesitation.

"Yeah? Well, Thaddeus fought him in the ring a couple of years ago and beat the shit out of him," said Stogie, chuckling at the memory. "How about the best lion tamer?"

"I've never seen one," admitted Jiminy.

"You were supposed to say Monk," said Stogie sullenly, "and then I was gonna tell you how Thaddeus pulled a couple of cats off him when they were attacking him. Hell, he could probably have found a way to beat the robot if he'd had to."

"I don't think anything could beat that machine in a fair fight," said Jiminy.

"Well, now," interjected Diggs, "Thaddeus wasn't so much concerned with fighting fair as he was with winning." He paused thoughtfully. "That's why I can't understand his leaving. What did he get for it?"

"Maybe he plans on coming back," suggested Jiminy.

"He will not come back," said Mr. Ahasuerus.

"Besides," said Diggs, "he ain't a man to carry a lot of emotional baggage around. When he walks out on a place, he's done with it. I've been with him longer than anyone but Tojo; I *know*."

Monk entered the mess hall and walked over to the little group.

"Anybody seen Batman?" he asked. "I was supposed to meet him here for lunch."

"He ain't been around," said Stogie. "Pull up a chair, Jupiter. I was just telling Jiminy about how Thaddeus saved your ass in the ring back in New Hampshire."

Monk pulled up a chair. "Let him tell it himself," he said. "He gets a kick out of it, especially if I'm around to hear." He paused. "Where the hell *is* Thaddeus, anyway?"

"He's gone," said Diggs.

"Gone?" repeated Monk. "Gone where?"

"He's left the show."

"Yeah. Where'd he go?"

"Earth."

Monk shook his head in amazement. "Can't imagine why.

Ain't nothing back there." He smiled. "Of course, there ain't nothing up here, either, but there's a lot more of it."

"Don't you understand what I'm saying to you?" said Diggs hotly. "He's gone forever."

"Big deal," said Monk with a shrug. "Tojo go with him?"

Diggs threw his hands up in exasperation and muttered an obscenity.

"Watch what you say to me, Rigger," said Monk ominously. "There's enough room in the Bozo cage for more than just me and Batman."

"Go fuck yourself, you crazy bastard!" growled Diggs.

Monk reached across the table and grabbed Diggs by the shirt. "Don't you ever call me crazy again!" he bellowed.

"You don't scare me!" said Diggs defiantly. "You were nothing before Thaddeus found you and you're gonna be nothing again now that he's gone!"

"Stop it!" commanded Mr. Ahasuerus, rising to his feet.

"You keep out of this!" said Monk.

The blue man reached out a long, lean hand and encompassed Monk's fist in his own. His fingers turned almost white as he applied pressure, and finally Monk cursed and released his grip on Diggs.

"I'll remember this!" he snarled as he walked to the door.

"I certainly hope so," said Mr. Ahasuerus coldly.

"And *you*!" he yelled at Jiminy. "Stop looking like my partner!"

All eyes turned to Jiminy, who had let his identity slip away during the tension of the moment.

"Well, I'll be damned!" said Diggs, surprised.

Suddenly the Jimorian was a Westerner again. "I'm sorry," he said. "I was startled." He turned to Mr. Ahasuerus. "Maybe we won't do so badly after all," he said admiringly. Suddenly he became aware of the fact that everyone at the table was staring at him.

"What is it?" he asked uncomfortably.

"When you changed back there . . ." began Diggs.

"Yes?"

"Damned if you didn't look just like Thaddeus!" concluded the gambler.

"That's what you looked like to me, too," said Stogie, his expression troubled.

Jiminy scratched his head. "That's curious," he remarked at

last. "I guess we're going to miss him more than I thought. How about you, Mr. Ahasuerus—what did I look like to you?"

"You looked like Mr. Flint," said the blue man calmly.

"You too?" said Jiminy.

Mr. Ahasuerus nodded his lean, bald head.

"You don't seem as surprised as the others," remarked Jiminy at last.

"Why should I be?"

"Don't you find it curious that I looked like Thaddeus?"

The blue man twisted his thin lips into a bittersweet smile.

"You always did," he said softly.

EPILOGUE: *2:08 A.M., August 17, 2009 A.D.*

The old man walked down the midway, his jacket slung over one shoulder in deference to the hot, humid Connecticut night. A warm breeze swept over him, tousling his thinning white hair, and he paused for a moment to wipe the sweat from his face with a shirtsleeve.

The Ferris wheel had been shut down for the night, as had the strip show and most of the games. A few hardy customers were still at the Bozo cage, and a number of young men were walking around the tents, looking for a little action—but for the most part the carnival had closed up shop for another day. It would open again in ten hours, turning its painted, slightly seedy face toward the hundreds of spectators who would find, as they always did, that it promised far more than it ever delivered.

The old man approached the specialty tent and nodded to the barker, a somewhat paunchy middle-aged man who was totaling up a pile of ticket stubs.

"How'd we do tonight?" asked the old man.

"Sold out all three shows," said the barker. "This new sharpshooter sure draws them in better than the last guy." He smiled. "I still don't know if it's because of his skill or his tight pants."

"What difference does it make?"

"None, I guess," chuckled the barker. "You know, I think he only missed two shots all night. He's about the best there is."

"One of 'em."

"You've seen better?"

"Once," said the old man with a nostalgic smile. "A long, long time ago."

He reached up and mopped the sweat from his face again.

"What's that?" asked the barker suddenly.

"What's *what*?"

"You've got something glittering inside your shirt."

The old man reached between the buttons of his damp shirt and withdrew a small golden object that hung around his neck on a small chain. "Just a whistle," he said. "A gift from a friend."

"I never saw it before. Is it a good-luck charm?"

"Something like that."

"It looks like there's some kind of inscription on it," noted the barker.

The old man tucked the whistle back inside his shirt. "Probably just says 'Made in Japan,' " he replied. He took a deep breath and released it slowly. "Come on. I'll buy you a beer."

"I've just got to empty the telescope boxes, and then I'll take you up on that. Care to come along?"

"Might as well," said the old man. "It can't be any hotter walking than standing still."

They walked down the midway to a small wooden platform that housed four inexpensive telescopes and a huge sign offering five minutes of stargazing for fifty cents. A young couple stood behind one of them, taking turns peering through its eyepiece. At last a sigh of disappointment indicated that their time had run out.

"Hey, mister," said the young man, holding out a dollar bill to the barker. "Can I get some quarters from you?"

"I'm sorry," answered the barker, "but we're closing for the night."

"Please!" begged the girl plaintively. "Just five more minutes!"

The old man nodded, and the barker turned over four quarters. The young man promptly inserted two of them in the coin box and put the other two in his pocket, then stepped aside as the girl once again looked through the telescope.

"It's beautiful!" she said. "You don't realize how many different colors there are when you just look up with your eyes."

"See any little green men yet?" asked the young man.

"No," she said with a smile, stepping back. "You try."

The young man placed his eyes to the telescope, while the young woman pulled a handkerchief out of her purse and gently patted her forehead and neck.

"It's fascinating, trying to imagine what we'll find when we finally reach the stars."

The old man smiled. "Oh, probably just a gambler and a couple of lion tamers, and maybe a beat-up old hootch dancer or two."

"No," she said, wrinkling her nose in a manner that the old

man would have found charming in his youth. "What do you *really* think we'll find?"

"Really?" The old man arched an eyebrow. "The same as you, I suppose."

"And what's that?" she asked, smiling.

"Glittering cities inhabited by wise and ancient races who have conquered death and are waiting for us to join them in a galactic utopia."

"How did you know?" she said, surprised.

"Just a guess."

Then it was her turn to look through the telescope again, and finally the lens clicked off and the couple walked away toward the parking lot.

"Boy!" chuckled the barker, starting to unlock the coin boxes. "They get younger and dumber every year! That was a nice line of bullshit you handed her."

The old man smiled back at him. "A carnival trades in bullshit."

"You must have been a real killer-diller with the ladies when you were younger."

"I had my moments."

The barker looked at the stars for a moment and shook his head. "What do you suppose is really up there?"

The old man glanced up at the sky, then sighed and gently touched the golden whistle with his fingertips.

"Nothing much," he said at last.

ABOUT THE AUTHOR

MIKE RESNICK was born in Chicago in 1942, attended the University of Chicago (where, in the process of researching his first adventure novel, he earned three letters on the fencing team and was nationally ranked for a brief period), and married his wife, Carol, in 1961. They have one daughter, Laura.

From the time he was 22, Mike has made his living as a professional writer. He and Carol have also been very active at science fiction conventions, where Mike is a frequent speaker and Carol's stunning costumes have swept numerous awards at masquerade competitions.

Mike and Carol were among the leading breeders and exhibitors of show collies during the 1970s, a hobby which led them to move to Cincinnati and purchase a boarding and grooming kennel.

Mike has received several awards for his short stories and an award for a nonfiction book for teenagers. His first love, though, remains science fiction, and his excellent science fiction novels—THE SOUL EATER, BIRTHRIGHT: THE BOOK OF MAN, WALPURGIS III, SIDESHOW, THE THREE-LEGGED HOOTCH DANGER, and THE WILD ALIEN TAMER—are all available in Signet editions.

Science Fiction from SIGNET

(0451)

☐ **LAST COMMUNION by Nicholas Yermakov.** (098226—$2.25)

☐ **EPIPHANY by Nicholas Yermakov.** (118847—$2.50)*

☐ **THOSE WHO WATCH by Robert Silverberg.** (120221—$2.25)*

☐ **STRATA by Terry Pratchett.** (121473—$2.75)*

☐ **STARBURST by Alfred Bester.** (091329—$1.75)

☐ **THOSE WHO CAN by Robin Scott Wilson.** (615956—$1.95)

☐ **GREYBEARD by Brian Aldiss.** (090357—$1.75)*

☐ **GALAXIES LIKE GRAINS OF SAND by Brian Aldiss.**
(070445—$1.25)

☐ **WIND CHILD by R. M. Meluch.** (115287—$2.50)

☐ **WIND DANCERS by R. M. Meluch.** (097866—$2.25)

☐ **KILLBIRD by Zach Hughes.** (092635—$1.75)

☐ **PRESSURE MAN by Zach Hughes.** (094980—$1.95)*

☐ **THUNDERWORLD by Zach Hughes.** (112903—$2.25)*

*Prices slightly higher in Canada.

Buy them at your local bookstore or use this convenient coupon for ordering.

THE NEW AMERICAN LIBRARY, INC.,
P.O. Box 999, Bergenfield, New Jersey 07621

Please send me the books I have checked above. I am enclosing $_____
(please add $1.00 to this order to cover postage and handling). Send check
or money order—no cash or C.O.D.'s. Prices and numbers are subject to change
without notice.

Name_____

Address_____

City _____ State _____ Zip Code _____

Allow 4-6 weeks for delivery.
This offer is subject to withdrawal without notice.

Ø

SIGNET Science Fiction You'll Enjoy

Great Science Fiction by Robert Adams from SIGNET